Vacancy

A Novel

Bryan Coburn

Vacancy

This is a work of fiction. Names, characters, places and incidents either are product of the author's imagination or are used fictitiously, and any resemblance to any actual persons, living or dead is merely coincidental.

Author photo by Jeff White Photography
www.jeffwhitephoto.com

For Evan, Emma, my family and friends. Special thanks to my Jenn for her enduring encouragement.

Vacancy

1

Opening his eyes, he was greeted by darkness. Through blurry-eyed vision he turned to look at the alarm clock on the nightstand beside his bed. The green glowing digital numbers were flashing 12:00. Only the light seeping in around the edges of the floor-to-ceiling heavy curtains at the end of his room told him that it was daytime. He reached for his watch squinting to read that it was 7:13. He had woken up late for work again. Although his alarm clock had a battery for when the electricity went out, the battery must have died, again. His shift started at 7 am.

"Hope I don't get fired," he said to himself with a grin.

To get a better look at the day, he walked across the room and pulled one side of the curtains across just enough so that only his head was revealed. Another perfect summer day, deep blue skies with only a few small white clouds. He surveyed the grounds beneath him. No activity. He pulled the curtain completely closed again, and turned back to his room.

His room had the standard hotel bachelor-style layout, furnished with a queen-sized bed, small sofa, coffee table, TV with stand, small dining table, and kitchenette. The kitchenette had a sink, microwave, a two burner stove top, and a bar fridge.

He grabbed a can of grapefruit juice and a pitcher of milk from the fridge. His breakfast was always the same: instant oatmeal accompanied by a glass of grapefruit juice and a cup of instant coffee. He had chosen the oatmeal as a practical option due to its prolonged expiry date. Having used the last of the milk, he rinsed out the pitcher, and placed it back onto the counter. From a cupboard he took out a tin of powdered milk and placed it beside the empty pitcher as a reminder to make a new batch that evening.

He sat down at the dining table and ate his breakfast, then quickly washed his dishes and placed them back into the cupboard. After brushing his teeth, he changed into his uniform, made his bed, and was ready to start his day.

He went out into an empty hallway. Rows of closed guest room doors stretched out in front of him. He pulled a small notebook out of his back pocket and flipped through the pages until he found the day's date. Handwritten in pen was a list of tasks he had made for himself.

"Let's see what I have to do today," he said aloud reading the page as he went down the hall.

The hotel was quiet. The only sound was his shoes scuffing the soft carpet as he walked. He stopped. Now there was no sound at all. Standing there alone in the middle of the hallway, he took a second to appreciate the silence.

The hotel, The Grand Summit Place, was the newest and most prestigious property in a large, ever evolving four season resort area best known as a superior skiing destination. The Grand had the reputation of being the elite place to stay in the region. Less than three years old, the five story, 475 room hotel still had an atmosphere of newness. The housekeeping and maintenance staff had worked diligently to keep the entire property in the same condition as it appeared on opening day. The new carpet smell still lingered in some areas.

He had worked in the housekeeping department as a houseperson at The Grand since it opened. The houseperson was responsible for maintaining the cleanliness of all the public areas in the hotel including the hallways, lobby area, conference rooms, public bathrooms, and the activity areas such as the pool, exercise room, and arcade. Hotel management had the benefit of selecting young, attractive, perky, staff to work in many of the more visible positions, especially the front desk. He was more of an introvert and was quite content working behind the scenes, and having minimal interaction with the guests.

During his time at The Grand, he had learned to live with the fact that most of the employees were younger than him, even though he was only in his mid thirties. Some staff were using it as a summer job, and some others coming from all over the world for the life experience of working at a ski resort. The remaining staff were locals who did not have many other options for employment. The hotel retained a small core of

2

permanent year round staff like him. The running joke among the staff was that it was not the wages, but the resort environment and the perks such as free ski passes, golf memberships, and discounted room rates for family members that kept the full-timers around.

He began every morning by walking the entire building, starting from his room on the top floor, which was at the end of the hallway. He would then proceed down the hallway on each floor until he reached the far end of the building on the ground level. The hotel was shaped like a stretched-out accordion, and as such, the hallway running through the middle of each floor was configured to have a series of doglegs so that every hundred feet the path would bend on a slight angle. Originally, walking the building gave him a chance to make sure any garbage left out in the hallways at night was picked up before the guests got up in the morning, so all the guest would see was a spotless hotel when they left their room. It also provided an opportunity to spot any repairs or maintenance projects needing attention, such as burnt out light bulbs, chips in the walls, or water leaks. As of late, he had considered abandoning the routine, but continued with it just to watch for any structural damages that might have occurred.

As he got halfway down the fifth floor, he passed by a newspaper resting in front of a guest room door. He reached down, straightened it up and continued on. The front page had a big picture of car completely covered in snow, and the previous night's hockey scores.

At the end of the hallway he stopped in front of one of the guest rooms. From his pocket he pulled out a plastic key card and swiped it into a slot on the door handle plate and pulled it out again. A little window above the handle lit up red. He swiped his card again. Red light.

He reached into his pocket and pulled out a similar card and swiped it. This time the window lit green.

He pushed down on the ornate handle and walked into the suite. It was one of the nicest and most costly suites in the hotel with a separate bedroom and a second level. A ceramic tiled floor at the front door led him past a full kitchen on the right and a small bathroom on the left. The tiles ended at the carpeted living room area. In the middle of the suite an open staircase led up to a loft.

All the lights were off. He did not turn any on. The room was dim with the early morning light.

He approached the bedroom, stopping to lean against the door frame. The drawn curtains held out all daylight. Peering into the darkness, he paused to contemplate his predicament, his motive for being in a guest room when he should be attending to his appointed houseperson duties.

He could make out the white satiny duvet on the bed. It seemed to have a luminous quality in the lightless room. The bed was fully made. The suite was empty.

The room attendants had already been in to clean it, making the room spotless, putting fresh linen on the beds, dusting, vacuuming, doing the dishes, and cleaning the three bathrooms. Each bathroom would have complimentary soap, shampoo, conditioner, and hand cream. Each would be made up with an exact number of bath towels, hand towels, and face cloths, all folded according to corporate specifications.

He turned around and went up the stairs leading to the loft. He noticed that the handrail had a thin layer of dust. The loft had a king-sized bed and a small en-suite bathroom. On one side, a half-wall overlooked the kitchen area, on the other side a pair of sliding glass doors led to a balcony. He walked up, pulled the curtain aside, and looked out over the area below. Satisfied, he slid one door open and walked out.

This vantage point offered a sweeping view of the rear grounds of the hotel and the surrounding area. Sprawled out beyond the hotel was a small upscale retail village, with family restaurants, cafes, boutiques, pubs, and ski equipment shops. Guests could sit outside on one of the many patios and enjoy their meal. It was not uncommon even in the winter months to see skiers enjoying a pint of beer sitting around a table outside a pub.

Beyond the retail area, a canopy of green forest stretched out as far as the eye could see, and was only broken up by a few roads, and the odd condo complex, or cottage. The closest actual town was twenty minutes away. The largest city was a two hour drive away.

Vacancy

It was easy to see why this area was a natural setting for a four season vacation spot. The resort was situated between the Arklay Mountains, and a large lake, Lake Arnette. The mountain range, modest in height, was not as high as the Rockies, or even the Appalachians, but was high enough to provide the best ski runs in this area of the country. The base of the mountains and the beaches of the lake were separated by a mere fifteen minute drive.

The hotel itself was positioned perpendicular to the mountain. Two hundred yards from this part of the hotel was the end of a ski run. The ski lift stood still. The lift chairs gently rocked with the summer breeze, waiting patiently for the winter to arrive. A multitude of ski runs lined the mountain in both directions.

He stood and scanned the entire area, the mountain to the left, the village in front of him, and Lake Arnette to the right. Everywhere was quiet. He turned around and went back into the bedroom, closed the balcony doors, and pulled the curtains fully closed again.

He made his way back down the loft stairs and left the suite. He went to the suite directly across the hall to follow the same routine. This room was identical to the room he just left, but faced the other side of the hotel. Like the room he just left, it had been cleaned and sat vacant.

He walked up the loft steps. After first stopping to look out, he went onto the balcony. Below him was the entrance to the hotel. An executive golf course was across the road. The deep green grass glistened with dew in the sunshine. Beyond the golf course was mostly untouched land. The mountain range continued, stretching out of sight. This side also was quiet. He noticed that this room also needed a good dusting. He left the suite and went back into the fifth floor hallway.

He took the stairs down to the fourth floor. Each footstep echoed through the empty concrete stairwell.

Walking down the fourth floor hallway, he stopped when he got to the elevator lobby. Four stainless steel elevator doors sat closed, waiting to be used. He inspected the area, and then continued on. He was already starting to get hot. The cooling system was turned off and the air in the hallways was weighty with the August humidity.

Part of the routine of walking the building was taking the stairs. This allowed him to make sure that the stairwells were also clean, and if not, it would be a job for later in the day. He proceeded down to the third floor and walked the entire length of the hotel again, then went down the stairs to the second floor.

Every door he passed was closed. In the past as he walked by suites, he would hear the TV, or guests talking, or even the shower running, but now every suite was quiet.

The top three floors were simply one very long corridor lined with hotel room doors. The middle of the second floor however, opened up into the main lobby area. A walkway bridged through the centre. Smoked glass railings lined the walkway, creating a balcony that overlooked the space below. This was a good vantage point to stop and discreetly ascertain how busy the lobby was during peak times. He did not need to stop, there was no need to do so.

The entire lobby area was empty. No activity at the front reception counter. The valet desk was also unattended. A large lounging area featured a group of oversized leather sofas facing a massive fireplace made from river stones native to the region. At the other end of the lobby was a small bar. The wall-mounted flat screen TVs behind the bar were turned off. The bar area was vacant and dark. He walked past a circular stairway that led down to the lobby. He continued on his route, crossing the walkway which led to the other half of the second floor with more guest rooms and the fitness centre.

He walked past the glass doors that led to the gym. The gym was opened twenty-four hours so guests could exercise at their convenience any time of the day or night. The gym was empty, the lights off.

At the end of the second floor, he took the stairs down to the ground level, and yet another hallway of hotel room doors. He soon reached the lobby. The early morning light radiated through the floor-to-ceiling glass windows and warmed the area. The pillars under the second floor walkway casted shadows like sentries on guard duty. Lanterns on the walls exuded an amber glow.

He walked to the back of the lobby and looked out through a pair of glass doors that led to the hotel's rear grounds. A plexiglas canopy led guests to the pool house with change rooms. The hotel featured a year round outdoor pool which was just as popular in the winter as it was in the summer. A heated cobblestone path ensured that guests going to the pool area from the lobby would not get cold feet during the winter months. The grounds also featured quiet sitting areas, a goldfish pond, picnic areas and several ornate gazebos made of cedar.

Just from looking outside the window, he could tell that it was going to be a hot day. It was going to be one of those perfect summer days people dream about during the cold winter months as they plan their summer holidays. He looked at his watch and sighed. It was ten after eight. The grounds were deserted, the pool, unoccupied.

He turned on his heels and continued with the last part of his walk, down to the end of the first floor passing the public washrooms, the conference area and the in-house restaurant called The Innsbruck. All the lights were off in these areas to save electricity. Large windows in the restaurant and the conference lounge allowed for natural lighting but the rooms still seemed dim.

Like The Grand Summit Place, The Innsbruck was the top of its class in the area, attracting not only guests of The Grand, but guests from neighbouring hotels and locals looking to impress with an expensive evening. The Innsbruck's style was part European ski chalet, part Muskoka cottage, and influenced by The Pottery Barn. As a result, the decor was all earth tones, rich wood grains, deer antler chandeliers, and old skiing photographs and signage.

All in all, the hotel was in good shape this morning. During the busiest times it was common to find empty pizza boxes left outside a guest room, drinks spilled down the stairwell, or wet pool towels piled in the hallway. Once he had even found a bag of dirty diapers abandoned in the ice machine room.

Having come to the end of the first floor, he turned around and headed back down towards the lobby. He stopped, and went through a door that led to a stairwell. He walked around the stairs, crouched down and pulled out a cardboard box full of cleaning supplies that he had hidden from view under the bottom step. This was a convenient location to quickly grab any items he might need. He took out a couple cleaning rags, a half empty can of furniture polish, and a spray bottle of a blue window cleaner.

He stood up and walked over to an emergency exit door that led to the rear grounds. He looked outside. Branches from the lilac bushes that bordered the door were overgrown from neglect, their leaves almost completely covered the window obstructing his view. Yard maintenance was not one of his duties, but he would have to get out there and trim the bushes himself, again. He pushed on the crash bar to make sure that it would still open from the inside if needed. The door opened. He pulled it forcefully to make sure that it was fully closed and would be locked from the outside.

He turned around, went back into the hallway and returned to the lobby. He started cleaning at the front reception counters, wiping down the marble surfaces with a spray of the blue chemical. He dusted off the blank computer screens, the keyboards and phones that reception staff would use to greet guests when they checked in.

Beside the reception desk, a large flat screen monitor was mounted on the wall. It would display daily activities and showed promotional videos boasting of the hotel's amenities. It had been turned off for weeks.

The door behind the reception desk leading to the front office was closed. He did not bother to go in the office.

He progressed through the lobby, polishing all the cherry wood coffee tables and book shelves, dusting the lamps, and fluffing the cushions on the leather sofas. He was always surprised at the amount of dust that could settle on the furniture in the course of a day. Doing a quick visual sweep to make sure he had not missed anything, he left the lobby.

He walked past the elevator foyer, took out his key card, and used it to open a wide door labelled "Staff Only." The room was small and was filled with supplies for the housekeeping staff assigned to that floor. Each floor had a similar storage room. White pressed linen sat neatly folded in stacks on a row of shelves; pillow cases, bed sheets, fitted mattress covers, fluffy bath towels, and face cloths all waiting to be picked up by the room attendants to be used in the guest rooms. The outer curved ends of the folded linen and the top sheet in each pile had a thin brownish layer of dust that had settled over time.

The service elevator for staff was also accessed in this room. He pressed the call button to get the elevator. During busy times of the day, he could stand there waiting for five minutes for the elevator, while the room attendants moved from floor to floor with their housekeeping carts.

The elevator door opened immediately. He walked into the grimy service elevator, and pressed the button labelled P2. The once white linoleum floor was grey and cracked from overuse. The faux wood grain walls were permanently scratched and scraped revealing the bare metal beneath. It was a stark contrast from the guest elevators that were cleaned three times a day and looked just as they had on the day they were installed.

The hotel had two levels of underground parking for guests. P2 at two floors below ground, was the lowest parking level and housed many of the staff facilities such as the laundry room, maintenance room, and employee lunch room. The housekeeping office was just outside the entrance to the service elevator.

He used his key card to get inside the locked housekeeping office. He flipped the light switch. The florescent lights flickered a couple times, before filling the room with bright light. He walked past the punch clock staff used every day to check in and out. The punch clock's electrical cord dangled to the ground unplugged. He stopped at the housekeeping manager's desk, opened the top drawer, and took out a set of keys. He used one to unlock a wood cabinet on the wall behind the desk. Inside the cabinet were several rows of small gold hooks. Most of the hooks held a plastic key card labelled with the name of a housekeeping staff. Only a couple hooks were empty. At the start of each day staff would be given their card. He grabbed one labelled, Moira Brown Room Attendant.

"She won't be needing this anymore," he said to himself.

He put the key card into his pocket. Then he took an envelope with "erased" written on the front in black magic marker and sat down in the manager's chair. He reached inside his pocket and pulled out the key card that had denied him access to the room earlier and put it in the envelope which already had several

9

cards inside. He returned the envelope to the cabinet. Swivelling his chair around, he reached under the desk and pressed the power button on the computer. The computer screen lit up revealing the image of the corporate logo with a log in section. "Barbara", was already typed in the box beside "USER NAME". He typed a series of numbers for the password. The screen changed again, and he started playing video solitaire. After five games, he shut the computer down.

He grabbed a vacuum cleaner, went to the first floor and made his way to the conference area. The conference area had a large central foyer with several sets of double doors on one side leading to different sized meeting and banquet rooms. Only darkness could be seen between the cracks of the closed conference room double doors. On the other side of the foyer, a wall of windows overlooked a covered patio area with glass doors leading outside. Leather armchairs grouped in pairs, lined the walls of the foyer. A cherry wood table with a tiffany lamp resting on top completed the stage for a cozy impromptu discussion spot.

The resort was a popular conference destination for major corporations who flew in management teams from all over North America to learn the latest business strategies. Some companies would invite high profile customers in hopes of landing huge sales contracts. Regardless of the conference purpose, the common agenda was to attend seminars during the day and hit the open bar at night, with attendees rolling into bed around three in the morning.

While vacuuming the conference area, every time he passed a glass patio door, he pulled on them to make sure they were locked tight.

Before leaving the area, he stopped outside a door with *Guest Computer Centre* etched on a shiny platinum nameplate. The room was an amenity that allowed guests free twenty-four hour computer access. He swiped his key card, opened the door and turned on the lights. Inside, four computer workstations sat empty, the screens blank. He was ready for another short break. He sat down on a desk chair. With both feet he pushed himself and glided across the room over to the water cooler. A coffee mug sat on top of the water jug for his own personal use. The cup dispenser attached to the cooler was empty. He filled the cup, quickly gulping the refreshing water. He cursed when he saw the last of the water gurgle down into the cooler reservoir. His second helping completely drained all the remaining water. Bending over, he unplugged the cooler. The hotel did not have a full water jug to replace the one he just emptied.

He sat relaxed with his legs stretched out into the middle of the room. He had the urge to play another game of solitaire, but felt that it would take too long to start up the computer so he just sat there daydreaming. A few minutes later he got up, and pushed the chair back into position in front of its desk. As he went to leave, he flicked the light switch off, and turned to look back into the dark room. From under one desk he could see a small red light on one of the computer terminals. He turned the lights back on. Crawling under the desk, he pushed the switch on the power bar. The computer light went dead. He looked around at the other computers to make sure their power bars were off as well. He was trying to minimize his electricity usage any way he could.

As he left the computer room, he felt a slight pang of loneliness which was unusual for him. The role of houseperson suited him, since the job required a lot of time working independently. Normally he was quite content to work in solitude, but every once in awhile he felt the impact of spending hours without any kind of interaction. To solve the lonely feeling he decided to head back to the reception office.

He used his key card to enter the front office behind the reception counter. The lights were off. The small room was dimly lit by row of windows at the far end that overlooked the carport out front. The office was cramped with empty work stations, computers and a large photocopier. It had three phone stations for staff to accept reservations and requests from guests. A name plate that read Manager on Duty rested on top of the largest desk.

He turned his attention to an elaborate computer terminal. He turned the power on. After a few seconds, the screen lit up. *Megaton Sound System* in large gold lettering filled the screen. A new window appeared, asking him to *Choose Environment.*

He selected the box that read *All Public & Staff Areas,* and then selected *"The '8os"* from a list of genres.

The screen changed again to display:

Artist: The Flaming Frogs   Song: Rat Race

Instantly, overhead speakers in the ceiling began to play:

"Soulless cities,
Soulless cities scrambling,
Scrambling in a work-a-day world
Caught up in the rat race
Caught up in the rat race
When will it end?"

Usually he was not the type to have music playing in the background as he worked. He genuinely preferred the silence which he found soothing. Some of the room attendants were the opposite; they constantly had to have music playing when they were cleaning suites. Some would turn on the TV to a music video station the minute they entered the suite, sometimes having one TV going in the living room, and another TV on in the bedroom in the larger suites. Others would turn on the radio feature on the alarm clock. Today however, he felt the need for the accompaniment of music, and he knew that the upbeat tempo and lively synthesizer of the songs from the 1980s would improve his mood. He instantly felt better as the song ended and the next one began.

"All alone in suburbia
Pretty, perfect houses
Pretty, perfect lawns
Pretty, perfect lives
Feeling all alone in suburbia"

He looked at his watch. It was almost lunch time. Usually he liked to go to his own room for lunch, but today he decided to continue enjoying the music, so instead he planned to have lunch in the main lobby. It had been weeks since he had taken his lunch break in the staff room. When he thought about it, it had been a couple weeks since he had even gone in the staff room. He made an entry in his notebook to go down there and do an inspection and cleaning, not that it would be messy though.

He took the elevator up to the fifth floor to his room, grabbed a frozen microwave meal from his fridge freezer and a bottle of water and went back down to the ground floor. He used the microwave in the reception office.

Back in the empty lobby, he sat down on one of the oversized leather couches, pulled the cherry wood coffee table over closer to him and placed his meal and drink at arm's length in front of him. All around, dust particles danced like glittering stars in the sunshine from the huge windows overlooking the back property. The warmth of the sunlight on his bare arms and face added to his upbeat mood as another song played overhead.

He thought it was a Don Henley song , but he was not sure. As he listened to the lyrics he marvelled at how the words took on a whole new meaning now. The song talked about the end of summer in a beach town, with the streets, lake and beach being empty.

His meal finished, he leaned into the soft, puffy back of the couch, and stretched his legs out straight onto the top of the coffee table.

"Just a five minute power nap," he thought, trying to persuade himself, then closed his eyes.

Fifteen minutes later, he opened his eyes, refreshed, but slightly groggy. He sat up, picked up his garbage, and wiped down the coffee table before pushing it back into its proper position.

For the rest of the day, he decided to conduct guest room inspections. He was systematically going through all the rooms in an orderly rotation to ensure that they were all up to corporate standards of cleanliness and presentation. He pulled his notebook out of his back pocket and looked at the rooms he had to go through today; 313 to 333. He created this rotating cleaning schedule so that no rooms would get overly unkempt, and he could ensure that every room was eventually checked.

Although he was a houseperson, he was also trained as a room attendant and could assist with cleaning suites when needed.

The room attendants generally frowned upon the term "maid," although he did not know why.

He took the service elevator up to the third floor housekeeping storage room. Five grey Rubbermaid housekeeper's carts where lined up single file against one wall. Four of them were completely bare and although at first glance they looked new, closer inspection would show that they were far from new, and instead had been totally cleaned and emptied. The cart closest to the exit door was fully stocked with cleaning supplies, toiletries, neatly stacked towels, and bed linen. He grabbed this cart, manoeuvred it out the doorway into the hallway and pushed it past a number of closed doors until he was in front of suite 313.

Even though the room was vacant, he always felt like he was intruding. Maybe it was the darkness. Maybe it was the fact that he truly respected the guest's room as their private living space, and some of this respect lingered with him even when the room was vacant. Other staff were not so reverent. If the guest was not in the room, some staff had been known to try on their perfume, or help themselves to some chips or candies that might be sitting out in a bowl, or even have a small sip of wine. Of course this was not an issue lately.

He swiped the plastic key card. The small window turned green, and he entered the room. This suite like his own, provided basic accommodation: a queen sized bed, small kitchen area, and living room all in one room. The room had already been cleaned and awaited its guest's arrival. The bed was made, with the pillows neatly propped against the headboard. The white duvet covering the bed was pulled tight to eliminate any wrinkles. He removed the pillows. Tiny particles of dust flew into the air as he smashed pillows together. He then shook the duvet. He carefully put the pillows back in place and ironed the duvet flat with his outstretched arm.

He went out into the hallway and grabbed a spray bottle and a cleaning rag. All the surfaces in the room had a thin layer of dust on them, enough that he could write his name in. He tried to estimate when the room had actually been cleaned last, but he gave up trying. He then vacuumed the entire room including the bathroom floor.

The toilet had a series of descending white scale rings from the water's slow evaporation over the time of disuse. He scrubbed the toilet bowl and then double checked to make sure the bathroom had the proper amount of towels.   The Grand Summit Place was part of a collection of upscale resort properties owned by an international corporation. As a result, each hotel had to follow the corporate standards that dictated everything from staff uniforms, to company brand named toiletries. Even the pictures that adorned the hallways were specifically chosen.

He made one final inspection of the room. He stopped at a pad of paper by the phone that had a hotel pen on it. He positioned the pen so it ran diagonally across the pad with the hotel logo facing upwards. Satisfied with the overall cleanliness, he sprayed a mist of air freshener, turned out all the lights, and closed the door behind him.

After going through a few more rooms, at four he decided to quit for the day despite not getting all the rooms on the list completed.

"There is always tomorrow," he said to himself.

He returned his cart to the housekeeping   storage room, and then went back to his own suite.

As part of his employment agreement, he was provided with an unused guest suite. The suite was in disrepair and had the undesirable quality of being situated at the far end of the building with the only view being the roof of the hotel's restaurant. When he was given this room, there were several holes in one wall, and a huge red wine stain on the carpet. The holes had since been repaired but the carpet still needed to be replaced. Instead of fixing such rooms, management opted to rent them out to staff at a reasonable rate.

One of the qualities of being a resort hotel is that many employees were single, would only be around for one season, and they did not want to get involved in a long term rental lease out in the community. As a result, many employees had short term accommodations arranged by the resort's human resources department in the form of a room in one of the hotels, or they would share a chalet with other staff.

15

Once in his room, Martin changed into more comfortable clothes: a pair of shorts and a t-shirt. In the past when his shift was over he would have a shower, but that was when the day's chores involved handling dirty linen, wet bath towels, and countless garbage bags filled with guest's discarded food, coffee cups, pizza boxes and other refuse.

It had been a long day. He decided to have a frozen TV dinner in his room. It had all the makings of a full meal including turkey, gravy, mashed potatoes, vegetables and a chocolate brownie for dessert.

Despite being a "TV" dinner, he sat down at his kitchen table with the latest copy of his favourite magazine, *VideoGamerz*, the January edition. He flipped through the dog eared pages for what seemed like the thousandth time.

When he finished his meal he looked at his watch, 5:30. He had a few more hours of daylight left, but more importantly, two hours until 7:30.

2

His first task after his meal was to go to the engineering office to get a new battery for his alarm clock. He took the service elevator down to P2. When he got off the elevator, every parking spot was empty, dozens of empty parking spots in both directions. The engineering office was at the far end of P2. It was not until he rounded a corner and was close to the end of the garage that he saw a small collection of parked vehicles. As he passed a couple of cars, he stretched out a hand and dragged a finger along the hoods, leaving a thin, clean line in the dust that had settled there. The line looked like the path left by a skier after a fresh snowfall.

As a result of being here since it opened, he knew the layout of the hotel better than anyone. He had been in every suite, storage room, utility closet, and maintenance room in the hotel. He had even been in remote places like the bottom of the elevator shaft and the boiler room. He always liked to see how things worked, and would observe the maintenance staff and even the service repairmen as they attended to the various mechanical operations of the hotel.

Using his key card, he opened the door to the engineering office and switched on the light. The office also served as the maintenance workshop. It was well equipped with every power tool needed, including a drill press, table saw, bench grinders, a band saw, and a planer. Large work tables sat in the middle of the room. Tall red metal chests filled with hand tools lined one wall. Everything needed to maintain the hotel was kept in this room, from paint to lumber, to light bulbs. A number of repair jobs sat waiting to be completed: a stand up vacuum cleaner with a frayed electrical cord, a dining room chair with a broken leg, and a picture with cracked glass in the frame.

He went to a shelf and helped himself to a box of 9 volt batteries. He also took a box of Ds.

Vacancy

He sat down at the manager's desk. A thick binder labelled "Repair Log Book" sat on top of the desk. He opened it up and found the last entry; Jan 3. Several repair jobs were written on the page. The bottom half of the sheet was empty. The rest of the pages behind it were blank. He read over the list of repairs, and copied them down into his own notebook. Some of the last entries had his initials in the "Done" column, but there were still a dozen repair jobs that needed attention. He left the workshop, shutting the lights off first.

He looked at his watch, and jogged towards the staircase. After two flights, he was back on the ground floor directly across from the arcade. The room was dark. He turned on the lights. All the games sat lifeless. The blank screens on the video games reflected the fluorescent lights from the ceiling. It was a depressing sight, like seeing an amusement park in the fall after it had closed for the summer. To remedy this, he reached up to a small metal door in the wall, and flicked a couple breakers in the electrical panel. The room immediately became animated with flashing lights and an energetic orchestra of electronic sounds.

It was a small room with two pinball machines, a couple of racing games complete with driving seats and steering wheels, and four stand up video games. There was also a prize game with a claw that could be manoeuvred to grab a stuffed animal from a pile inside the glass booth.

He went to the token machine. The door was slightly ajar. He pulled it open and took out a handful of tokens.

He sat down in a plastic contoured racing seat, attached to the *Cruizin World* racing game. He put a token into the slot and grabbed the steering wheel. He had, at one point or another, tried every car in the game. Tonight he chose an orange VW Beetle and raced through a desert course in Africa. He came in first place and got the sixth best high score. He entered LSTMAN when prompted to put his name in to the top ten score list. When he did, the top ten list showed ten identical names: LSTMAN.

He spent the rest of his time going from game to game. He had mastered all the video games, but he liked pinball the most. There was something appealing to him about the simplicity of the solitary silver ball rattling around the confined space.

When it was 7:20, he stopped playing and shut down the games using the electrical panel then turned off the lights. He took the five flights back up to his floor. At this time of day, he did not dare risk taking the elevator.

Once on the fifth floor, he approached the door directly across from his own room, took out his key card and opened it. Being the middle of summer, there was over an hour of daylight left, but the room was beginning to darken already. He turned on the lights for the entrance.

The vacant suite was larger than his, with a separate bedroom, a main living room and a separate small den with a TV area and a couch. The den was an interior room with no windows, and could be sealed off from the rest of the suite by closing the door. This is where he would spend the next few hours. Just outside the den sat a red portable Honda generator. A thick black extension cord ran back into the den, and was plugged into a power bar behind the TV cabinet. He started up the generator which was supposed to be a quiet model but still made a lot of noise.

He checked his watch; 7:29. He walked out of the suite and stood in the hallway with the suite door open, and waited. Within a few seconds all the lights in the hallway turned off, as did the light in the suite behind him. It was exactly 7:30. He did not know why he did this every night, but he liked to witness the power go off. It was childish, but the novelty had not worn out yet.

Back in the suite, it seemed to be even darker than it had been when he first entered it five minutes earlier.

He reached into his back pocket and pulled out a small Maglite flashlight and returned to the den closing the door carefully behind him. The sound of the generator was hushed to a quiet hum. With the door closed the room would be pitch black. He turned on a floor lamp that was plugged into the power bar and turned on the flat screen TV. There was no picture, no sound, just a plain blue screen. The words "Cable - No Source" appeared in one corner of the screen. He bent over and turned on his XBOX 360 video game system.

For the next couple of hours he entered the world of *Grand Theft Auto*, becoming engrossed in the digital world and forgetting his own: running around a city full of people, doing errands for crime bosses and corrupt public officials, racing around the busy streets at high speeds smashing into other cars and pedestrians that got in his way.

When he started to feel tired, he saved his game and turned everything off using the power bar switch. He used his flashlight to guide him out of the room and turned off the generator.

The entire suite was now dark. He had one important evening routine to complete before going to bed. With flashlight in hand he walked to the opposite end of the living room to a wall of curtains. He picked up a pair of binoculars that were sitting on a small end table, and then turned off the flashlight. He reached out and pulled the curtains open to reveal the sliding glass doors leading to the suite's balcony. He slid the door across and walked out. He was hit with the warm, welcoming summer air and felt exhilarated.

Leaning against the balcony railing he surveyed the landscape outstretched before him. From this vantage point, he could see for miles into the distance. And all he could see was darkness. No street lights. No houselights. No car headlights. Once the sun went down, darkness took over.

Normally on a summer night, the resort's quaint retail village was a beehive of activity. Music from the patios and the laughter of tourists enjoying themselves would reach up to the top of the hotel. A cheery radiance from the lights of the restaurants, pubs and open air patios, would fill the sky with a yellow haze. Now, the hotel grounds below and the village beyond lay silent and dark. The various colourful buildings had been diminished to mere black silhouettes.

The features of the landscape were transformed into rough dark shapes. The rounded mountain range became a black outline ending at the dark bluish, night time sky. The only lights in view were the twinkling stars in the sky.

What he was looking for was any type of light in the darkness. No lights meant no signs of life. These days of course, a light source was more likely to be in the form of a bonfire or the faint glow of candlelight in a distant window. Tonight, like a long string of other nights, he saw no lights at all. He knew that any light source would stand out in the darkness regardless of how far away it was. He stood there waiting and watching. A few minutes later, satisfied that there was nothing out there, he turned around and went back into the suite closing the balcony door behind him and drawing the curtains fully closed again.

He switched on his flashlight, and placed the binoculars back onto the table ready to be used again the next night. He left the suite. The windowless hallway was even darker than outside. If he turned off his flashlight, he would be enclosed in complete blackness. He turned the beam onto the door of his room and entered.

To complete the routine, he went onto the balcony of his suite. This side too was dark. He waited, eyes squinting to see any trace of light in the landscape, any signs of life in the darkness. All the houses and buildings were now hidden in the sea of darkness. No lights from vacationers enjoying themselves on their cottage decks, or sitting around a campfire in the back yard, or sailboats lit up cruising Lake Arnette.

The solemn scene was in strange contrast to the warm summer air that invigorated him. The weather continued as it always had, oblivious to what was going on. He stood waiting, observing, and enjoying the fresh air. In the past, he could look out into the horizon and faintly see the sky illuminated by the distant town lights. Now even that area was dark.

Satisfied that there were nothing to see, and growing tired he went back into his dark room, pulling the curtains completely closed behind him. He was not sure how he would react now if he did see a light. It had been a few months since he last saw one. Thinking back, he wished he had marked the date on his calendar, but if he was guessing, it was probably sometime in late March.

He lit a candle, then stripped down to his boxers and t-shirt and sat on the side of his bed.

He put his key card into the drawer on his bedside table. Before he closed the drawer, he took out his name tag and wiped it on the sleeve of his shirt to give it a shine.

Etched with black letters was written:

The Grand Summit Place
Martin
Houseperson

The name tag had sat in the drawer unused for a few months. There was no need to wear it. He put the name tag back into the drawer.

Martin put fresh batteries in the alarm clock. The clock came to life, flashing 12:00. Checking his watch, he changed the clock to the correct time and set the alarm so he would not wake up late again.

From the kitchen cupboard he pulled out three large prescription bottles. He took one pill from each bottle, and swallowed them with a gulp of bottled water. At the age of eight Martin was diagnosed with a rare blood disorder, and since then he had to take medication every day. In the end, it was probably the blood disorder that saved him.

With the alarm set, he got into bed, and turned his flashlight off. The room was illuminated only by the glow of the alarm clock.

Tonight, like most nights, once he went to bed he had nothing else to occupy his mind, so he thought about the series of events in the past few months. The reason why there were no lights anymore.

The reason why he was alone.

3

The virus spread quickly. In less than four months, the world's population was decimated. The number of survivors is unknown. A census is difficult when no one else is around to count.

The virus started out in a small tropical island, popular as a vacation destination. Thousands of tourists from all over were avoiding the dreary, damp days of fall to vacation in paradise. There was a never ending cycle of guests who would arrive, stay a week, go home then be replaced by new guests. The infection spread this way as the travellers returned to their normal lives of going to work, attending school, shopping, visiting relatives, participating in activities. The opportunity for the pathogens to spread, even during the course of a single day, was exponential.

The first death occurred at the end of October. An otherwise healthy father in his thirties died ten days after having returned home from visiting the island for a family vacation. The cause of death was listed as a severe respiratory infection. The man had contracted a strange infection while on the island, but when his family displayed similar symptoms yet remained somewhat healthy, the father's death was downgraded to an unfortunate accident. News of his death did not go beyond the obituary page of his local newspaper.

The death of a popular, young Hollywood star a few days later however, was international news. Within minutes following the death of the actress Solara Carnegie, various internet news sites were reporting her passing. Newspapers and TV stations followed suit. An autopsy completed immediately the following day revealed that she had died from an unfamiliar infection.

Earlier deaths with similar characteristics came to light. A small number of people had died quietly in hospitals all over the world, but the deaths had not been linked together. The International Centre for Disease Reporting determined that the infection was a new virus strain and was able to trace the origins of the virus back to a specific resort Solara had stayed at on vacation.

ICDR officials conducted an on-site investigation at the resort and learned that a group of travellers who had arrived with symptoms of the common cold were at the resort the same time as Miss Carnegie. One overly concerned guest was seen by the house physician and was told that she had influenza. The ICDR was able to get a culture sample from the guest's visit to the doctor and determined that the guest actually had contracted human metapneumovirus. Investigators were still puzzled however; human metapneumovirus is a common, generally benign viral infection that mostly affects young children. Solara's autopsy showed fungal lesions in her lungs and brain which did not fit with the characteristics of human metapneumovirus.

Further investigation at the resort area revealed that neighbouring land had been clearcut to make way for the development of another resort. The clearcutting involved the removal of a forest of red gum trees and almond trees. Investigators deduced that as the trees were cut and removed from the area; spores from the trees became airborne and travelled into the resort area. These spores were then inhaled and colonized the nasal cavity and lung tissue of the guests. The investigators were also familiar with this infection, known as cryptococcus, that it can be life threatening, though rare but not contagious.

Tissue biopsy samples from Solara's lungs were used to determine that a genetic recombination had occurred with the cryptococcus and the human metapneumovirus creating a new viral strain. The new virus would feature the worst of the two infections, deadly and highly contagious. It could be transmitted like the common cold by sneezing, coughing or touching surfaces that have the virus on them.

Miss Carnegie's death announced the existence of the new virus to the world. Officially the virus was given a clinical name by the International Centre for Disease Reporting which consisted of a series of forgettable numbers and letters, but the media almost instantly started calling it "The Solara Virus" in honour of the actress. This moniker caught on with the public and the virus became known as Solara or simply The Virus.

As soon as news of the virus was made public, thousands of travellers came forward to disclose that they too had been to the resort and had since returned home with Solara symptoms. Culture testing confirmed that those who had visited the island had contracted the virus and had been unknowingly spreading it in their communities. Unlike influenza which mainly affected the very young and the elderly, people of all ages were being infected with the new virus.

The actress's death captured people's attention. She had been a spokesperson for healthy living. She did not use drugs or alcohol, and was a vegetarian. The fact that she was young, only in her twenties, combined with her healthy lifestyle made people around the world fearful of the new virus.

From the beginning, international health officials tried to reassure the public that Solara would behave like any other virus and follow a predictable path. They simplified the standard infection process into four stages, beginning with the incubation period when one is first exposed, and ending with the recovery phase with the person returning to normal health. The two middle stages were characterized by differing severity of symptoms.

It was a confusing time for many amid the early days of the infection. The experts were saying one thing, but the virus was behaving differently. Solara quickly proved that it was a unique virus. The incubation period for Solara lasted up to ten days instead of the usual five days as with most viral infections. During this time, the infected did not have any symptoms and were not aware that they had contracted Solara, yet were still contagious and unknowingly spreading the virus. When the second stage developed and symptoms appeared, they were identical to those of the common cold; a runny nose, fever, sore throat, nagging cough, headache, and fatigue. Since it was cold season, many were unsure if they had caught a cold or indeed had Solara. World health officials declared a worldwide crisis that the infection was on a pandemic scale. Yet the symptoms were more of an annoyance than what could be perceived as a dangerous virus. For the afflicted, the worst that could be said about Solara was that it seemed to last longer than the cold, but was otherwise a tolerable inconvenience. Also, in the two weeks after Miss Carnegie's demise, less than a handful of Solara related deaths were reported.

The public became bored and lost interest in news stories about the virus. Since it was no longer a hot topic, the media responded by ceasing any updates about the virus. Since there were no media updates, the public assumed that the virus was not as severe as originally stated.

Initially, no vaccines prevented the Solara infection. Similarly, existing antiviral medications to combat the symptoms were ineffective, and current treatment strategies for Cryptococcus involved weeks of administering anti-fungal medication and in extreme cases using intravenous therapy. All health officials could offer was advocating preventative measures such as effective hand washing techniques, the use of sanitizing hand gel, or avoidance.

Pharmaceutical companies did not hesitate to capitalize on the opportunity to be the first to create a vaccine. It did not take long before one corporation successfully produced a viable vaccine. Governments and health officials out of fear of losing their jobs, and facing outcries of inaction were eager to have a solution for the public. The new vaccine was promoted as a saviour. Skeptics who raised questions about the short testing time were rebutted with the response that the vaccine was a variation of an existing vaccine used for the SARS coronavirus outbreak and just needed some minor tweaking to make it effective against Solara. The public was told, "Trust us, we're experts." Millions of batches of the vaccine were purchased by governments all over the world.

As the virus continued to spread, like a fair weather sports fan, the media jumped back on the bandwagon to provide news items about Solara. Each day the public was inundated with updates in newspapers, television, radio, and the internet about the number of confirmed cases in different countries. The media had the unintended role of both spreading information and creating paranoia.

There was a rush to take the vaccine. Clinics were set up in local community centres, veteran halls and even shopping malls.

In larger cities there were reports of people lining up for hours to get their shot, some getting in line in the darkness of the early morning long before the doors would open. The demand was so high, that in some areas, restrictions had to be put in place so that only the elderly and children were given the vaccine at first.

At some point, it became apparent that the vaccine was ineffective. Those who had been inoculated were still catching the virus. Eventually it was revealed that the vaccine had been rushed through a modest clinical trial that did prove positive results at the onset. Unfortunately during the testing phase, the virus was in an undetectable incubation state and the pathogens remained dormant in the participants for several days, resurfacing only after the vaccine had been declared a success.

The vaccine created a false sense of security, and actually accelerated the spread of Solara. Anyone who was inoculated returned to their daily lives spreading the virus instead of staying home to avoid others. When they did display symptoms of Solara, many truly believed they were immune, and concluded that they had caught the common cold or the seasonal flu.

During the second stage, the symptoms seemed to linger without getting better or worse. What was not known however was that the infection was slowly multiplying throughout the lungs while showing no adverse signs.

When the third stage arrived, it was heralded by the need for immediate medical attention. In the third stage, the infected would suddenly wake up feeling feverish, have breathing problems, muscle stiffness, and feeling fatigued to the point that they could barely move. It was during this stage that lung damage began to occur from the fungal masses that had been slowly replicating. During progression, some masses would break off, enter the bloodstream and travel to other organs in the body including the brain.

The severity of the third stage surprised the public and medical officials alike. By early December, the demand for medical attention was overwhelming. Compounding the challenge was the fact that patients were presenting with different stages of Solara. Doctors had the unenviable task of triaging the infected and sending those with minor symptoms back home untreated.

Healthcare systems at every level were not prepared for the sudden influx of patients. Family doctors could not accommodate their own patients. Emergency rooms were full beyond capacity. Serious cases in the ER were admitted to the hospital, at first to the Intensive Care Unit, but when the ICU was filled, other departments within hospitals were taken over. Individual hospital rooms would be occupied with up to a half dozen patients, some in beds, some on stretchers or cots. When hospital rooms were full, the sick occupied stretchers in the hallways. Many were too sick to be discharged home, and so remained in hospital. To combat the spread of infection, most hospitals banned visitors from entering the facility.

As hospitals became full, community centres and hockey arenas were converted into makeshift infirmaries with row after row of cots set up for the infected. For millions around the world, Christmas Day was spent in the hospital or at a temporary infirmary. When the word spread that the hospitals were full, many people felt that using the community hall did not sound like an appealing alternative. Many simply stayed home instead of seeking treatment.

Then came the fourth stage, the final stage, death. There was no recovery stage with Solara. It came suddenly without warning. There was no obvious transition into the final stage. While the second stage of the virus lingered for over two weeks, the third stage was over in a couple days. The final cause of death was a combination of respiratory failure and central nervous system breakdown. Thankfully, death for most came after they had already slipped into a coma.

By the end of December, the final stage was striking in large numbers. The military had the grisly task of going from house to house collecting bodies. Transport trucks with refrigeration trailers were used to efficiently collect large quantities of the deceased from places such as apartment buildings, hospitals, and the makeshift infirmaries where multiple deaths occurred in a short time span. In larger urban areas, bodies were temporarily stored in warehouses until time allowed for proper burials. The reality was that there were too many dead, and too few remaining to clean up.

With the ban on visitation, those who were in hospitals died amongst strangers. There were a rare few who were *lucky* enough to have an ailing family member occupying a hospital bed beside them.

In the end, the effects of the virus where nothing like what people would have expected from watching movies or reading books. The virus did not turn ordinary citizens into crazed, murderous zombies who attacked and fed on the living. The highways were not clogged with vehicles, as people tried to flee the cities; the dead drivers slumped over the steering wheel, the passengers stiff in the back seat. People did not die in the streets coughing up blood on the asphalt.

In the real world people died in the consoling confines of the hospital, or spent their last hours at home in the comfort of their own bed.

In the real world, the end was peaceful.

4

Martin woke up on time the next morning. Lying there, he reflected on how the virus had affected him. He searched for a memory of the first time he had heard about the virus, but no concrete date came mind. Sometime in the fall, he thought. In hindsight, it should have been a significant event, but then again, there were other recent viral scares that had come and gone, Krippen, H1N1, SARS, Motaba. None impacted him personally.

"We were caught up in getting ready for ski season," he had told himself countless times.

In the beginning, like most other people, he discounted the potential impact of this new virus. It seemed to be affecting people far away from the idyllic setting of the resort he called home.

He recalled a conversation he had with a valet, Eli, after Halloween when the virus was first making news. Martin was clearing the fall decorations out of the lobby: giant orange pumpkins, dried corn stalks, and platters of large crimson and yellow maple leaves arranged like potpourri. Eli had a unique way of looking at things which made him more interesting to talk to than most of the other staff.

Eli had told him, "Think about it Martin, the hotel business is all about high turnaround. They want the place full all the time. They want people coming in, staying, leaving, and then replacing them with all new guests. On the weekends you got the families driving up here from the city, you got the university kids, and then you got riff raff from all over using the discount coupon they printed off the internet. Then they go home, and their rooms are filled on Monday with the suits here for their big corporate conference. Then the cycle starts all over again on Friday night. The same rooms being used over and over again. It's only like, what, November third or something, ski season is about to start. We are going to have a full house right into April, one hundred percent occupancy. Last year we had snow until, like, the first week of May for Christ sake. This place is going to be crawling with the virus for a good five months. We're like sitting ducks man. And you live here. At least I go home and get out of here at the end of the day."

Eli liked to go on rants sometimes.

Martin remembered the date of the first snowfall last year, November fifth, he had written it on his calendar. The ski slopes opened the very next weekend.

He liked Eli. He was a young snowboarder who had been at The Grand for a year. He finished high school and was just working at the hotel to be close to the slopes. Eli lived in a ski chalet five minutes away, renting it with four other guys. They all worked at various places in the resort, one at the ski rental shop, one was a ski lift operator, and two others worked at a pub. All of them, like Eli, were young and delaying university so they could live the snowboarder life for the time being. There always seemed to be a guy couch surfing at Eli's place, a friend from back home or a pro up for the week for a competition. Some of the young guys had been living at the resort for a couple years.

He had been at Eli's chalet a couple times, once for a Wii and weed party. He played Wii but passed on the marijuana. Another time he was there for a poker night.

Despite Eli's doomsday prognosis, most of the staff were swept up in the excitement of the season. The guests always filled the hotel with an elated energy, and last year was no exception. Despite the shadow of the virus, the hotel was always full. People who did have flu-like symptoms thought that fresh country air and a couple days of relaxation at the resort would make them feel better. For many guests, the virus was the furthest thing from their minds as they focussed on enjoying the vacation they had booked months previously. Compounded to this was the fact that the virus was still in the first stage which presented with not much more than the sniffles and a slightly sore throat.

Once the virus became more widespread however, Martin's interest, like many others' increased. He read news stories daily

31

in the national newspaper. He looked at updates on the internet and found a website with an interactive map that showed confirmed cases around the globe. Once he had jokingly said to a co-worker, "I might move to North Dakota or Prince Edward Island, no one has the virus there yet."

He still thought this was somewhat funny, and it drew a faint smile as he lay there in bed. But he had made that joke in November, when the death toll was minuscule and people were still downplaying the virus' severity.

Later on, this same website showed the number of deaths per country, state or province, and when the numbers were significant, the report was narrowed down to cities around the world.

The scenario at the hotel played out like out Eli had predicted, people from all over came to stay, bringing the infection along with them like the luggage they were dragging into the hotel. While they were at the resort they were spreading it to the village nearby as they visited the shops, the pubs, and the restaurants. And as they travelled to the resort, they were spreading the virus at all the stops they made along the way, from the gas stations, to small town grocery stores, to the McDonald's they ate at for lunch.

By the end of November, staff started to become sick too. The most vulnerable were staff who had frequent one-on-one interaction with guests such as waitstaff at the restaurant, front desk reception staff and room attendants who spent most of the day inside the guest rooms. Eli had taken to wearing black leather driving gloves all the time. He said it was to protect him from the contaminated surfaces in the cars he parked.

Martin had seen many different people come and go. Due to the nature of the business, the hotel was a seasonal employer, letting most staff go during the slow months of spring and fall and hiring a full staff compliment for the winter and summer months. He learned not to get too attached to any co-workers since they might not be around for long. In the beginning, he had made some friendships, only to be disappointed when they moved on. Now, he was friendly and amiable, but limited his emotional attachment with co-workers.

In early December, Martin attended a meeting for all staff. Management was stressing the importance of team work and personal sacrifice for The Grand during the crisis of staff shortages. All available staff were required to work in any department when asked.

At the end of the meeting he walked out with Eli. Eli was upset. "Do you believe that shit? I like being a valet. Rich people pay me to park their Porsches and Range Rovers. They think I am going to be a bus boy in their crappy restaurant, or, like, vacuum the conference rooms? I sure as hell ain't gonna be scrubbin any toilets, cooped up in a guest's room with all the germs doing maid duties. No way, man, I'll walk."

A couple days later he saw Eli wearing shorts and a Grand golf shirt, folding towels by the indoor pool.

Other staff were helping out too, reception staff were cleaning guest rooms, and managers were working the front desk. Since he was always healthy, Martin filled in for all roles: maintenance, reservation agent, room attendant.

Lying in bed now more than half a year later, his thoughts turned to Frannie, the first staff member to die due to the virus, and how Nadine had told him about the death. Frannie and Nadine both worked as room attendants.

He relived the scene of when he first heard. The memory was now like a movie clip in his mind.

He is standing alone in the service elevator holding a cardboard box filled with rolls of toilet paper.

The door opens.

Nadine walks in crying, " Frannie died," she blurts out.

He utters a muffled, "oh", nothing else. He's not sure what else to say.

He does not move. In the silence, he just stands there leaning against the faux wood grain wall, staring at the top of the cardboard box.

The elevator moves, then stops and the door opens. He pushes past Nadine. It is not his stop but he gets off quickly anyway just to break the unbearable awkwardness.

33

He didn't know how to handle that situation, how to respond appropriately to the news, or how to comfort Nadine. He was always socially awkward. He remembers being hit with a suffocating sensation that made his head go foggy when he heard "Frannie died."

Frannie had caught the virus early and was off work for about three weeks straight before she died in the hospital. He had talked to her a few times before, but just in passing, just being friendly. He knew she was young, in her early twenties, with a couple kids. A single mother struggling to make ends meet on a minimum wage job. Frannie was always talking about her kids, fondly giving updates to anyone who would listen as to the funny things they would do. Martin didn't know what happened to her children after she died, maybe the grandparents took them in their care. He knew the kids' father was not in the picture.

"Christmas around the corner, what a shame," he thought at the time.

Like the rest of the resort staff he was shocked. There were reports of deaths in other regions but staff still thought that death would never come to the resort.

Frannie's death brought the reality of the virus to The Grand. He began to wonder if other people who were off sick would die too. Would he ever see some of his co-workers again? Would he get sick? He was still feeling normal while most of the staff were showing some symptoms of the virus.

As days passed, more and more staff would go off sick, some would return in a couple days, some would be off for a week then return out of necessity to pay the bills. A couple of the younger ones who were hired just for the ski season, went home to their parents to recuperate, never to return.

Martin's thoughts jumped next to another memory from that time.

He walks out of his room into the hallway. Three doors down, a paramedic is backing out of a room. This is Nick's room, another employee who lives at the hotel. The end of a gurney comes into view. On the gurney is a black vinyl bag, obviously a body bag. Martin can make out the shape of upturned feet, like they were under a black bedspread.

Paramedics usually work in pairs. This one is alone.

The gurney is too long to fit into the narrow hallway. The paramedic squeezes past the gurney back into the room. He lifts and pivots the end off the floor, so that the gurney is now in the hallway. He drops the end with a muffled bang on the carpet. Martin watches the paramedic's back as he walks away, pushing the gurney down the hall.

One of the last times he saw Eli was on a lunch break. Deaths were becoming more frequent and common place everywhere.

Eli had told him one of his concerns. "What gets me is the whole like, logistics of the cleanup, the collecting of the bodies of people who have died at home. In November some buddies and I made a trip to Toronto to a ski and snowboard show. I'm sittin in the car and I'm thinkin about how the virus has caused some deaths, and I'm wonderin what happens if this becomes major? As we're drivin, I'm seein all these high rise apartment buildings and condos. They're like, 20, 30 stories high. There must be a few thousand people living in each building. Just one building! And like, there are tonnes of these buildings all over the goddamn city. Realistically, to check every single unit, to remove bodies for even one building it could take days. You expand that by the number of buildings in all of Toronto and it's like, impossible, even if you had the whole army on the job. Then you start thinkin about every house, we're talking about thousands of houses. And that's just for one city. Then we're drivin home, passing farms, little piddley towns, villages, smaller cities. The whole time, I'm thinkin, all these people, what's gonna happen to them? All the people in every province, or I guess state in the US. It blows your mind. The problem is, there may be no one left to do the cleanup."

Eli continued, "And if there aren't enough resources to clean up the bodies, then there sure as shit, aren't going to be enough resources to keep the peace. Soon things will get out of hand. People will start looting, setting things on fire. With no police presence, it will be a free for all. People will change. To survive

35

people will do anything. You may not know who to trust. Think about it."

Eli was fired a couple days later. For his personal safety, Eli insisted on walking around wearing a dust mask to reduce the amount of germs he breathed in. From the beginning management banned the use of any type of respirator, saying that the sight of hotel staff wearing such apparatus sent the wrong message to guests indicating that The Grand was not a safe place to stay. After several warnings, Eli was terminated. He however was more than happy to return to his hometown to be with his family.

Before Eli left, he said "Martin, I leave The Grand in your capable hands. What is there, like, six staff left including you?"

Martin replied, "Ya, I think so. At least everyone left is still healthy."

Eli was quick to add, "For now."

5

Slowly the number of people showing up for work at the hotel dwindled. Many were either at home sick or had left to be with loved ones. Although management did not want to report it, the news of staff deaths still leaked out through the grape vine.

As the weeks passed, the number of guests staying in the hotel also declined as people's priorities changed. People were either too sick to travel or opted to stay home with an ailing family member. As occupancy rates plummeted, many staff did not see the relevance of coming to work. Some could see the writing on the wall, and did not want to spend their last days cleaning bathrooms, or parking cars for the few guests that did show up at The Grand.

It was a quiet Christmas. Less than twenty rooms were occupied over the holiday season. Usually, the hotel was sold out from December twenty-third to January second.

By January third, only five staff members were coming to work: Yvonne, the Financial Compensations Lead; Shaun, the manager of The Innsbruck; Liz from the reception desk, Ed from maintenance, and Martin.

As for guests, there was only one family in the hotel who had been there for a week to celebrate New Year's. All of the family members showed early signs of the virus. The parents were hoping that a holistic approach of fresh air, relaxation, and healthy eating, would help combat the virus. As the only guests in the hotel they were treated like royalty and said that it was the best vacation they had in a long time. The remaining staff became close to the parents, their eight year old son, and their four year old daughter. When it was time to leave, the family was restored mentally, but the virus was still present in all of the members.

After the family departed, only Martin, Yvonne, and Ed seemed healthy. Liz and Shaun were starting to show symptoms of the virus. Liz told the rest that she would not be coming back until she felt better. Optimistic like so many others, she still clung to hope that she would get better and be back to work soon.

Shaun was usually a bundle of inexhaustible energy. He often put in twelve or fourteen hour days during the busy season, sometimes helping out by waiting tables, bartending, or even cleaning the kitchen at the end of a long day so his staff could go home on time. He always seemed to have as much energy at the end of the day as he had when he walked in the front door in the morning. With the onset of the virus however, he was lethargic and had regular coughing fits. Regardless, he was dedicated to The Innsbruck and continued to show up for work. Despite having no staff, he still felt a responsibility to keep the restaurant open just in case customers did show up, but the family who were staying in the hotel, were the last customers to visit the restaurant in over a week.

The day after Liz gave word, Martin went to talk to Shaun in his office. He found Shaun asleep, his head on his desk. It was only two in the afternoon.

Shaun did not come back the next day. Yvonne called Shaun at home. She woke him up. He told her he was going to sleep for awhile and might come back in for the evening to check on things. He did not come to work that night. When Yvonne phoned him the next morning there was no answer. She tried again later in the day, but there was still no answer. They all knew that if there was even a slim chance that he could make it in, Shaun would drag himself to work.

Although none of them had been to his place, Yvonne knew his address from filling out his paycheque stubs, but no one volunteered to check in on him. No one said it out loud, but Martin, Yvonne, and Ed, knew it was over for Shaun. They never heard from Shaun again. The restaurant stayed dark from then on.

At age 58, Ed was the senior maintenance employee and knew everything about the hotel. Management valued his ability to fix things that normally would require calling outside technicians or tradesmen. Overweight, Ed shuffled along through his duties at his own pace. He had the belief that if you were going to do something, you might as well do it right. Like Martin, he was dedicated to his job and stuck around to ensure that the hotel remained running. During the last weeks, Ed taught Martin about the operations of the hotel, showing him the heating system, the plumbing, elevator mechanics, and the electrical configuration.

Martin had spent a lot of time with Ed over the years at work. They would often stop and talk as their paths crossed. Although Martin did not smoke, sometimes he would sit outside with Ed while Ed had a cigarette and talk shop.

Ed lived in the neighbouring town of Paradise Falls, a half hour's drive away. Martin had been to Ed's house once for a BBQ and met his wife Mary. Ed and his wife had two adult children who had moved out of the area, and now had families of their own.

Two days after Shaun left, Ed announced that he would not be returning to work. Although Ed himself was healthy, his wife was sick. He wanted to be with her for her last days instead of wandering around the bowels of the hotel. Ed's son had also come home with his wife and their baby. Ed's daughter had passed away mid-December. Ed wanted to be with all of his remaining family members.

Ed spent his last day at the hotel reviewing all the mechanical workings of the building with Martin. Ed predicted that if things continued as they were, the electric company would eventually stop functioning, and everywhere would be without power. One of the last things he did was to show Martin how to use the large generator which would kick in as soon as power was lost. Ed carefully explained how it worked and how to keep it going.

At the end of the day, Ed pulled his Ford Ranger pickup truck to the front of the hotel. Yvonne gave Ed a hug goodbye. Martin extended his hand, but Ed pulled him in and gave him a big bear hug. As he got in his truck, Ed looked up at the hotel one last time, then got in the driver's seat and closed the door. Martin saw a tear running down the big man's cheek. Ed drove down the road and gave a friendly honk with his horn. Yvonne and Martin waved goodbye then went back inside the hotel in silence.

Yvonne had been with the hotel soon after it opened. She was hired in haste after the original Financial Compensations Lead quit to move onto a more lucrative position two months after the hotel opened. With the chosen candidate gone, the General Manager was desperate and selected Yvonne from the pool of candidates that were rejected at the beginning of the hiring process. Front line staff had misgivings about Yvonne. She had one of those job titles that no one knew what it meant, and most staff did not know what she did.

She was divorced with no children. Although she was only 56, a diet consisting mostly of cigarettes and Coke made her overly thin and look at least ten years older. Years of smoking had etched permanent creases around her mouth. Her cheeks were sunken, and her skin was an ashen colour. Gossip around the hotel said she was an alcoholic. During the weeks that the virus spread through the hotel, Yvonne remained healthy. Staff said that between the alcohol and the cigarettes her body was probably pickled, and her lungs impenetrable to the virus germs.

At the end of December, she decided to move into the hotel for convenience instead of commuting the twenty minute drive back and forth every day. With the other management staff absent, she was asked to assume the role of Manger on Duty by corporate headquarters. She reluctantly accepted on the agreement that she could have a one bedroom suite free while she stayed there. Since the hotel was almost empty anyway, her wish was granted.

Since moving in, she kept to herself which was her nature. In the past, instead of interacting with other staff, she would spend the day at her desk, only leaving to have smoke breaks. She would miss frequent manager meetings with the excuse that she had too much work to do. She even ate lunch at her desk, and had a small microwave put in her office to heat up her lunch.

When remaining staff were asked to fill in for those who were absent, Yvonne would only help out at the front desk. She refused to help clean guest rooms, or cook in the restaurant kitchen. And, she only helped out when prodded. Yvonne would never volunteer to assist.

Two days after Ed left, Martin found Yvonne sitting at the lobby bar reading a novel, and having a glass of wine. It was only 3:30. She kept the wine bottle close, within grasp. It was half empty. Martin did not know if she opened it that day or if she had found it that way on the bar shelf. There was a couple balled up napkins beside the bottle.

Martin walked up to her. "Hi Yvonne, how about I make us some supper," he offered.

Yvonne put her finger on the page to mark where she was reading and turned to Martin. "Hi, um sure, but don't go to too much work on my account."

She then turned back to her book without saying another word.

As Martin headed off to the restaurant he heard Yvonne blow her nose.

In the walk-in freezer he found a large bowl of fettuccine alfredo covered with plastic wrap. "Shaun" was written in black marker on the wrap. Martin assumed that Shaun had put it aside to eat later. It would still be good since it had been kept in the freezer. Martin heated it up on one of the restaurant's gas stoves, and also toasted a loaf of garlic bread which he also had found in the freezer.

Within forty-five minutes he was back at the bar eating dinner with Yvonne. They made small talk about the hotel and the situation, but Martin could tell that she would rather be left alone. Yvonne was reading her book and eating at the same time. Five minutes after they finished the meal, Yvonne announced that she was going to go up to her room to relax. She took her book and a new bottle of wine.

Martin did not see her again until the next morning when she was going to her office just after ten. Martin went outside and shovelled the sidewalks out in front of The Grand. He wanted to make it safe for anyone who might show up. The roads had not been plowed lately, but they were clear enough that vehicles would still have no problem driving around. As far as Martin could tell, the resort's plowing crew was unaccounted for. He noticed that the County's Road Maintenance department was still periodically plowing the county roads, but not as diligently as usual. He assumed the entire department was probably down to one dedicated worker. Martin did not see a single person or vehicle the entire time he was outside.

When he came inside there was no sign of Yvonne. At five o'clock he called her extension to offer to make supper again.

There was no answer. He called up to her suite. She told him she had already eaten, and was going to just stay in her room and rent a movie off the TV. She sounded like she had a sore throat, her voice was even more raspy than normal.

Martin spent the evening reading by the fireplace on one of the plush leather sofas in the lobby. He was still holding onto hope that someone might walk through the front door.

Once it got late and he was ready to go up to his room, he locked the front doors. With no staff to monitor the entrance overnight, he did not want to leave the front doors open. First however, he set up a patio table under the carport with a note and a walkie-talkie so if anyone came they would see the table. The note gave instructions on how to use the walkie-talkie to contact hotel staff so the guest could be greeted at the door. Martin would keep his own walkie-talkie sitting on his bedside table all night. This way Martin could let any visitors into the hotel.

The next morning Martin did not see Yvonne at all. Around 10am, he went to her office but she was not there. Unsure of her whereabouts, he resumed his duties. He did not want to wander all over the building if she was simply outside for a smoke, or doing laundry. An hour later he returned to her office to find that she still was not there. He was starting to get worried. He then checked the smoking area outside but she was not there either and there were no signs that she had been out at all that day. Usually there were fresh footprints in the snow, or fresh cigarette butts thrown on the ground.

Using a house phone near the elevators, Martin called her room. He let it ring a dozen times. She did not answer. He went directly to her room and knocked on the door.

"Yvonne? It's Martin."

He waited twenty seconds. No answer. He knocked again, louder. "Yvonne?"

Still no answer. She could be asleep with her bedroom door closed, he reasoned.

He used his key card to unlock the door. He opened it a few inches and called into the room. "Yvonne?"

There was no answer. There were no lights on in the room. Martin opened the door fully with swelling apprehension.

Daylight strained through the drawn curtains giving the room a gloomy, unsettling appearance. He liked the rooms when all the lights were on, it was more congenial. He had not been in Yvonne's room since she moved in. The room was a mess and reeked of stale cigarette smoke. A collection of empty wine bottles were lined up on the kitchen counter, along with dirty plates. He did not see Yvonne in the immediate area of the living room or kitchen.

Yvonne had a one bedroom suite with the bedroom separate from the open concept living room and kitchen area. Her bedroom door was wide open and ten feet away from where Martin stood. He slowly approached the threshold to her bedroom. Inside it was dark. She had the curtains pulled completely across the windows. From the doorway he could see that Yvonne was still in bed. She was covered by a single, thin, white sheet, pulled all the way up to her chin. She was curled up on her side, her back to Martin. The sheet clung to her thin frame like a shroud. The thick duvet, and other layers of the bedding were piled up on the floor in front of her bed.

"Yvonne, you ok?" he said, barely more than a whisper, as if not wanting to startle her, not wanting to break the silence.

She did not respond.

He reached out to touch her, hesitated with his arm half extended, then pushed on her bony hip. "Yvonne?"

She did not move. She was stiff. He took a step back hoping to see her side rise as she breathed. The sheet did not move at all. She was not breathing.

His heart racing, he rushed out of her suite and closed the door behind him. He sat down in the hallway and leaned against the wall. He was sweating. He did not know what to do.

He sat there for a couple minutes in shock, then went into the room across the hall and sat on the couch. Using the yellow pages he looked up funeral homes in the area. He spent the next few minutes phoning all five funeral homes listed in the local yellow pages. No one answered. Each time he got an answering machine. For one place he got a recorded message informing that "the mailbox is full please hang up."

Then he tried calling 911. The phone rang several times before the operator picked up. He was put on hold. He waited on hold for five minutes, all the while in disbelief that he was on hold for 911. When he did get to explain his situation to the operator, he was told that the deceased were not a priority, and there would be no assistance. The operator also told him that she did not have any current information on services in his area. She then abruptly hung up the phone.

Martin leaned back on the couch. He had never had to dispose of a body before. There were always other people to do that, emergency response personnel, funeral home owners. In the past few weeks he had cleaned up after someone had died in a room, but that was after the body had already been taken away. He thought of just leaving her where she was. He sat there until his anxiety made him too jittery to sit still any longer. Then he resigned himself to the fact that he would have to deal with the situation. He stood up.

"Just another dirty room," he told himself.

He went down to the housekeeping storage area and got one of the large Rubbermaid carts and returned to Yvonne's room. The cart looked like a plastic bathtub on wheels. He pushed it right through the front door and positioned it parallel to her bed. He pulled the sheet over top of her head so he did not have to look at her face. He rolled her over onto her back and pulled her legs out straight by the ankles. It felt like grabbing onto a couple 2x4 pieces of lumber. He pulled the fitted mattress sheet completely overtop of her, leaving the bare mattress on both sides of her. He rolled her over onto her stomach cocooning her in the sheets, then pulled her right into the waiting Rubbermaid cart. Her rear hit the bottom of the cart with a thud. She was now lying in the cart in a "V" shape with her head and feet sticking upwards. He threw all of the remaining bed linen on top completely covering her. It now looked like he was simply pushing a cart full of dirty linen, like he had done hundreds of times before.

He took the cart to the main floor and headed to the restaurant. He continued on through the immaculately clean kitchen. In this particular instance with its stainless steel work tables and white tiled walls, it made him think of the morgues he had seen on TV.

He stopped in front of the large, floor-to-ceiling walk-in freezer. He pulled on the metal handle and opened up the door. A cloud of icy fog rushed out past him. The freezer was a large room twelve feet long by eight feet wide with galvanized metal walls. Chrome wire shelving racks lined the walls. The racks were still full of boxes of bulk quantities of meat, vegetables, and partially prepared entrees and appetizers.

Martin pushed the cart into the centre of the freezer. He took one look back at the cart as he left. As he closed the door, a vacuum force from inside pulled the door firmly shut. In the last second, the crack between the door and the outside freezer wall turned black as the interior light went out before it shut completely. Yvonne was in her frigid tomb.

Martin left the restaurant and walked into the empty silent, lobby. Except for Yvonne and Ed he had not seen anyone else for over a week now.

He went up to his room and looked out from his balcony. He did not see any signs of life outside. The surrounding area as far as he could see was deserted. The roads were empty of cars. He did not see anyone walking around. The ski hills were empty and the lift chairs sat motionless.

He was alone.

6

Martin spent most of the next day cleaning Yvonne's room. He pulled one of the Rubbermaid carts directly into her room. She had accumulated a lot of garbage in the short time since she had moved in. Several plastic grocery bags, knotted at the top and bloated with trash were jammed in the cupboard underneath the kitchen sink. A small blue plastic recycling bin in the corner of the kitchen was overflowing with water bottles, a rolled up magazine, and old food that had been scraped on top of the recyclables.

Despite having a dishwasher in the room, Yvonne had used all the glasses and plates until they were all dirty. All the dirty dishes were spread throughout the entire suite. One wine glass was on the top of the toilet tank, another one in the glass shower stall. He found a dinner plate on the bedside table that she had used as an ashtray. An empty Canadian Club whiskey bottle sat beside the plate. It too had been used as an ashtray, the butts in the bottom of the bottle swimming in the last ounce of whiskey. He even found a cereal bowl outside sitting in the snow beside a lawn chair. The cereal bowl too had been used as an ashtray.

He collected all the garbage. Some had been shoved under the bed. As he threw black garbage bags into the Rubbermaid cart, empty bottles would clang together. He packed up all her clothes and the few possessions she brought with her and put them in a bag to be disposed of with the rest of the garbage. He saw no need to keep her items. The smell of smoke had permeated everything she owned.

Before he left he put on an air ionizer machine to eliminate the offensive odour of cigarette smoke. He would come back in a couple days to make the bed with clean linen and add fresh towels once the air quality was restored. The room would then be guest ready once again.

In the past if this happened, the guest would be billed a cleanup charge of $300 for smoking in the room. This did not happen very often, the type of clientele The Grand attracted was more respectful.

As the last remaining staff member, Martin spent the first couple days after Yvonne's death hanging around the lobby to watch for either staff or guests who might show up. No one came. The reception phone did not ring. He would check for messages, but there never were any.   By day three of being alone, Martin was starting to accept the fact that maybe no one was coming.

Being the only employee he would have to assume all roles: houseperson, maintenance, reception, manager on duty, valet, even restaurant staff if needed.

Four days after Yvonne died, Martin was dusting the elevator vestibule on the fourth floor. Martin polished each elevator door with stainless steel cleaner until they were gleaming. He then vacuumed the area. As he turned his attention to the next task of dusting the blinds, he spotted a car parked by the front entrance under the carport. His heart started racing. During busy times, this was a common sight, but not now.

Even though he had only been alone for a few days, the sight of the car was unsettling. Martin did not see anyone near the car, and he could see that the car was empty. He had no idea how long the car had been sitting there. He was surprised that the first emotion that came to him was not relief but dread. Deep down, he liked being alone in the hotel.

The front door of the hotel was unlocked so Martin assumed that the occupant or occupants of the car could now be inside his hotel waiting to check in.

Martin pushed the button for the elevator. It seemed to take forever to come up to him. When the elevator arrived, Martin rushed in. As the elevator descended he paced around the confined space.

When the elevator door finally opened he ran out but slowed down his pace to hurried steps so as not to appear panicked as he made is way down the hallway. He found the lobby empty. He stopped by the reception desk and scanned the area. He could not see anyone around. He went out the front doors. The sky was filled with steel grey clouds. The day had alternated between freezing rain and wet snow. As a result, slush had collected at the bottom of the car's windshield.

The car was empty, as was the front sidewalk.

Martin walked back into the hotel and called out, "hello?"

No answer.

He would have to search the floor. As the seconds passed the uncertainty of the car's occupants filled him with anxiety. Who was in the car? How many people were there?

He went into the middle of the lobby. Two hallways exited the lobby, one on his right and one to his left. He had already come down the one on his left from the elevators. He turned and went down the hallway to his right. Due to the shape of the hotel, he could only see thirty feet ahead of him before the hallway veered off on an angle. When he came to the first bend, he saw a lone man walking towards him. The man was wearing a long black wool coat, and carrying a small leather suitcase.

"Hello!" the man called from twenty feet away. "I was beginning to think this place was deserted. It looks deserted."

"Oh, sorry," Martin said, as he looked beyond the man to see if there was anyone else.

The man realized what Martin was doing. "Only me I am afraid," he said.

A wave of relief flushed through Martin. The stranger did not look hostile, in fact he looked like the type of guest that frequented the hotel. He had the appearance of a businessman or company executive, slightly overweight, balding, middle aged, well groomed.

"Sorry sir, I was on another floor. I am the only one..." Martin paused, he did not know how to phrase the rest of the sentence. "I am the only one still working," he continued. "Are you looking for a room?"

"Yes," the man replied. "My name is Stewart Redman, pleased to meet you."

"I'm Martin," he replied and shook the guest's extended hand. "I can check you in sir, if you would like to follow me back to the front desk," Martin instructed.

Martin led him down the hallway towards the lobby.

"Thank you, I knew this was a resort area, and it was on my route. I thought it would be a good rest stop. I saw this place from a distance. On this gloomy day, I could see that the lights were on. It stood out like a beacon, so I made my way here.

When they got to the front desk, Martin turned on the reception desk computer. "You'll be the only guest here. What type of room would you like, Mr Redman?" Martin asked.

Stewart did not seem shocked by this revelation. "Well, I guess I get the pick of the litter," he said jokingly. "And, you can call me Stewart."

"You're right. All the rooms are waiting and ready to be occupied. We have the standard hotel suite, plus suites that range in size from one bedroom, one bedroom with a den, two bedrooms, and one bedroom with a loft. And of course the largest room, the Presidential Suite."

"Well, I'm only passing through, but I think I will take the Presidential Suite. Why not? Who knows how much longer money is going to be useful so I might as well spend it now. I cleaned out my bank account three weeks ago before something happened, like the banks closing or if we lost power. I'm not sure if the banks could even tell me how much money I have if they did not have access to their computers."

Martin nodded as he booked Stewart into the Presidential Suite and gave him a key card.

"This time of year the rate is $1000 a night, but under the circumstances I think I can give you a deal. How does $500 sound?"

"That sounds fair," Stewart agreed.

"Let me get your bags, and then I will take your car to the underground parking garage after you get settled in. I am happy to give you the full service, despite the current situation," Martin offered.

"I will only need the green suitcase tonight," Stewart instructed. He handed Martin the keys. "Underground parking? Perfect. It'll do her good to get away from the snow and freezing rain for the night."

"Nice car," Martin commented looking at the light blue vintage sports car parked out front. "When I first saw it, I didn't have time to appreciate it, I just saw it as someone was here."

"Thanks, 54' Mustang," Stewart informed him.

Martin went out to the trunk. It was full. Besides the green suitcase, there was a duffle bag, a red plastic gasoline can, and several overflowing grocery bags. Martin could see that the back seat was also full of bags, and a couple cardboard boxes full of canned goods. A bigger suitcase sat on the front passenger seat. The suitcase was heavy so Martin put it on a baggage cart along with the bag Stewart had been carrying.

On the elevator ride up to the fifth floor, Martin said, "I hope you are not disappointed with the Presidential Suite, the name is misleading. It's just a moniker for the largest room in the hotel. It's not opulent like you see in the movies. Try and think more in terms of a rustic ski lodge type presidential suite."

"No worries. I just want to be able to tell my folks I stayed at the Presidential Suite. I'm on my way to see them. Tomorrow I will drive the remaining four hours to their place in Stovington."

The Presidential Suite was in the centre of the hotel on the top floor. Martin opened the door for his guest when they arrived.

"Wow!" Stewart exclaimed when he entered.

The front door opened into a large open concept living room. On the opposite end of the room a wide river rock fireplace stretched from floor to ceiling. Flanking the fireplace were equally impressive floor to ceiling windows. A door in the bank of windows led to the balcony that stretched the entire length of the suite. Three large black leather sofas were arranged in a "U" shape to face the fireplace. The room had its own bar in one corner, and in the other corner was a small baby grand piano. Martin showed Stewart around the rest of the suite including the kitchen, a TV room complete with a 56 inch flat screen TV mounted on the wall, and all three bathrooms. The master bedroom was at one end of the suite, and the two other bedrooms were at the opposite end of the suite. Each bedroom had its own gas fireplace.

"I like this arrangement," Stewart said when he saw how the bedrooms were separated, "Gets you and the wife away from the kids."

The master bedroom en suite bathroom had a large whirlpool tub, as well as a glass-walled shower big enough to accommodate two people.

"Welcome to The Grand Summit Place," Martin said when he was ready to leave Stewart in his room. "Why don't I make you a nice meal? You just relax. I will call when dinner is ready," Martin said as he exited.

"Thanks, I will freshen up, maybe have a shower," Stewart replied.

An hour and a half later, Martin had moved the car down to the parkade and had prepared a meal for the two of them. When Martin called Stewart to inform him that dinner was ready, the guest graciously invited Martin up to his room.

Stewart greeted Martin at the door wearing blue jeans and a black sweatshirt emblazoned with *Boston Bruins Stanley Cup Champions.* He was walking around in his bare feet.

"Thought I would invite you to dine with me. Make the most of the Presidential Suite. We could probably both use the company. Am I right?" Stewart asked.

They went to a long dining table in the kitchen. Martin had prepared fillet mignon wrapped in bacon, roasted baby potatoes, carrots and a garden salad.

"Wine ?" he asked.

"Definitely," his guest replied.

Martin took a bottle of red wine from the bar and poured Stewart a glass.

Martin looked down at the wilted lettuce. "Sorry about the salad, we're almost out of fresh vegetables except for some potatoes that have grown tentacles. I really had to pick through the lettuce to get any good leaves," he apologized.

"Sometimes the manager would bring in fresh produce himself from local farms, but this is the last of it, and the restaurant has not had a delivery for over three weeks."

"No problem, I am happy to have anything homemade right now. This is fantastic. Thanks." Stewart replied.

"Making the meal was easier than it looks, most items on the menu are pre-made, or come from the supplier ready to be thrown in the oven then served." Martin said.

"The restaurant actually closed down about ten days ago. Well, not formally closed down," Martin corrected himself. "Staff stopped coming to work. The manager was sick, but he dragged himself in to try to keep it open, but then one day he went home early and I have not heard from him since. There were no customers anyway, so I guess it doesn't matter."

Martin then told him about Yvonne and Ed and how now he was alone. "I have not seen anyone at all since Yvonne passed, no visitors, no staff, no tradesmen, not even anyone around the ski village and this place is usually booming this time of year. I have been just keeping busy, trying to work like usual, and maintain the hotel, waiting for guests, until I hear different from head office or somewhere."

"Well, I am not sure if anyone is going to bail you out," Stewart said. "I have been on the road for two days. I live in Madison, or at least lived in Madison and worked for an advertising agency on the twenty-third floor in a building downtown. Just like here, people stopped coming to work, and the office closed down a couple weeks ago. Most other places are closed now too."

Stewart took a bite of his steak, and continued, "I'm single, divorced about twelve years ago with one grown son on the other side of the country. He was single with no kids. He passed away in early December. I did not get to see him before he went."

Stewart paused, took a sip of his wine, "I have nothing to keep me in the city, so I decided to pack up some clothes, favourite possessions, and go see my parents. I call them every day. They're feeling under the weather but are tough. They are an amazing pair, both in their late seventies but very active. A few years ago, they decided to start eating healthy, and I guess it worked for them. My father has some hearing and vision loss, but that never stops him. He is still puttering around the house, working on the deck, or doing renovations or painting. Sometimes he does things just by feel, that's how bad his vision is. Last summer I pulled up in their driveway, he was outside working in a flower bed. He did not hear or see me pull up, but there he was outside pulling weeds. My mother is the same. She totally retiled her main bathroom herself and it looks great. Looking back, I regret not spending more time with them, or living closer. At least now I have that chance."

"How about you, don't you have family, somewhere else to be?" Stewart asked.

Martin answered without hesitation, "This is my home. I have lived at The Grand as part of a room and board agreement for over two years now. I don't really have anywhere to go. Never married. My father died six years ago. I was never close to my mother. She is remarried and lives ten hours away. I'm an only child. I have a few friends, but they are all really co-workers." He paused, then added, "Besides, who wouldn't want to stay in a five star resort?"

"It is a beautiful place," Stewart agreed.

"Excellent meal, why don't we retire to the living room, it's more comfortable there," Stewart suggested.

Martin quickly cleaned up and put all the dishes in the dishwasher as Stewart moved onto one of the sofas in the living room.

"Can I get you anything from the bar?" Martin asked.

"What do you have?" Stewart inquired.

Martin went behind the cherry wood bar in the corner of the living room. The shelves were stocked with unopened twenty-six ounce bottles of white rum, vodka, gin, Canadian whiskey, and scotch. In the mini fridge was a six-pack of Wellington Special Pale Ale, a six-pack of Coors Light, and a six-pack of Guinness. The guest would be charged the full price of any opened bottle or six pack. Martin lifted all the alcohol onto the granite countertop of the bar to display for his guest.

"Let's start with a Guinness," Stewart said.

Martin poured the dark brew into a glass. Then opened a bottle of Wellington S.P.A. for himself, and sat on a couch opposite Stewart.

Martin turned on the flames in the gas fireplace. It added an instant cozy feeling.

"Being here, I have been isolated from any news. The satellite provider for the area must have shut down, so we don't get TV at all here. Same goes for the internet. Can you tell me anything?" Martin asked.

"Well, since leaving home two days ago, I haven't seen many people along the way. In cities, because they have a higher population, more people are around, but not many. Most small places are like ghost towns, stores closed, no one driving around, sometimes you will see someone outside their house, but otherwise you don't see a soul. You may see house lights on, but then you wonder if someone is still alive, or if they just passed away with the lights on. Or you see the TV on in the living room, but there's no show, just static. Outside you see the driveway has not been shovelled and the car is completely covered in snow."

Stewart finished his beer with one large swig, "I've passed a couple of other cars travelling, but mostly I'm the only car on the road. I came across a small family owned gas station in the middle of nowhere and filled up my tank, plus the owner gave me a ten gallon gas can which I filled up and put in my trunk. I also bought a bunch of canned goods, boxes of cereal, snack cakes, bread, and bottled water. I took all the milk he had and put it in my cooler. He said he is just going to wait it out and help anyone who comes along. His family already passed away, and he is sick too. That was the last person I saw. That was yesterday morning."

"Why don't we crack open the scotch, what kind is it?" Stewart asked.

Martin picked up the bottle, and read the label, "um, Glenmorangie?" he said, not sure if he pronounced it properly or if it was quality scotch.

"Ahh, the good stuff," Stewart said.

Martin grabbed two goblets and poured a dash into his glass and a healthy amount into Stewart's.

"Not much of a scotch drinker," Martin admitted and sat back down.

"This may sound stupid, but see any signs of violence?" Martin asked.

"Well, that's a natural question. As you know, I've spent a lot of time on the road. On the whole, I've not seen any signs of violence. Most places appear untouched. During the last month some of the major cities had some rioting and looting, but these are the same places that have people looting after winning a Super Bowl, or their team makes it to the World Series. You know, mob mentality, a lot of people just looking for an excuse to destroy property. There were reports of home invasions too. People looking for food, stealing cars, that kind of behaviour. I travelled through some mid-sized cities, population around a hundred thousand which had some damage done to businesses, some had cars burnt out."

"But just this morning I passed through a small town about four hours from here. It had some vandalism. It was one of those small towns built around a crossroad with only a few houses, a variety store, a car repair shop, a diner and not much else. I wanted to stop at the variety store hoping it was still open and get some more supplies. When I pulled up in front of the store though, the windows were all smashed in, broken glass all over the sidewalk, a couple crushed empty beer cans, and some candy wrappers. I didn't even get out of the car. I could see inside that the store had been ransacked. Merchandise strewn all over, some shelves toppled over on the floor. But lots of food still left behind, canned goods, chocolate bars, bags of chips, bottled drinks. It could have been the work of a couple local kids having some fun, but I doubt it. The town seemed deserted. The virus would wipe out a small place like that in no time. More likely it was someone passing through. Maybe they took a few items, loaded up with beer and junk food, or only what they could fit in their car and for whatever reason decided to get their kicks by destroying the place. I was thinking of getting a gun. Might be wise. If these types of people are around, they are not to be trusted."

Stewart stretched his legs out onto the coffee table. "I know what you mean though. Maybe I've watched too many apocalypse movies, and while they seem farfetched, the thought still crosses your mind that gangs could form, roam around killing, raping, pillaging, all that stuff they put in movies."

"That's what I was thinking," Martin said, " movies like The Book of Eli, or Mad Max, or The Road, gangs terrorizing innocent survivors."

"Well, I don't think it will get to that extent, but very soon, any survivors will be living in a lawless society. I have not seen any military presence or even a police car lately. It's in your best interest to be cautious regardless of how ridiculous it sounds. I think it's best to head to a remote area with fewer people around, and a lower potential to run into undesirables. That's why I am going to see my parents, they live outside a small rural town. But, at least we don't have to worry about zombies," Stewart joked.

Stewart poured some more scotch into his glass. Martin had not touched his scotch at all. "Let me get you a beer," Stewart said when he noticed the untouched scotch, then emptied the contents of Martin's glass into his own.

"How are you feeling, I mean physically, you seem to be ok, no virus symptoms?" Stewart asked.

"Feeling fine. I have a blood disorder. Had it since birth, so somehow I guess that saved me," Martin said, then paused, "so far, but I still feel normal. How about you?"

"I have always been into alternative medicine, so right from the beginning, I consulted a naturopath, and started taking immunity boosters. I was skeptical about the virus vaccine right from the start and never got my shot, and looks like I was right after all. I have been taking the naturopathic remedy for the past few months and feel almost normal. I also tried to get more exercise, eat better and spend less time at my stressful job. I have a bit of a scratchy throat, but, I've felt that way before, and just doubled the dose and perked up. I just want to go see my parents before, well, you know."

Martin perked up, "Ok, maybe you will understand one of my reasons for staying then, since you mentioned your holistic philosophy. Around the start of the virus, I was reading this book, *Future Shock* by Alvin Toffler. It was written, like, forty years ago, but it's one of those books they say everyone should read."

"Oh, ya, I remember reading that back in university. Don't remember much about it," Stewart interrupted

"It's about coping with technological change, but what I got out of it was how change in general affects us. The author talks about how the normal life events such as a death in the family, moving, getting a new job, even going on vacation, causes stress. These things interrupt our routine lives and throw us into new scenarios. We have to make new decisions and come up with new coping strategies. He says too many new decisions could cause psychological damage for some people."

"Wait let me get my book, the quote can explain it much better than I am."

Martin ran down the hall to his room and returned five minutes later with the book in hand.

"I highlighted all the good quotes," Martin started to read:

If we are hit by so many novel situations that programming becomes impossible, life becomes painfully disoriented, exhausting and anxiety-filled. Pushed to its extreme, the endpoint is psychosis."

"So, I'm thinking, Solara forced all survivors to deal with multiple major life events all at once, job change or actually job loss, and not only death of a single family member which happens in normal life, but death of all family members, plus friends, co-workers, even strangers. All this in a short time span. Everything in the survivor's regular daily routine would have disappeared with no support or guidance."

Stewart listened intently, drinking his scotch.

Martin continued, "this idea of dealing with so much change scared me, so for my psychological wellbeing I decided to stay in my familiar setting of the hotel, keep to my routine as much as possible. So now, I don't have to make the decisions that other survivors have to make, like where will I sleep, what will I eat, who will I meet up with, all that stuff."

Martin flipped ahead to another page. "He even talks about disasters."

The disaster victim finds himself suddenly caught in a situation in which familiar objects and relationships are transformed.

"Skipping ahead a couple sentences..."

The environment is filled with change and novelty. And once again the response is marked by confusion, anxiety, irritability, and withdrawal into apathy.

Martin put the book down. "I think when he says *irritability*, he is just being polite or like, scholarly. In a disaster, or end of the world type scenario, I am sure that people will be more than irritable. I'm thinking certain people could be more like violent, savage, a higher extreme than just irritable. These people are who I am trying to avoid, if they are out there. So, I am staying right here, instead of wandering off into the unknown."

"You make a good point. This is the biggest crisis mankind has ever had to face, and for the most part we are forced to face it alone," Stewart said when he thought his host was finished. "Not everyone would be able to cope with all the changes. Heck, some people can't even cope when their cable TV goes out for the weekend. At least, I have a safe destination I am heading to."

"Well, I took advantage of the world coming to an end. Like my car?" Stewart asked.

"Um, ya," Martin replied.

"Just got it. I know it's not what you would expect. All the guys at the office have Jags, or Mercedes, or BMWs, or some big name SUV. I had a Lexus. But, I've always wanted an old Mustang. There's this classic dealership I would pass by every day on the way to work. The last couple months they had this Mustang sitting in the showroom. Then I thought, hell, I'm going to buy it. Might be my last chance. So a month ago I purchased it. I realize I could have waited, and probably just stole it when the virus took all the sales staff and the dealership closed, but I'm an honourable man. I paid cash for it. I love the car. It doesn't look quite as good now with the snow tires on, but I certainly needed them the last couple days. Madison doesn't get much snow, but it's been tough going to get here. You can tell that some of the roads have not been plowed lately, some side streets not at all, just a big snow bank at the entrance to the street. No accidents though. Maybe when I get to my parents I will start a collection of cars I have always wanted."

Stewart raised his glass, "Now, more than ever is the time to live in the moment, before those moments come to an end."

Martin could tell that his guest was getting tired. Stewart was slouching down, his head resting on the back of the couch. A combination of the long day of driving and the alcohol was taking its toll.

"Well, I think that's it for me," Stewart said following a yawn. He slowly sat forward, and with effort, got to his feet. "Think, I will have a soak in the Jacuzzi tub, another glass of scotch, then

hit the hay. Thanks for everything," he said with gratitude as he walked out of the living room towards the master bedroom.
  Martin said goodnight and left the suite.

7

After Martin woke up the next morning, he went straight down to the restaurant to make Stewart a big breakfast. Standing in the walk-in freezer, he glanced around taking a mental inventory of what was still available in the numerous cardboard boxes. The boxes had the tops cut off to show their contents, clear plastic bags of carrots, asparagus, spinach, baby roasted potatoes, french fries, and other vegetables. The Rubbermaid cart was still sitting there. Martin opened a box labelled 200 Sausages, it was half empty. He took out a dozen. He located a box of diced hash browns but it was on the other side of the cart Yvonne's body was in. He made a mental note to get rid of that sometime.

He reached over the cart, over Yvonne, frozen and buried beneath the layers of her bed linen. He grabbed a bag of hash browns. The freezer was quickly filling up with an icy fog. It was getting too cold to linger any longer.

He left the freezer and went into the walk-in refrigerator. Several cartons of eggs were still left. The restaurant boasted on the menu that all the eggs were fresh, purchased from local farms. The expiry date on the cartons said Jan 16. "Still good" Martin said to himself in relief, "Two more days until they expire. I'll be eating eggs for breakfast, lunch, and dinner for the next couple days," he mused.

When everything was cooked, Martin ate his portion standing up, his plate on one of the stainless steel prep tables in the kitchen. He washed it down with a cup of coffee. He liked Stewart, but he just did not feel like making small talk with his guest over breakfast. He would rather just deliver the breakfast, leave his guest alone, and then Martin could get on with his day. Martin filled a small carafe with coffee, poured some orange juice into a wine glass and set everything up on a room service cart.

When he got to the door of the Presidential Suite, he arranged all the cutlery and dishes in a presentable fashion. It was 8:45. It was that difficult time in the morning that made staff unsure about knocking on a guest's door. There was the possibility that the guest could still be sleeping, and would begrudge being woken up, but staff had to get on with their job which meant a long list of rooms to clean, and they needed to get started. Quite often though, the guest was already up eager to get the most of their stay.

He knocked on the door, "Room Service," he called out.

No answer.

He knocked again.

No answer.

"Maybe he's still asleep, or because the room's so big he can't hear me knocking," Martin reasoned.

Then something Stewart said the night before popped into Martin's mind, "Got a bit of a scratchy throat."

Martin used his key card to enter the room next door. He dialled Stewart's room number and let it ring. He lost count of the number of rings, then hung up. He tried again, just in case he had misdialled, but there was still no answer. Martin started to get worried. He had that sense of déjà vu. He started to perspire.

He was still trying to rationalize however, "maybe Stewart is just in the shower. He didn't seem sick last night. He can't be sick."

Standing in front of Stewart's door again he unlocked it with his card. The lights in the living room were off. The fireplace was still going. The room was dead quiet. There was no sound of the shower going. The living room appeared as it had when Stewart was heading to the master bedroom to retire for the night.

"Stewart?" he paused, "Mr. Redman, I have breakfast for you."

The master bedroom door was open but the lights were off. He approached the entrance to the bedroom with dread.

Two different scenarios entered his thoughts, one was that Stewart was dead in his bed, just like Yvonne, the other was that Stewart was dead, but still in his Jacuzzi tub. Stewart had said that he was going to have a soak before going to bed.

Martin's heart was pounding.

He stopped five feet from the doorway.

He wanted to turn and run, run from the suite. He wanted to hold off on knowing what the situation was. He wanted to cling to the idea that Stewart was still sound asleep in his bed, that he would just wake up on his own and talk to him later in the morning.

Leaving the room without knowing the truth however would be worse than just pretending that everything was ok. He took a few steps forward. He could feel a stream of sweat running down from his armpits. At the threshold to the bedroom he mustered the courage to take his gaze from the carpet and look at the bed. A window illuminated the room. The bed was empty. The sheets had been pulled up, and flattened out, the way guests will try to tidy up before they check out.

There was enough light to see that none of Stewart's possessions were visible, no clothes lying around, no suitcase. The en suite bathroom door was open, and the light was off. Martin glanced into the bathroom, none of Stewart's toiletries were lying around, only the hotel's face cloths, towels, and a used bar of the complimentary soap.

"He's gone?" Martin said aloud in disbelief.

He walked to the other end of the suite. Stewart was not in any of the other rooms.

Martin was so positive that Stewart was still in his room that it never occurred to him that he might have left without telling him.

He went into the living room and sat on the back of one of the couches to pause for a moment, then clued in that Stewart had left without paying.

Martin could not believe it. Stewart did not seem like the type of person to sneak out. He had even boasted about how honest he was and that he had paid cash for his new car instead of stealing it.

Then the thought crossed his mind that maybe Stewart left the money like how guests leave a tip.

Martin looked around the room. On top of the bar he saw a stack of money sitting on a piece of paper. He picked up the paper. Written on a sheet of notepaper was:

Martin, I would like to sincerely thank you for your hospitality. I decided to leave early and did not want to disturb you. I have left what I think is enough money to cover my stay, plus a tip. With any luck, maybe I could return to the hotel and see you in better times. Take care.

Stewart Redman

If I see you on my way out, then disregard the note.

Martin put the money in his pocket and left the room.

He still wanted to make sure that Stewart had indeed departed. He went to P2 where he had parked the Mustang the day before. He did not have to go far to see that the car was gone. The entire parkade only had a few cars.

Martin went to the reception desk, turned on the computer and completed the checkout transaction for Stewart's stay. Martin put the cash into the register. He was still hopeful that other staff would return or that maybe someone from corporate headquarters would show up to check on the property.

8

Back in December there was a power outage and although it lasted only an hour, Eli immediately thought the worst. The loss of electricity came at a time when businesses were starting to close down due to attrition. As soon as the lights went out, Eli said to Martin, "Oh my God man, that's it. The hydro company is kaput. I bet it's unmanned. Everybody off sick. We're never going to have power again. What if we have no power ever again? Who's going to know how to turn the turbines back on at the hydro station? Who's going to fix the power lines if they fall down during a storm? Not anyone can do that. They got those repair crews from the hydro company to fix that shit. What the hell are we supposed to do now?"

Then Eli rambled on about people being spoiled, "Twenty-first century man takes all this stuff for granted. All the conveniences in our daily lives we use without thinking, without appreciating. You flick a switch, the lights come on. You turn a tap, hot water comes out. You open the fridge, there's cold food. Then you got all the modern toys: laptops, flat screen TVs, air conditioning, iPads, smart phones, all that shit. Everyone's gonna go mental without their toys."

To Eli's relief, the power did come back on a couple hours later.

However, the entire region lost power for good in mid-February.

Although Ed and Eli had predicted it, the loss of power caught Martin off guard. Martin was vacuuming a guest suite when the electricity went off. Initially, he thought he had blown a fuse. He checked the electrical breaker box in the room, but all the breakers were still on. He poked his head out the room door and saw that the entire corridor was ominously dark. If the entire floor had no power, then Martin knew that the rest of the hotel must have lost power as well.

His first reaction was to sit and wait it out. Power outages were not uncommon in the area. Ed explained that it was due to the age of the hydro lines and transformers, and that the rural areas were not high on the utility company's list for upgrading. Often the power would go out, then would be restored a few minutes later. This is what Martin anticipated, as he sat there in the now dim guest room.

After ten minutes of waiting, Martin remembered the generator. He ran down the stairs and started it up. Even as he descended the steps he still felt certain that the power would come back on like normal. He had watched Ed use the generator before and had learned how to operate it. The generator was almost as long and as tall as a minivan. It had the capacity to provide the entire hotel with electricity during a power failure so there would only be a minimal interruption in electrical service for guests. Guests paying for five star accommodations did not tolerate inconveniences like no electricity. In the occurrence of an outage, staff could quickly start the generator, resulting in only a couple minutes of actual power loss to the hotel. On a full tank of fuel, the generator could handle the hotel's total electrical load for seventy-two hours.

It was not until the sun set that night, that Martin knew the entire region had no electricity. All he could see was darkness in every direction he looked. No lights anywhere. Martin went to sleep with a flashlight by his bed.

By the next day the power still had not come on. Martin assumed that like The Grand, staff had stopped going to work at the power company. Without staff to operate the power station the transmission of electricity stopped abruptly. Martin assumed the same thing probably was happening in other areas of the country too. Any survivors would be left without electricity indefinitely. Martin had no way of knowing if power would ever be restored.

He knew he had to conserve power, and that the supply of diesel on hand would not be enough to keep the generator running for very long. He would have to make preparations in the event that he would be without power for a long time, possibly forever. He would have to get a large amount of diesel fuel for the generator or do without electricity.

Martin knew of a local fuel company that made deliveries of diesel around the resort. After looking up the address in the phone book, Martin drove to Frank's Fuels in a Chevy pickup that had been left behind in The Grand's parkade by a staff member.

An eight foot high chain-link fence surrounded the property of Frank's Fuels. Martin used bolt cutters to cut the padlock on the front gate. The snow in the driveway was easily half a foot deep, and tall drift had formed on the other side of the gate. The cumulative weight of the snow would make it difficult for Martin to open the gate by hand. He got back into the pickup and pushed the gate open with the front bumper as he drove into the lot of Frank's Fuels.

There were no staff cars in the parking lot, but a couple company pickup trucks, a propane delivery truck, and a small fleet of assorted sizes of tanker trucks were quietly sitting in the deserted depot yard. An even layer of untouched snow covered the entire property, no vehicle track marks, no foot prints.

The office looked like a converted school portable. He trudged through the shin high soft snow to get to the office. He tried the front door. Locked. There was a small window in the door that already had a crack in it running from top to bottom. Martin smashed the window with his bolt cutter. He reached inside, unlocked the door, and went in. The room was already dusty. It looked like no one had been in the office for a few weeks. He was hoping that the keys to the fleet of trucks would be kept somewhere in the office.   He went to a cabinet hanging on the wall, and found a number of keys. There seemed to be enough keys to match the number of trucks parked outside. He grabbed a set of keys labelled Small Tanker.

He walked up to one of the smaller sized tanker trucks, leaving a path   in the foot deep snow behind him. Frank's Fuels was stencilled in faded orange and green lettering on both sides of the long cylindrical tank on the back of the truck. On the rear of the tank was the warning, "Diesel Delivery Keep 20 Feet back". A gage at the side of the tank told him it was full. The truck was an old Peterbuilt, maybe from the 80's, with a standard transmission. Martin had never driven a truck this big before.

It was a difficult journey home. He stalled the big truck numerous times. It took him forty minutes to make the twenty minute drive back to the hotel. His body ached from being jolted every time he stalled. He parked the truck beside the generator in the lower level of the parking garage.

In the first few days after the power went off, Martin was running the hotel business as usual. He did not alter the hotel's electricity usage at all, but he quickly learned how much energy the building consumed. Being February, the temperature was still around zero degrees outside. After a couple days of heating the hotel, and with The Grand operating under normal conditions, the generator unceremoniously ran out of fuel one day around 6 p.m., returning the hotel to darkness.

In response, Martin adopted several power saving measures. He completely turned off the giant HVAC unit that provided the heating, ventilation and air conditioning function for the entire hotel for intervals of four hours at a time. With the heating system off, Martin was walking around the building wearing his winter coat and gloves. Some days he could almost see his breath while still inside the confines of the hotel. He was surprised how quickly the temperature dropped once the heat was turned off.

He began the practice of shutting all power off before dusk and not turning it back on again until after daylight. He went further by keeping the power off in all guest rooms, even during the day. If any room needed electricity, Martin would manually switch the breakers in the room's own electrical panel. His room was the only one in the building that had constant power, mainly for his bar fridge. The restaurant's walk-in freezer and refrigerator were the only regular large consumers of electricity left permanently on. He also shut service down to all elevators except the service elevator. As a result of his conservation practices, he was getting multiple days out of a single tank of diesel from the generator. With the tanker truck handy, he could replenish the generator's fuel levels at any time.

9

Sitting at the dining table, staring into space, the piercing scream of the boiling kettle woke Martin from his thoughts about the winter months. He unplugged the kettle and made himself some coffee and two packages of instant Quaker oatmeal. As it turns out, Stewart was the last person Martin saw or spoke to. Martin used his fingers and counted back the months aloud, "Stewart was here in January, it's now August; so, August to July, June, May, April, March, February, January, seven months. God, seven months, I've been alone."

He had to stop the playback of the memories. By this point, he was no longer grieving, but still, he tried not to let his attention linger on the deaths, the list of people from his past he would never see again. For this reason he liked to maintain his work schedule, to keep his mind and his body busy. After he was alone, he quickly realized that time could go by slowly if you did nothing. There was a lot of time to fill in the course of a day; hours, minutes, seconds, but there was plenty of work to keep him busy. Once he got some chores done he could relax at night knowing that he had done something constructive and earned the rest.

He pulled out his notebook to see what he had planned for today. Without managers around, he had to create his own schedule and would write down tasks to do in future dates as he went along. To keep the hotel running there were certain things he could not forget. Some tasks required regular maintenance checks.

Once his breakfast was done he left his room to start the work day. He walked down the hall to the elevator. The hotel was already starting to get warm. It had been a hot, humid summer so far. He was feeling the effects of shutting off the air conditioning as the humid air sat thick and stale in the hallways.

The heat inside would definitely be unbearable for guests if there were any staying in the hotel.

He took the stairs all the way down to the lowest parking level. He stepped out of the stairwell to a mechanical droning sound thumping through the concrete chamber of P2. He passed empty parking spot after empty parking spot until he came to the end of the garage and the source of the noise. The generator was running full tilt. Beside the generator sat the Frank's Fuels tanker, unmoved, since he had parked it there in February.

He checked the fuel level on the generator. It was low, as he expected. He transferred diesel from the tanker to the generator's fuel tank until it was full. Martin had a personal contest to make the fuel in the generator's tank last as long as possible before refilling, and as weeks passed he had to devise new ways to use less electricity each time. It was getting to the point however that there were not many energy saving measures left to implement.

His concern was that when the tanker was empty, he would have to drive it back to Frank's Fuels. His ultimate motivation for conserving power was actually to avoid driving the big truck anytime soon.

He took out his daytimer, and put a check mark beside his hand written note "Generator", and then flipped seven days ahead to August 23, and wrote "Generator".

Working around the diesel fumes gave him the urge to go outside for some fresh air.

He took the stairs up the two flights and exited onto the main floor. He stopped in front of the double glass doors in the lobby that led to The Grand's private pool. Peering through the glass he scanned the hotel's rear grounds and the retail village on the other side. He saw no signs of human life. This was a routine he went through before ever going outside.

Feeling safe, he opened the door and followed the cobblestone path that led from the doors to the fenced in pool area. It was a beautiful summer day, presenting the ideal conditions for suntanning around the pool. The sky was a deep blue dotted with just a few small fluffy white clouds. His face was immediately warmed by the sunlight.

Normally on a day like today the pool would be filled with families. There would be a buzz of excitement captivating the area from happy guests enjoying their vacation. Sounds of children laughing and splashing would echo off the side of the hotel. Now the only sound was a faint summer breeze rustling the leaves of the trees.

A hundred or so lounge chairs placed around the pool sat empty. They framed the pool following its free formed curving outline, each chair conveniently placed a couple feet away from the water's edge so parents could lay back and keep one eye on their children in the water and the other eye on the magazine they were reading as they relaxed on their reclining pool lounger.

The forgotten lounge chairs were now starting to show small patches of black mould on their white plastic surfaces. The pool was in a similar state of neglect, its water now murky with a greenish hue. A family of ducks had taken up residence and shared the pool with the debris of fallen leaves, floating garbage, and sunken, bloated earthworms.

The pool was a popular feature of the hotel even during the winter months. Martin tried to maintain the pool after the guests stopped coming, but with a month of no guests, he shut the expansive pumping system down. He rationalized that if things turned around, he could always restore the pool. He also felt that in the aftermath of the virus the last thing anyone would be worried about was having a clean, outdoor swimming pool.

A few steps from the door sat a small opened walled hut, complete with bamboo pillars and palm leafs covering the roof. The bare counters would normally be covered with fluffy, thick pool towels neatly stacked. Guests would stop at the hut on their way to the pool and be handed towels by a young attractive pool attendant. Martin had never been asked to be the pool attendant.

He walked into the empty hut, opened a small cabinet under the counter and grabbed a spray bottle of cleaner and a rag. He looked for the lounge chair that seemed to have the smallest amount of black mould growing on it, and wiped it clean. He sat down, pulled the back rest up, and then stretched his legs out straight in front of him. He was glad he had decided to wear shorts today. The August sun was hot. He closed his eyes. His face started to feel like it was glowing from the sun's rays.

He stayed there for a few minutes relaxing. It was quiet, tranquil. He was content. He wrote "clean deckchairs" in his notebook as a future task. Since he was setting up his own work routine, he decided he would remain outside, but was not in the mood to scrub black mould off of the chairs for the next couple hours.

Looking through the black iron fencing that surrounded the pool area, he could see the hotel grounds needed some tidying up. To get to the grounds, he had to go back into the hotel. The pool area was completely fenced in to guarantee the privacy of the hotel guests and to ensure that only guests of The Grand Summit Place were enjoying the pool. He went back into the hotel lobby and took a different set of double doors that led out to the rear grounds of the hotel.

The hotel's back property ran the entire length of the hotel and stretched to a manmade creek a hundred yards away. A quaint wooden bridge led visitors over the creek to the retail village on the other side. On the edge of the village, visitors could have a game of beach volleyball in the sandy volleyball pitch, or play chess on a man sized chess board complete with three foot tall chess pieces.

Cobblestone paths meandered through the grounds of the hotel, leading visitors past well manicured hedges and native trees with small plaques in front of them telling the curious the tree's Latin and common name. Benches and picnic areas were thoughtfully placed here and there amongst the boxwoods, globe cedars, and perennial flower beds.

The resort had its own landscaping maintenance crew to oversee of all of the properties and to keep everything perfect, but without human nurturing, the foliage was turning wild. The grass was overgrown, the hedges were misshapen, and a blight of yellow dandelions dotted the once perfectly manicured lawn. By this point, the grounds had not been touched since fall of the previous year. All the greenery was left to the unkind elements of the frigid winter, sloppy spring, and hot summer.

Martin spent the next hour collecting garbage that had blown around. Periodically, he would look beyond his immediate area for any movement in the distance.

By the time he was done, the back of his neck was sunburned. He had forgotten about using sun block, and now every time he turned his head, the back of this shirt collar rubbed the sunburn with a scratching sensation.

He went back up to his room had a late lunch, and put some cream on his neck.

He spent the rest of the afternoon inspecting and cleaning four suites on his never ending list of rooms to go through.

The weather put him in the mood to have a barbeque. A patio attached to the hotel restaurant was usually set up as an all day BBQ buffet in the summer months. Martin turned on the propane and lit the BBQ to warm it up. As the flames danced, he scrubbed the grill, and could immediately smell the leftover grease sizzling on the lava rocks.

Entering the restaurant kitchen, he went into the walk-in freezer. He pushed the grey Rubbermaid cart to one side to get to the shelf that had boxes of meat stacked on top of each other. He opened up a box and picked out a large steak. Each steak was vacuum sealed in a plastic bag to preserve freshness. He would have liked to have a hamburger, but without any buns, all he would be eating would be the patty. Before he closed the door he stopped to look at the white sheets covering its contents in the grey cart. He sighed and closed the door with a resounding thud. He still had to dispose of the cart's contents, not a job he was eager to tackle.

As soon as he stepped outside he immediately knew that starting up the BBQ was a huge lapse in judgement. Smoke was billowing up into the sky from flames fuelled by the leftover grease of barbeques past. He was also hit with the sweet smell of cooking meat remnants, and wondered how far away the scent would carry.

He ran over to the grill, and turned off the propane tank. The flames from the element flickered out, but the flames on the rocks continued to dance away in stubborn defiance. He closed the lid to extinguish the fire. One last puff of smoke rose then died, dissipating into the air. He was sure that no one was around to see the smoke or smell the barbeque, but he still did not want to take any chances. He had no human contact for months, and he did not know what people would be like now. Would they kill for food? He did not want to find out.

Dejected, he returned to the restaurant and used the gas stove to cook his steak and boil some carrots. It was definitely not the same as a real BBQ meal.

After eating, and cleaning up, he still had over an hour before the electricity shut off.

Three nights a week Martin worked out in the hotel exercise room. In the past, staff were banned from using the Fitness Centre. Management felt that it was unbecoming for hotel staff to be seen using the gym equipment by guests. But now, Martin took the liberty to use the gym whenever he wanted. His interest in exercise was partially influenced by the movie Zombieland, which he had watched a couple times before Solara hit. He remembered the advice given by the lead character that cardio training is beneficial in a post apocalyptic world. The theory was that superior cardio vascular endurance would help if zombies where chasing after you. Though it seemed silly, Martin thought this was a good idea. He of course knew that the virus did not turn people into zombies in real life but he was not certain that people would not become hostile when their basic needs were taken away from them. If he ever had to evade someone on foot, his training could save his life. So, a couple weeks after being alone in the hotel, he started using the exercise room.

For the next hour he rotated between using the weight machines, the stepper, the treadmill, and the elliptical machine. The exercise room was on the second floor, and all the cardio machines were lined up in front of a wall of one-way glass windows overlooking the rear grounds and the village. Martin liked this view because he could also look for any activity outside while he was exercising.

Over the weeks he had grown stronger and his endurance had greatly improved. By the end of the workout however he was exhausted and ready to relax. After having a shower in the guest change room and towel drying the shower stall afterwards, he changed back into his work clothes and left the gym.

Before heading up to his room, he made sure all the exterior doors were locked, stopped at the bar and grabbed a vodka cooler.

Soon after he reached his room, the power went out for the night. It was still light out, but the sun was beginning to descend. With the curtains closed the limited natural lighting made his room dim.

The sun had not quite set, but it was dark enough that any lights in the distance would show up. He would start his lookout early tonight. The combination of exercising and being out in the hot sun had made him tired.

He went onto his balcony and sat down on a patio chair. He searched the immediate area and looked into the horizon and saw no lights of any kind. As he sat, the sky slowly turned from a dark blue to a deep purple as the sun disappeared behind the mountains.

He then went to the room across the hall and repeated the activity. Again no lights of any kind to be seen. Satisfied yet again that he had proof that there was no one else out there, he went back to his room and took his medication.

This is how he spent a Friday night on a beautiful warm August evening. He was in bed by 9:30. But tomorrow was Saturday and he gave himself the weekend off from hotel duties. Tomorrow he would leave the confines of the hotel and go pick up some groceries.

10

Civilization has always been built around a basic daily schedule of either work or worship, which would then dictate that day's identity within the week. Solara effectively dissolved the workplace and houses of worship, therefore disrupting the elements that determined the identity of the day. In the new world, a Monday was no different than Wednesday or a Sunday. The days could easily blend together becoming a blur. It did not take long before days lost their relevance, and therefore the week as an increment of time lost its relevance.

Before Solara, the workers at The Grand followed a clear, repeated routine. Fridays and Saturdays were special as families would arrive for the weekend. On Sundays, staff frantically cleaned all the rooms after the guests departed to get ready for new arrivals. During the weekdays, the hotel was busy with clientele partaking in a business conference. Once the virus took hold and Martin was alone, he quickly realized that days of the week essentially had no individuality. Martin however liked to keep order, so he continued to acknowledge time by checking off each day on a calendar hanging in his room. He was certain that he would have lost track of the actual date long ago without the use of his calendar.

For the past few years, Martin had worked almost every weekend. Due to the nature of the business, the weekends were the busiest days of the week, and like most staff, he was required to work weekends without question. Now that he was in charge of his own schedule, and with no boss, and no guests to cater to, Martin switched it around so he only worked Monday to Friday.

He still had some duties to do on Saturdays and Sundays, which either related to upkeep of the hotel or his own survival. Reserving supply runs for the weekend made it seem like he was doing something exciting on his day off.

On this Saturday morning, he planned to go to a local variety store for food. Before leaving his room, he went into the coat closet and grabbed a black canvas gym bag. Lifting it caused the contents to make a loud metal clang.

He stopped at the valet office in the lobby which served as a handy central location to keep the keys to all the vehicles still in the building. A few hundred gold hooks had been screwed into a large bulletin board to accommodate enough keys for all the guest rooms plus any visiting restaurant patrons. Now most of hooks were empty, with only about a dozen sets of keys left. A portion of the keys belonged to guests who had either passed away in their suites or taken away ill never to return. Some keys belonged to staff members who had abandoned their cars at work. Some like Martin, lived at The Grand. Two others, had to be driven home mid shift by someone else after they became too sick to drive home themselves. For these two, Martin had to break into their personal lockers to get their keys, which were added to the collection of keys hanging up.

Martin took a key embossed with a Porsche emblem, then went down to the underground parking garage where all the cars sat. Some of the vehicles had not been driven any distance for months. The thick layer of dust was proof of this. Martin made a mental note to spend an afternoon washing all the vehicles. He had parked all of them in the same remote section of the lower level of the parking garage, a section that was hidden from plain view and required a jaunt around a couple corners before the group of vehicles were seen. He wanted to keep them all together, yet hidden away since he was the only staff left to watch over them.

Martin stopped in front of a black Porsche SUV with dark tinted windows. Cayenne Turbo S was written in stylized silver cursive letters across the middle of the tailgate. He pressed a button on the key and the tailgate opened and slowly rose. He dropped the gym bag into the luggage area and closed the hatch door. Today he was going for a supply run and needed a larger vehicle. Of course he could have chosen the hotel's Chevy utility van, but he opted for the Porsche. He had driven the Cayenne once before just around the parkade, but today he wanted to get supplies in style.

A few weeks ago he had covered both front headlights and rear taillights of all the vehicles with black garbage bags and duct tape to hide the lights from being seen when he drove around outside. He did not want anyone seeing the daytime running lights which were a feature of most current models and also the tail lights every time he applied the brakes. He doubted that the owner of the $130,000 Cayenne would approve, but then again the owner was a guest who had died in December.

Martin slid into the two toned black and tan leather driver seat. He was sure that the Porsche designers had a more exotic name for the colour of the seats, but to him it was just black and tan. The Porsche logo was stitched into the head rests of all the seats. He was impressed with the attention to detail, even the dashboard and the steering wheel were covered in leather.

He started the Cayenne. The engine roared to life, ensuring him that he was not driving an ordinary SUV. The cavernous cement walls of the parkade amplified the sound of the engine as he drove through the levels to reach the exit door. He stopped, screeching the tires and got out. He had secured the bottom of the delivery door using an industrial strength padlock fastened to an eye bolt drilled into the ground. He unlocked the padlock, and set it aside. Using the remote control, he opened the door and drove out. Once outside, he stopped to make sure that the door completely closed behind him. The electric door would be difficult to open, and would delay anyone trying to break in long enough until he got back in a couple hours. The public entrances were safely secured with the same padlock method he had used here.

Usually it was not until he ventured outside that the reality of the current situation struck him. Inside the hotel remained the same as always since Martin was there to maintain the cleanliness. Outside however was completely different. Everywhere was showing the signs of neglect in the absence of human attention. Grass was overgrown. Garbage had blown and collected in trees and bushes. Weeds proliferated. Sand used during the early winter months to cover the snow and ice still sat on the edges of the roads and boulevards. Since the Township's roads department no longer existed, there was no spring clean up after the winter road maintenance efforts.

He turned and drove on the road that led past the entrance driveway to the hotel. It was a strange sight to not see any vehicles parked out front, or guests rushing in and out the front doors. Even in the slow times there was always some activity, even if it was just a bored valet pacing back and forth. Now the scene at the entrance was somewhat depressing. It was much more cheerful inside the hotel.

Across from the hotel entrance ran the thirteenth hole of the resort golf course. The grass on the fairway was overgrown to a length that would normally be considered the rough. Now the rough, which edged the fairway was over a foot long. He passed a green which in normal times would have the appearance of a carpet, but now was also overgrown, and was drying out in the heat of the sun with patches of brown. The flag stick still stood defiant in place, the flag waving in the wind with stubborn pride. It was customary for any golf course to have a large grounds crew working on the course every day from before daylight to after dusk . They would work diligently from soon after the snow melted in the spring to just after the first traces of snow in the fall. The golf course as it was now, was in a state of disrepair that would now take years to recover if things ever returned to normal.

The resort area itself was the size of a small town. During peak season the roadways were crowded with tourists zooming around and it could easily take up to ten minutes to get from one end to the other. The roads were now ghostly quiet. He saw cars, but they were parked quietly in front of dark chalets, condo units or in the parking lots belonging to other hotels. All the cars had a layer of dust on them. The properties of all these places were in the same state of neglect as the golf course.

It was a beautiful Saturday summer morning. He passed several houses. He should have seen fathers mowing their lawns, or kids playing catch on their front yard, or people out jogging, the normal scenes on a weekend morning. Instead he passed one lifeless house after another. The roads were empty and quiet.

Out of habit he stopped at an intersection despite the fact that the traffic lights blankly manned the crossroads.

Ten minutes later he pulled into the parking lot of a small plaza. The plaza had only four stores, a flower shop, a liquor store, a variety store, and an antiques store. The parking area in front was empty. The setting was nothing like Martin had seen in post apocalypse movies. There were no signs of looting. None of the windows were smashed. There was no garbage from stolen merchandise strewn everywhere outside. No dead bodies lying on the sidewalk. Instead, the front doors were still secure, the glass intact. Only a thin layer of dirt on the windows that had blown off the road indicated that the stores had been vacated for a while.

The plaza was on the main road leading to the resort and had been built long before the retail village was ever constructed. The plaza showed its age. It looked outdated and tacky compared to the trendy upscale boutique style shops in the resort. The dated façade of the plaza turned off tourists who preferred corporate owned retail stores. As a result, most tourists drove right by the plaza. The main customers were locals who had grown accustomed to paying the overinflated prices due to the plaza's close proximity to the resort. The only tourists that came to the mall were young adults, barely of drinking age, looking for a bargain on beer and whiskey.

A yellow plastic mobile sign with black removable letters sat on the edge of the road advertising:

LIQUOR ST0 E CANADIA BEER 24 BOT LES $15

Some of the letters had fallen to the bottom of the sign.

He drove around to the back of the plaza to the delivery lane and parked. The land behind the plaza was a swampy forest of mixed trees and wild bushes. There were no houses or buildings in sight.

He was still cautiously paranoid about anyone seeing him. He knew that if he continued to be cautious and discreet this practice would help to avoid any unwanted encounters. So his continual plan was to stay hidden and on alert. He had no reason to not trust survivors, but he did not want to find out the hard way that people had changed.

Martin got out of the Cayenne. From the gym bag in the trunk he took out a crowbar and bolt cutters.

Martin surveyed his options of gaining entry to the stores. This was his first trip to this location for supplies. Out of respect, he did not want to break the glass in the front doors. So far he had not seen any signs of looting or damage to any of the places he had been. He wanted to maintain the civility in what for all intents was now a lawless society. His goal was to get inside with the least amount of damage.

All the back doors were windowless, made of steel, and had a thick metal protector plate that overlapped the lock so no one could jimmy the latch. The only windows were small, about three feet long, and had metal grating over top of them. He spotted a metal ladder bolted to the wall leading to the plaza's flat roof. The bottom of the ladder was still five feet off the ground. Martin pushed a wheeled dumpster over to the ladder, jumped on the lid, then stepped onto the bottom rung. Once on the roof he crouched down and duck-walked to the front of the building. He wanted to survey the area from this height. He looked all around and saw no signs of life. He could follow the road for miles in both directions and also see other roads in the distance. He did not see a single car travelling anywhere.

He only needed to get into the variety store. He had no need to get into the others. Skylights provided natural lighting to the stores below. He went over to skylight above the variety store. The plastic dome was yellow and cracked with age. One side was hinged so that the entire dome could swing open, but a padlock held it securely in place. He rubbed away some grime on the dome and peered inside. The black and white linoleum tiled floor looked a long way down. He stopped to consider the possible outcomes if he dropped down. What if he broke his ankle or something when he landed? He sat down with his back resting on the skylight to review the situation. He had not thought this out very well. If he had one of those roll up chain ladders this would be no problem.

"I'm no cat burglar," he thought.

He abandoned the idea of getting in through the roof and went back down the ladder to the ground. He sized up the rear window and judged that he could probably squeeze through. A closer inspection showed that the metal security bars on the outside of the window were only held in place by a single bolt at each of the four corners. He grabbed a socket wrench from his duffle bag and removed the four rusty bolts. With the last one removed, the grate fell to the pavement below with a loud clatter.

He peered through the filthy glass, It appeared that the window was unlocked, the latch inside was free. He pushed on the window. It swung open. The window stayed in place upright. He went back to the SUV and grabbed few reusable shopping bags, then threw them into the open window. It looked like the window led to a small room, probably an office. A desk was sitting directly below the window. He boosted himself up, and head first, climbed inside. With both hands planted on the desk he pulled his legs through, and was soon kneeling on top of the desk.

On the desk, paperwork sat waiting to be completed. Beside the papers sat a white coffee cup. Green and brown fuzzy mould had grown in the bottom, replacing the last sip of coffee that had been left in it months before. A calendar on the wall was still set to January, the bottom of the page was starting to curl up.

He left the office and went into the retail area. All the shelves were still fully stocked with merchandise. Except for the lack of electricity, the store had all the appearances of being business as usual. One wall was entirely made up of glass door refrigeration units, their contents shaded by the dark interior. All of the perishable items like milk would be spoiled by now without electricity. Regardless, the expiry date had long since passed. Martin was not sure if all the drinks went bad, but he took a couple bottles of cola, two cases of bottled water, and some cartons of orange juice. He then filled his grocery bags with canned vegetables, Chef Boyardee Ravioli, peanut butter, fruit cocktail, soups, and boxes of instant mashed potato mix. The next stop was the junk food aisle, potato chips, Twinkies, chocolate bars. He selected a couple magazines as well. When he was done, he had five large size shopping bags overflowing with items plus the cases of water. He estimated the value of the items, and left $60 under the cash register. He knew that the owner was probably long gone, but it felt like the right thing to do.

He decided to leave the easy way, through the back door that was beside the office.

It took him two trips to get all his groceries from the store to the Porsche. He put the bags of groceries into the cargo area then slammed the door shut.

As he rounded the SUV, he noticed that the store window was still wide open from when he broke in. He did not want to leave it this way. He would need to come back again for more food eventually and did not want animals raiding the store. He knew that raccoons for sure would have no problem getting inside through the open window.

Back in the office, as he was closing the window, a quick flash of movement in the vacant land behind the plaza caught his eye.

He froze.

He had not seen anyone for months. A million thoughts ran through his mind including scenes from various movies of roving gangs of violent, sadistic, starving survivors.

Whatever made the movement was far off but coming closer, making its way through the bush, coming towards the building. Towards him.

The shape appeared from behind a cedar tree. It was a deer, a hundred yards from the back wall of plaza. Deer were common for the area, and he had been seeing more of them lately. He stopped to enjoy the moment.

Then behind the deer he saw a shadow, a dark shape creeping slowly. He could not make out if it was human or animal. Then another similar shape alongside it. The shapes were getting closer, following the deer, stalking it.

The deer sensed something and darted towards the plaza.

The shapes were now in chase.

Martin did not move from his spot and instinctively crouched down, his eyes now level with the bottom of the window.

He considered running to the SUV, but had a vision of being trapped in the SUV, blocked from driving away, the attackers shattering the driver's window and dragging him out onto the pavement below. Or if they were hunters, they could easily shoot him.

He decided to stay in the store. It was more secure. He could observe the predators while still locked safely inside the store.

The deer came into a clearing just on the other side of the SUV. The shapes behind approached the clearing as well but separated from each other. One branched off following the cover of the brush, but still coming towards the plaza.

The lead pursuer was visible now, a coyote or wolf of some kind, no too small to be a wolf. Its head held low in stalking mode. It was moving slowly, following the deer's path, but also edging closer, herding the deer. The deer sensed the danger. A third predator appeared. This one just stayed back and was now positioned in the middle of the other two coyotes.

He saw the action unfold before him as if watching a scene in a wildlife show on TV. The lead coyote ran flat out, the deer darted in the opposite direction, and veered towards the middle coyote but saw it, and continued running away from the lead coyote. Then the third, the hidden coyote, sprang from a bush twenty feet in front of the deer, the direction the deer had planned to flee to safety. The deer stopped, changed direction and ran towards the back of the plaza, and onto the asphalt. The hidden coyote soon gained ground and pounced on the deer's hindquarters bringing it down skidding on the pavement. Soon the other coyotes were on the spot.

The SUV was ten feet from the back door of the store, but the coyotes were only ten feet beyond the SUV, hovering over their kill. He would have to run in their direction to get to the driver's door of the Porsche.

Martin watched, his heart racing. He was starting to get a trapped, panicked feeling. He did not know what to do. As he was thinking, the coyotes started howling. An eerie sound, like babies wailing. It sent shivers down his spine. In the distance another howl responded. The coyotes started tearing into the fallen deer's flesh.

He went to the back door of the store and opened it without making a sound. He peered his head around the frame looking towards the coyotes. One sensing his presence stopped feeding and turned its head towards the door. It went on alert, stood up. One partner looked up too. Martin slammed the door shut as hard as he could to try to scare the animals away. He went back to the window. The coyotes were still on alert. The loud bang of the metal door slamming did not send them fleeing. They were not going to run off and abandoned their meal.

Then he saw more shapes coming from the bushes, more coyotes to join in on the feast, four more adult coyotes, and a few younger pups.

With humans gone, deer had freely drifted away from their usual feeding areas. Martin had seen a few wandering onto resort property lately. The absence from their traditional areas had probably impacted their predator's diets. The coyotes had expanded their hunting territory to find their prey. The coyotes were starving. He could tell by looking at their thin torsos.

Martin moved into the retail area. For some reason it made him feel safer. Being amongst all the cheery, brightly coloured packaging of the chocolate bars, Doritos bags, and Keebler Chocolate Chip Cookie bags, he felt removed from the savage reality of nature outside. He sat down on the grimy tiled floor behind the cash counter to think and review his options.

He did not want to stay at the store any longer than he had to. He wanted to go back to the hotel, back to his home, back to the security of his room on the fifth floor.

But, should he wait until they left or try to make a run for it to the SUV? How long would they be out there? He did not want to risk running to the car with the coyote pack only a few feet away. They would see him for sure. The coyotes could still be hungry. He had heard that in extreme situations, they have attacked humans.

He went back to the window in the office. They were still feeding. There was now a pool of blood on the pavement around the deer.

He decided to wait a while longer. With the decision made he started to feel calmer. Maybe they would just feed then turn back into the forest.

He returned to the store area. Martin slid the glass door open of a refrigeration unit, and paused to review the ample selection. The wire shelves were still full of a wide assortment of drinks in cans and plastic bottles, Coke, Pepsi, Sprite, root beer, juice, Gatorade, and water. He grabbed a can of Coke. On his return to the back office to watch out the window, he helped himself to a package of Twinkies. The Coke was warm and unsatisfying.

Even after he finished his snack the coyotes had not moved. A couple were still feeding, some were lying on the grass beside the carcass. Red paw prints were all over the pavement, like they had stepped in paint and walked away, except this was not red paint. One had left the others and was roaming around the far end of the plaza as if on patrol. Martin watched. It circled back and went out of view as it headed towards the wall of the plaza. Then he heard the distinct clang of metal hitting the ground. An aluminum garbage can. The coyote yelped with delight, having discovered something, maybe a rat, or food that might still be edible.   Martin knew then that they had found a good scavenging spot and would not leave anytime soon.

Then a thought occurred to him. Maybe the store owner had a gun somewhere. He searched around the office looking in the desk, then the filing cabinet drawers. No gun. No gun behind the cash register counter either. Chances are that this place had never been robbed, and the owner did not need a gun.

Pacing around helped him think. Then he spotted a firecracker display. There were firecrackers of various sizes but he selected a couple packages labelled Black Cat with red and yellow packaging, a fierce cat's face looking back at him. He ripped open the waxy package. Inside were two rows of three inch long fire crackers, their wicks woven together in the centre. He took another package an opened it up.

From the candy rack he found a small plastic pail stamped with the Double Bubble gum logo. He dumped its contents of bright pink gum packages into a half empty box of chocolate bars. Carefully, he twisted the wicks from all the firecrackers together to make one wick, and placed them in the bottom of the pail with the wick bent upwards. In total he had forty-eight firecrackers.

As he left the retail area he grabbed a lighter from a rack beside the cash.

Slowly he opened the back door of the store and set the pail on the asphalt. He knew this type of firecracker exploded almost instantly. Bending over, he quickly lit the wick. It immediately ignited. In one motion, he shouldered the door completely open, grabbed the pail by its flimsy handle and tossed it in the direction of the pack of coyotes.   Mere inches from his outstretched hand, the fireworks blew. A machine gun of cracking sounds rang out, amplified by the bucket and the echo off the cinder block wall of the plaza.

He bolted to the Porsche. He quickly covered the distance to the SUV and slammed the door shut behind him as he jumped into the seat. Through a haze of grey smoke he could see that the parking area was empty except for the abandoned deer carcass. He looked towards the forest, the last of the coyotes were scattering through the brush.

He was shaking so badly that it took several tries to get the key in the ignition and start the Porsche. The smell of burnt rotten egg firecracker smoke and the hint of the toxic melted plastic seeped through the air vents. Still panicked, he hit the curb as he rounded the corner to the front of the plaza, and drove up on the grass. He righted the steering wheel, then turned back on the pavement. He stopped to calm himself down before he ended up driving into a ditch on his way home.

He was safe now. When he felt calm, he turned onto the road and headed back towards the hotel. Twenty uneventful minutes later he was safely back inside The Grand's underground parking with the garage door securely locked behind him. Once parked, he rested his head back on the driver's seat, closed his eyes and sighed relief. He was soon back in his room with all his groceries. It was only 4 p.m. He did not leave his room again that day.

11

On Sunday morning, Martin woke up anxious. He had gone to bed early, emotionally exhausted from the ordeal at the plaza. As he lay there staring at the stucco ceiling, he went over a task he had been ruminating over since he left the variety store. A plan he lamented, but knew had to be done. The last thing he wanted to do was leave the hotel again, so he wanted to complete the task and get right back home as soon as possible. This time, every step was plotted out to limit the element of risk. The location he was headed to was familiar. A place he had been many times before.

After a quick stop at the valet office he headed down to the underground garage. This time he chose a dark green Land Rover Discovery. He knew the history of the Land Rover as a rugged, reliable workhorse of a vehicle that had seen service in African deserts, and were used by the British during World War II. The owner of this Land Rover lived in a metropolitan area two hours away and the most strenuous thing it was probably used for was going back and forth to soccer games and Starbucks.

After twenty-five minutes of driving, he passed a sign, Welcome to Hemingford. The next right turn was into the empty parking lot of King's Sporting Goods. It was a one stop shopping paradise for everything an outdoorsman would need: sporting goods, hunting, fishing, and camping gear. It even had a boat repair garage with four service bays. Although the region was famous as a skiing destination, hunting and fishing attracted visitors all four seasons. Even when the shore of the lake was frozen over, anglers came for the ice fishing.

Martin pulled the SUV in front of one of the service garage doors.

Similar to the plaza the day before, the store was intact. The large plate glass windows were not smashed. The doors were closed shut. The interior was dark. It was as if at any moment staff would turn on the lights and open the front door for the day. However, it was 10:15, normally the store would have been open already for over two hours to accommodate the fishermen eager to get an early start. Of course there were no staff left alive to open the front doors and Martin was the first customer in the past seven months.   Still, due to the store's unblemished appearance, Martin could not shake the feeling that he had arrived too early and was the first customer of the day.

This time he did not overly care about being respectful to the property. With a hammer from his duffle bag, he smashed one of the small rectangular windows that made up one of service bay doors for the garage. He cleaned off the broken jagged edges still caught in the frame and managed to squeeze through the tight opening.

Once inside, he used the rope pulley to open the garage door. Months ago he had noticed a mechanic open the door this way. Martin had marvelled that they had not advanced to electric door openers. Now he was glad they had stuck with the old, reliable mechanism.

He backed the Land Rover into the garage then closed the door again.

Ten feet away, a boat was up on a hoist. The scenario was obvious, the customer had passed away after leaving it for repairs. The mechanic died before completing the job, leaving the boat where it still sat six feet off the ground, and would sit for who knows how long.

A door at the far end of the garage led to the service centre reception room. Luckily this door was unlocked making it easy for Martin to get into the store. The room had an order desk and a small waiting area with a couple of warn out couches. The other end of the waiting room opened into the main retail area of the store itself.

King's had been open for over twenty years, and looked dated compared to the antiseptic cookie cutter national sporting goods retail stores spread throughout the country in malls, and big box super centres. King's, the size of a small department store, was cluttered, musty, and had a lot of out of date stock. Most customers viewed it as the perfect outdoors store where they could still find the hard to get items that the newer stores did not sell. Over the years, the owner had added display items, here and there, so by now the most of the store's walls and ceiling were covered with fishing, hunting, and sports paraphernalia. A large birch bark canoe was hung from the ceiling. Displayed haphazardly throughout the store were various mounted fish; rainbow trout, northern pike, largemouth bass, walleye, some with a red and white lure sticking out of their mouth for effect. A stuffed bison stood by the front door.

On his days off, Martin liked to borrow one of the company trucks to go fishing at Lake Arnette and King's was his favourite place to buy tackle. He could easily spend a couple of hours looking around. Today however, he was in a hurry, he wanted to get back home as soon as he could.

He walked past the fishing section. Two aisles of hundreds of different types of rods stood upright pointing at the ceiling. He turned to the back of the store. A large wooden sign with *Hunting* painted in a camouflage paint scheme hung from the ceiling on chains.

Behind a long counter, a large selection of rifles stood upright in a long stretched out row. At each end was a mounted stuffed deer head, with matted fur, and black vacant eyes. There were many rifles to choose from but Martin knew nothing about firearms. He had never shot or even held a gun. But he did know that he wanted a rifle with a scope and not a shotgun.

He went behind the counter and selected a couple of rifles from the rack. Both rifles had a scope attached. He held each one in place, butt against his shoulder and looked through the scope towards the front of the store. He was surprised how instantly he was overcome by the gun's power, and the impulse to press the trigger and shoot, shoot anything. He had the urge to shoot a hole in one of the blue plastic water jugs on display twenty feet in front of him, or shoot through the pane glass window at the front of the store. He chose the rifle that felt the most natural in his hands.

He also wanted a crossbow. Like the rifles, there was a large selection, more than he would have ever expected. He picked out one of the compact pistol-style crossbows.

He had no idea what size ammunition to buy for the rifle, but went in to the back storage room behind the gun counter where the extra stock of rifles still sat in their boxes. He found a box with the same model rifle as the one he picked out, a Browning BAR Safari. The side of the box showed the calibre ammunition. The box boasted of the Browning's 22 inch blued finish barrel, and the gloss finish walnut stock. He took the new rifle and returned to the gun counter.

He had already spotted all the ammunition on display underneath the glass top of the gun counter. He grabbed four boxes. They were much heavier than he thought they would be.

He soon realized that he was not going to be able to carry all this in his arms. He went to the sports section and found a big CCM hockey equipment bag. He walked past a life size cardboard cut-out of Don Cherry, adorned in a red plaid suit coat, and holding a bottle of cold medicine.

He took two boxes of crossbow bolts and threw them in the hockey bag.

From the apparel section, he picked out a complete camouflage outfit, army pants, a camo t-shirt, and a camo coat.

At the front of the store he spotted a tall rack filled with various packages of beef jerky. He was excited because he knew that the jerky had a long shelf life. Sure enough, after checking the expiry date, he saw that most of the vacuum packed contents were good for another three years.

"Organic?" he said aloud in disbelief after reading one description. He was not sure how it was possible to make organic beef jerky, but that was what it said on the package.

The last item he grabbed was a telescope. This would allow him to see a lot further than the binoculars he already had.

With everything collected, he was finished with his shopping trip. The bag was so heavy, that he had to drag it behind him through the store back out to the garage where the Land Rover sat.

With difficulty he heaved the hockey bag into the back of the SUV. He started it up, walked up to the garage door and looked outside. He could see no signs of life, just an empty parking lot. Across the road, a darkened bungalow sat dormant. The front window reflected the blue sky and white clouds. Beyond the white picket fence, the grass was long and a dusty car sat in the driveway.

He stopped and pondered the scene. Normally, a car out front meant that someone was home. Now, he knew that there was no one there, no one alive at least. He wondered if the home owners were still inside, rotting, their bodies lying in their bed or maybe on the couch. Or did they die in the hospital and were taken from their home by ambulance and that is why the car is still in the driveway. Regardless, he did not want to find out. He did not want to go in the house, and had no need to enter it. Maybe, eventually when he had emptied all the stores and restaurants of their food in the area, he might have to go house to house rooting through cupboards for non-perishable food.

He pulled the garage door up, and drove the SUV outside.

When he looked both ways down the street, he saw no movement. He could see other stores, houses, and restaurants on the main street. The windows revealed the dark interiors of all the buildings. Even the illuminated signs that never got turned off sat blank and cold without their electric life. The street was vacant, no cars driving around, no one walking. The scene was unnatural, disturbing. He was hit with the urge to return back to the hotel where the atmosphere was comforting.

On the way home he passed a restaurant in mid construction, a franchise of a large chain of sit down dining restaurants with a rustic cabin like setting. The sign said it was to open in March, four months ago, just in time to catch the tail end of ski season, and be ready for the summer cottagers. The frames in the walls where windows were to supposed to go sat gaping open. The plastic sheeting that had been placed over the openings to protect the interior from the elements was now flapping in the wind. The construction would never be finished. The owner's dream of owning a restaurant would never be fulfilled.

Once back home, Martin was eager to try out the rifle. He set up a spot in the lowest level of the underground garage. He knew that rifle fire could be heard from miles away when shooting outdoors. He was still unsure if anyone else had survived, and did not want to attract unwanted attention by firing the rifle outside.

At a spot directly across from the Land Rover, Martin stood up a tall cardboard box. Using the Land Rover's rear cargo area as a table, he took the rifle out of its box and read the instructions on how to fill the magazine with ammo. He jammed the magazine into place then held the rifle up. Again he was hit with the power of the innate object in his hands. Looking through the scope, he focused on a picture of a cup on the cardboard box. The cup image was only about four inches tall. He squeezed the trigger. Nothing happened. The trigger would not even move. Then he remembered something about a safety switch. He had been so eager to start shooting, that he never thought it would be more complicated than just pressing the trigger. He looked at the instructions again, found the safety and turned it off.

He held the rifle up again, squeezed the trigger. A loud crack rang out, the sound amplified by the cavernous parkade. The recoil of the rifle butt struck his shoulder with such force that he was sure that he would have a bruise.

Excited to see the damage done, he ran over to the box like a little kid who had just gotten his first BB gun. The bullet struck just above where he was aiming. The force of the recoil had lifted the barrel of the gun off target. The bullet went straight through the box and embedded itself into the wall behind. He ran back to his rifle. This time he held it firmly, squeezed the trigger, and could instantly tell that there was less swaying from the recoil. When he ran back to box, he was pleased to see that this time he hit the target, there was a hole in the line at the top of the cup picture.

He took a few more shots at the box, but his arms and chest were getting sore, and his ears were ringing. For fun he wanted to try a target further away. He spotted an exit sign a hundred feet away at the end of the parkade. Using the scope, he got the sign in sight. He fired. A distinct metal ping rang out, a clean hit on the metal exit sign. He put the rifle down and went over. The sign now had a big dent in it, but the bullet did not go through. Martin was impressed with his prowess at using the weapon.

He packed his newly acquired gear back up and took it to his room.

His plan for the rest of the day was to just spend it relaxing. It was a beautiful summer day. The sun was shining with only a few sparse fluffy clouds to interrupt the enjoyment of the sun's rays.

Even though the outdoor pool was not in service, he felt that sitting poolside was the place to be. He even changed into his swim suit.

After a quick lunch, he set himself up by the pool. He turned a lounge chair around so that his whole body was facing the sun. Beside him sat a grey plastic bus boy's bin he borrowed from the restaurant. Normally used for collecting dirty dishes, he had filled the bin with ice, bottles of beer, and a couple citrus flavoured vodka cooler drinks. The ice cubes, retrieved from the walk-in freezer, were old and fuzzy with frost from freezer burn, and had formed into big clumps. To save energy, he had long ago unplugged the ice machines that were placed on each floor for the guests' convenience.

On the other side of his chair sat the pistol crossbow and a dozen bolts. Thirty feet in front of him he had placed a three foot high cardboard box. That would be part of an activity for later. Right now he just wanted to lay back and relax. Stretched out on the lounge chair he read through the magazines he had gotten the day before and drank his beer.

Soon, he could feel he was getting a buzz from the alcohol. As he was flipping through the pages of the magazine his mind wandered and he began to reflect on his situation. Before the virus, work for him was a 7 a.m. to 4 p.m. shift, five days a week at the hotel. After four he was free to do whatever he wanted, but he often would work later just to help out. Now, work had changed, existing had become a job. His free time was still spent being the caretaker for the hotel. He also had to organize tasks for his survival, such as getting food, supplies, fuel, and now weapons. All these months since he had been alone, he had stuck to his regular work schedule, and kept up on his work duties. As he sat there, he decided he would no longer commit himself to an eight hour shift of cleaning the hotel.

The Grand was in perfect shape thanks to him. He would still maintain the cleanliness of the entire hotel, but not make it a full-time job. If when he woke up he felt like cleaning that day, he would. If he just felt like sleeping in, or relaxing, then he would do just that. He was pleased with his decision. He felt more at ease than he had in months. He felt free.

He settled back, put down the magazine and took a generous sip of a vodka cooler. When he went to set it down, it fell over and the remaining contents of the orange drink spilled onto the cement. He did not notice.

He glanced up at the grandeur of the hotel spread out before him, "This is my castle" he thought with pride, and looking around the property, he added, "and this is my kingdom."

With a boost of bravado, he reached down for the mini crossbow. He grabbed a bolt and tried to put it in place. He turned the crossbow back and forth trying to figure out how to cock the bow. Once cocked, he raised it to eye level, and aimed at the cardboard box thirty feet in front of him. The target seemed to waver. He closed one eye to focus and the blurry target stopped moving. He pulled the trigger. The bolt shot off and whipped through a shrub five feet beside the box.

"Cool" he said aloud.

He shot off the rest of the bolts. Only two hit the target. The remainder went off in various directions. One had skipped off the cement and landed in the pool briefly disturbing the green film on the surface before it disappeared in the murky water and sank to the bottom.

He went to get up, but felt lightheaded.

"Screw it, get em later," he said aloud.

He laid back down, and fell asleep.

He opened his eyes to darkness. He abruptly sat up, alarmed and confused until he remembered the afternoon. He could still feel the buzz from the alcohol. He looked up at the cloudless black sky dotted with twinkling stars. He glanced around at his surroundings. The black silhouette of the towering hotel was a foreboding image. He looked towards where the village somewhere stood hidden by the night. In its darkness it looked bleak and uninviting.

He had no idea what time it was.

As he got to his feet he swayed with dizziness then staggered to the back doors of the hotel. The lobby was just as dark as the outside, but his eyesight was already starting to adjust. A sudden rush of nausea overcame him and he hurried to one of the big leather couches, laid down, and passed out again.

12

His back felt like it was roasting. Still on the couch in the lobby, sweating in his clothes, with the heat from the sun beating down on him, Martin woke up. The sun's rays came streaming in, amplified by the glass of the huge bank of eight foot high windows. The leather on the sofa was damp with his sweat where he was laying. He felt groggy and nauseous. He slowly rose. Spears of pain shot into his head. Clutching his stomach, bent over as he walked, he made his way to the elevator.

It was Monday morning, following his new work guidelines, Martin decided to take the day off.

Back in his room, he drained half a bottle of water without stopping, and then slumped into his own bed. He quickly fell back asleep.

He woke up for good at 3pm feeling fatigued and dehydrated. His head was pounding and his stomach felt raw, like he had vomited despite the fact that he had not. Compounded to the effects of the alcohol, he had not taken his medication the night before due to having passed out beside the pool. Although it was only three o'clock, he considered the day to be almost over. In a few hours when the electricity shut off, he would be relegated to his room avoiding the darkness of the hotel.

Despite all this, he felt elated, gratified by his decision to take charge of his work schedule. A week ago if he was in the same condition, he would have forced himself to spend the day working in the hotel, vacuuming, attending to rooms, and other tasks despite his hangover. A year ago, he would have had to answer to his manager about missing the day of work.

Since it had been almost twenty-four hours since he ate last, he went to the restaurant kitchen and cooked himself a full meal and washed it down with plenty of fluids, orange juice, tomato juice, and water.

He still had some daily duties he had to perform, such as doing a walking inspection of the hotel. Feeling less than energetic however, he stayed on the main floor making sure all the doors were locked. With the building secure for the night, he went up to his room.

He sat on his balcony and watched the sun set over the mountain. The fresh air only made him feel slightly better. No lights came on in the expanse of land below.

He went across the hall and sat on that balcony to look for any signs of human activity. No lights in the darkness below on this side either.

It was early, but he was still tired. He went back to his room, made sure the curtains completely covered his balcony door, and lit a couple candles on the bedside table. He took his medication and then went into bed.

Under the glow of candle light he took out *Fahrenheit 451*. He had been reading the classic Ray Bradbury novel on and off for a few months. Martin was just at the part when the lead character is fleeing the authorities after being caught in the illegal act of owning books.

Half an hour later, when he could barely keep his eyes open, Martin marked his place with a hockey card of Martin Brodeur that he was using as a bookmark. He blew out the candles and went to sleep.

13

Over the next couple months, Martin continued with his free spirited approach to scheduling his days. He found himself still completing hotel duties most days just to fill in time, but other days he just relaxed.

Martin regularly practiced firing the rifle and the crossbow and was becoming an excellent shot with the weapons. He was also becoming proficient at loading the weapons in a timely manner. He made a trip back to King's Sporting Goods to get more ammo and bolts. He even picked up a silencer for the rifle to stifle the sound when he fired. He had seen the silencer part in the manufacturer's catalogue, and King's happened to have the part in stock.

Whenever he left the hotel, he brought the rifle and the mini crossbow with him. He realized that as he became more capable with the weapons, his confidence about leaving the hotel improved as a result. However, he still preferred to stay inside the familiar environs of The Grand and was not interested in leaving except for the necessary trips for food or supplies.

Despite persistent surveillance of the region during the day and night, Martin still had not seen any signs of human life. Stewart remained the last person Martin had spoken to. He was however seeing more signs of wildlife. With the absence of humans, animal sightings on the property were more common. Deer were wandering the golf course, and a family of skunks had taken up residence on the hotel's rear grounds underneath a gazebo. A great blue heron, usually a rare sight, stayed for a couple days at the manmade creek by the resort village.

Soon after Labour Day there was a noticeable drop in temperature, as if the weather knew that the calendar date marked the unofficial end of summer. Fall was usually a somewhat somber time at the hotel as occupancy numbers dropped significantly and the building was almost vacant of guests except for small business conferences. At this time of year, it was easy to pretend that you were in the hotel alone, or even in the world alone as you walked the deserted corridors. Outside would be just as quiet, no one wandering the paths in the gardens, or soaking in the hot tub out back. During the course of a day during the off season, Martin could go for a couple hours without seeing another co-worker or guest. Martin had always been a private person and as such he was comfortable being alone. He had co-workers who could not stand working by themselves for more than an hour and would seek out another room attendant to chat with or visit the front desk staff. Now of course, Martin did not have to pretend that he was alone in the hotel, it was his reality.

As the weeks passed, he watched the landscape become a kaleidoscope of colours. Each fall the forests were transformed into puffs of orange, green, yellow, and crimson. Normally, the beauty of the fall leaves offered the last small window of business for the resort as tourists came to the area from the cities to see the fall colours. None would come this year.

Fall also meant that night time came earlier. Martin had to adapt to fewer hours with the luxury of electricity as he had to calibrate the automatic timer for the generator to make it shut off earlier and earlier as the hours of daylight dwindled.

Mentally, he adjusted. Despite the grey, rain soaked days of September and October, for the most part his mood was still upbeat. The cooler temperatures meant that the fireplaces could be turned on. The large fireplace in the lobby gave the room a comforting warm glow. Martin also liked to use the fireplace in his own room every evening as he settled in to relax for the night.

He took care of one job he procrastinated on for months. He finally removed Yvonne's body from the restaurant freezer. He pushed the Rubbermaid cart with her still in it through the ground floor of the hotel and right out the front doors. He then pushed it down the vacant street and onto a service road to a wooded area at the bottom of a ski run. The whole time, he was thinking how it must have been a strange site to see this hotel employee pushing a big cart full of white sheets down the middle of the road. Even though there was no one around to see him, he still felt subconscious.

He dug the grave the old fashioned way, with a shovel. When he felt the hole was big enough, he tilted the cart and unceremoniously dumped Yvonne's body in. He left the grave unmarked. He did not want to draw attention that someone was buried at that spot. He also reasoned that thousands, possibly millions around the world also were now in a similarly undignified, or worse, final resting place.

It was now mid October, a drab fall day. Standing on a balcony of a suite on the third floor, Martin was scraping bird droppings off the railing when something in the distance caught his eye. A movement of light registered in his peripheral vision. He turned to look. Off in the distance he saw a pair of white lights moving down a road. Daytime running headlights from a car or truck he quickly surmised. The day was so dreary that the headlights could be easily seen as if it were dusk instead of late afternoon. The driver of the vehicle probably did not even realize the headlights were shining since they came on automatically once the car was started.

Most of the trees had lost their leaves. The bare branches provided Martin with a mostly unobstructed view of roads, and buildings that would have been hidden by the canopy of trees in the summer. Only coniferous trees; the spruces, pines and cedars would temporarily obscure his view of the car. The headlights flickering as it passed tree trunks along its path. It was not driving very fast, but fast enough that no one could be following on foot. Martin thought of how in the movies large trucks, the back loaded up with passengers, would be driving a snail's pace so others on foot could follow behind. Gangs of violent, dishevelled survivors pillaging the countryside in their journey. Martin was sure that this was not the situation here, but still, the thought crossed his mind. In this case, the driver's slow speed indicated that they were not taking any risks and was unsure what would be on the road ahead.

Martin watched the car drive along. Sometimes he could see the lights, sometimes they would disappear behind the cover of a ridge or densely forested area for a few seconds, then would reappear. Then it stopped. The vehicle was still far off in the distance, but it did not reappear again. He stood watching. The minutes passed. The vehicle did not reappear again. He assumed it must have stopped for a break.

Nothing was happening. He was eager to continue his surveillance from his own balcony. First he went down to the parkade and shut the generator off for the night. He did not want to take any chances that the travellers would see the hotel lit up like Stewart had.

He took the stairs two at a time to get up to the fifth floor. Once in his room, he went straight out onto his balcony.

He pointed the telescope in the vicinity where he had last seen the headlights. From this vantage point, he could see that there were a few scattered cottages cut into the mostly forested area. The driver must have stopped at one of the cottages for a break, possibly for the night. It was a well chosen isolated spot in a sea of trees. He had a much better view from the fifth floor. The vehicle had come down a side road, instead of taking the main county artery that normally has high traffic use by both locals and tourists. The driver was being cautious Martin presumed, and probably did not want any unexpected encounters with other survivors.

When it came to supper time, he ran back and forth from his balcony window to his microwave while his frozen dinner was cooking. He ate fettuccine alfredo outside sitting on a lawn chair as he watched and waited. Donned in a winter coat and a toque to keep warm, he continued his surveillance as the cool fall wind whipped across the building.

As the minutes passed, daylight lowly surrendered its hold, and dusk shaded the area. Then the darkness of the night replaced dusk. It was still early in the evening, but night time came early this time of year. It was just past seven. There was still no sign of the visitor, or visitors, there was no way of knowing how many people were in the vehicle.

Martin wondered if were they sitting in the dark, or had they blocked off the windows so no light would escape if they were using candles or a lantern. Were they already asleep and waiting to surface again during daylight? It would be too risky to travel at night with the headlights.

Then it appeared, a small square of light, a window white from the illumination inside. He pointed his telescope at the cottage. It was still far off, and the telescope made it only slightly larger. Not enough that he could see inside the window. It remained the only light in the building, a single lonely light in the sea of blackness.

A few minutes later, he could make out the dancing red glow of a bonfire. He could barely make out the light of the fire through the trees but there was no mistaking that it was a bonfire on the cottage's property. It would be used maybe for cooking a dinner or maybe simply to provide warmth.

It was just after nine. It had been dark for a couple hours now. He marvelled how the tiny light source stood out even from this distance.

Martin watched for a long time. Eventually the fire was put out. Then the window light went out. The area was again covered in complete blackness, like a shroud. He watched still, wondering if a new light would turn on or if the visitor would drive off, but nothing changed.

He waited until after midnight, it had now been an hour since the light went out. Tired and sure that the travellers were also tired and probably long asleep, Martin went back inside. In the comfort of his warm bed, he did not sleep well. He kept wondering what to do next. He did not know what the morning would bring. They were definitely coming in the direction of the resort area.

14

Drifting in and out of sleep, Martin's imagination fuelled by his semi-conscious state, fabricated farfetched scenarios about the travellers. What if the car was full of violent crazies, wielding machetes, or guns, or baseball bats with spikes driven through them, like in Mad Max? What if they came right up to the hotel and tried to break in, smashing the front door to gain entry, and trashed the hotel looking for food and booze? What if they went to the resort village raiding the stores, then set fire to the whole place? The different thoughts played out in his mind in a dream-like quality, except the setting for the destruction was his hotel instead of some apocalyptic wasteland.

He woke up early. Rational thoughts returned once he was alert. He decided to continue watching from his balcony and hopefully get a better idea of who was in the car. With his telescope he may even get a good look at the driver.

He was still unsure how to react to the travelers. From appearances, if they seemed non-threatening, should he try to make contact with them and find a way to attract their attention? What if they drove right on by the village without even stopping?

Maybe, like Stewart, they saw The Grand in the distance and would want to explore it. Even without lights on, the five story hotel stood out in the landscape as the tallest building around.

It was not quite seven, the sun was just rising. Martin set up a spot in the corner of the balcony, so he would be hidden from view and ate his breakfast. It was chilly, but he could tell it was going to be a beautiful sunny fall day.

In the daylight, he could make out more details about the cottage. It was a small unassuming "A" frame shaped chalet. It was the only one with a car parked beside it. Most of the places in the area were vacation properties and had been empty during the outbreak of the virus. The vehicle was a silver coloured elongated car, probably a station wagon. There was no movement outside.

"Probably still sleeping," Martin thought.

He waited a few minutes, and then the lights came on in his room. In the excitement, he had forgotten that the hotel's power would come on automatically.

He dashed down the seven flights of stairs to P2 and shut the generator down for the day. To be safe, he did not want to take the risk that somehow the lights would be seen from the outside revealing to the driver that the hotel had electricity.

By the time Martin got back out on his balcony, the parking spot beside the chalet was empty. Frantic, he lowered the telescope to see if he could spot the car anywhere in the vicinity with his naked eye. Large sections of the road were hidden behind dense pockets of cedar trees. The car could be anywhere, and it would have been only a ten minute drive to get to the resort area.

He soon spotted the car making its way down the same sideroad it had appeared on last night. It was headed in the direction of the resort, but would still have to take a turn to come onto to the main road.

He tried to get a look at the car's occupants but the sun was reflecting off the windshield.

The road curved and the car came to a stop sign at the main highway. From his vantage point, Martin had a bird's eye view of the options the driver faced. Continuing straight and crossing the highway would lead to the Lake Arnette. Turning left onto the main highway, would lead towards the resort area. Turning right would lead them back in the opposite direction, the way they had come from in the first place, but would take them to the small town of Ogden Marsh.

The driver took a minute to decide, possibly to view a map. Then the car turned left, choosing to go in the direction of the resort.

Bright, information signs directed motorists to hotels, skiing parking lots, the shopping village, The Grand Summit Place, the Arklay Mountains Championship Golf Course, and other points of interest. This road curved then ran alongside the mountain and its ski runs, and eventually led past The Grand.

Martin watched intently. The car crept past the large ski lodge that served that part of the mountain. The car turned onto a small parking lot in front of the lodge and stopped. Inside the lodge's dark interior was a cafeteria, a small bar, and a ski rental shop. Several ski runs ended at the lodge. A hundred feet from the lodge, a chair lift sat idle. The lodge was a quarter mile away from where Martin stood on his balcony.

He could see the car clearly now, a silver Volvo station wagon. The occupants had chosen a reliable, practical vehicle. The back of the car was facing him and he could see through the rear window that the back seat was loaded up with cargo.

Martin trained the telescope on the car. The passenger door opened, a male figure got out. He looked to be in his late teens. He was dressed in a youthful style, had on baggy jeans, a baseball hat, and although it was cold outside, he was only wearing a purple basketball jersey overtop of a red t-shirt. The teen stood and scanned the area, then turned back around and spoke through his window at the driver.

The driver's door opened. A female stepped out. She was tall, had on blue jeans, and an oversized black hoodie, her blonde ponytail sticking out the back of a pink baseball cap. No one else got out from the car. Martin was relieved to see that neither of them were holding a weapon.

They both slowly walked along the front of the lodge to the far side and disappeared around the corner of the building.

Martin turned back to the car. He could not see any movement inside. Maybe it was only the two travelling.

He put the telescope down and watched. The lodge was close enough that he would clearly see anyone walking around.

A minute later the pair came around the side closest to Martin, completing a tour of the outside of the lodge.

They must have been scoping out the area looking for inhabitants, Martin assumed.

They turned and started walking up the grassy incline of one of ski runs. At first Martin was not sure why they would do this, but then thought of it from their perspective, and realized that from a higher vantage point, they would be able to see the entire area, including the various hotels, condo complexes and the retail village.

This was not a leisurely afternoon hike up the middle of the ski slope, they were walking along the tree line that edged this particular run. The couple must have known that it would not be wise to walk out in the open. Two figures hiking in the open area would be easily noticed even if the observer just casually glanced in that direction. By walking along the tree line they were more concealed.

They continued to make their way up. The male was falling behind, then stopped and plopped himself on the ground. The female backtracked to him. With his legs stretched out in front of him, he gestured her to continue up the hill with a wave of his arm. She continued the ascent alone.

Martin knew it would not be an easy climb. The slope got steeper as you got higher. The bottom of the run levelled out and was flatter to help skiers slow down.

The female was now at a point that was higher than even the top of The Grand's roof. Martin had to look up to see her.

She stopped and turned around to scan the entire area. She would easily be able to see any people walking around, or driving. She would probably also be looking for any building that would have signs of life inside, such as lights, or a smoking chimney. Of course what she did see was a completely deserted area.

Martin realized it was wise to turn off all the power at the hotel, for she would easily see the interior lights if they were still on.

He held the telescope up to his eye again and looked at the male. He did look young, late teens or early twenties. He had the makings of a light moustache, like he had not shaved for a couple days. He was lying propped up on his elbows with his legs stretched straight out, smoking a cigarette.

Martin turned to the female. She looked like the type of clientele that frequented The Grand, tall, blonde, with an athletic figure. She appeared to be in her late twenties or thirties, it was hard to tell with the large sun glasses she was wearing. But, she was probably too young to be her companion's mother.

About five minutes later she came down the slope to meet up with her companion.

Martin had a decision to make. His thoughts ran through his mind like a conversation. Should I go out and meet them? They look harmless. Should I offer to let them stay at the hotel? What if they got in the car and drove off, without even stopping anywhere at the resort?

He estimated that he had ten minutes to act. The amount of time it would take them to get back to the bottom and into their car. They may try to get into the lodge, but he wanted to be prepared just in case they went straight to their car and drove away.

Martin reviewed his prospects. He was quite happy in his current situation of being the sole occupant of the hotel, but guilt and charity were pulling at his emotions. These two were seemingly homeless, and he could provide a safe sanctuary. If they were heading to a destination, he could offer his hospitality, and in the process get some information about the outside world. He had the two main necessities of life; food and shelter, plus the basics of heat, electricity, running water. Beyond the necessities, the hotel offered the luxuries of a comfortable bed, fresh linen, a hot tub, sauna, exercise room. Martin imagined that in these times, even hydro, heat, and hot water could be seen as a luxury.

At least he could meet them and offer his hospitality and if they turned him down, he could just return to the life he had known the last few months. If they took him up on his offer, then he would have company for as long as they stayed. It had been months since he had spoken to another person, and he could use the company. It would be good for him, he convinced himself. Also, he had been working hard to keep up the standards of the hotel all this time, and he finally had the opportunity to welcome guests.

With his decision made, he bolted out of his room and down the stairs. On the way down, he realized that taking a car would be too time consuming. He had never anticipated needing a car in a hurry. It would involve getting the keys from the valet room, getting a car from P2, then going through the process of unlocking the garage door. These steps would take about fifteen minutes by which time they could already be driving away and he would have lost sight of them.

His plan was simple, go out the front door and run down the road. The lodge would always be in his sightline. By running, he could be there in five minutes.

Halfway down the road, it occurred to him that he did not bring a weapon. With this realization, his pace slowed to a walk. They would not be able to see him yet, a row of thick pine trees separated the sidewalk from the ski runs on the other side.

He decided to continue on, after all, they did not seem dangerous, except the kid looked like he might give Martin some attitude.

Martin could see them coming down the slope, their eyes focussed on the uneven ground before them. The male finished his cigarette and flicked the butt ten feet in front of him onto the grass. The female said something, which caused the kid to look back to her.

Martin came to the end of the tree line. He was now fifty feet from the lodge. Still hidden from sight, he turned his attention to the car. There were no other people inside.

He walked out onto the grass at the base of the run. He would now be completely visible to the pair and directly below them. They were still a hundred feet away.

They both spotted Martin at the same time and froze. They reacted like they were seeing an alien. They looked at Martin then instinctively looked around to see if he was alone or not.

Martin gave a friendly wave.

The male turned to the female but she was already walking down to greet Martin.

The travellers stopped ten feet in front of Martin.

Both parties stared at each other for thirty seconds studying their counterparts.

The female had a friendly face.

"Where the hell did you come from?" the male abruptly inquired, with a scowl on his face. He stepped forward a foot and pulled a hunting knife from his belt. He held it threateningly in front of him but did not move any closer.

Martin stood his ground and did not move. "Relax, I thought you guys might need some help."

The female reacted just as Martin had started to speak, "put the damn knife away, Travis."

"We don't know shit about this guy, maybe he ain't alone," Travis countered.

"I can help, or you can go on your way, and I will just turn around and go back home," Martin tried to say nonchalantly. "Just trying to help, I live here. If you want, we can go in the lodge, and talk, I have a key."

Travis turned to the female, she did not take her eyes off Martin standing there looking unassuming in khaki pants and a yellow golf shirt.

"Could be a trap," Travis said to her in a lowered voice, but Martin still heard him.

"Let's talk right here," the female said.

"Ok, I'm Martin." They were still too far away for a hand shake and the pair were not moving any closer, so Martin did not extend his hand.

"I'm Claire, Claire Rockatansky-Gibson, and this is Travis."

She pushed Travis's arm down. He put the knife away.

They both looked physically exhausted, their clothes were filthy, and their faces and hands had smudges of dirt on them.

Despite her current dishevelled appearance, Claire still had an air of sophistication.

Travis had long straggly hair. It was hard to tell if this was the way his hair always was, or if he just let it go since the virus.

"Look, I can offer you a hot shower, a hot meal, and, a warm, clean room. Your own room. You can even wash your clothes, " Martin added.

Claire's eyes lit up, but Travis still looked skeptical. He was acting defensive, like another lion had come into his pride.

"How can you do all this crap, why should we believe you, what do you want?" Travis rattled off.

"Looks like you could use some help, that's all, whatever. It doesn't really matter to me," Martin said.

Claire was already walking forward.

"When you say you live here, where is 'here'?" she asked.

Claire stuck out her hand, and Martin shook it in greeting. "First, how do I know that you too aren't alone?" Martin asked.

"Believe me, Travis is the only person I've seen for weeks," Claire said with regret in her voice.

"Well, I need to be cautious too, I have a lot to lose, and really nothing to gain, by helping you, I could have just let you drive on by."

"Ok, ok, anything you can offer would be great. What about you, you said you're alone?" Claire asked.

"Ya, just me," Martin replied.

"Where are we going?" Claire looked around at possible places that Martin could have appeared from on foot. Across the road from them were a couple privately owned chalets, then the golf course, and further up, The Grand.

"I live there," he said pointing, "The Grand Summit Place, the hotel."

This time it was Travis who perked up, but tried to hide it. Martin caught the initial reaction on Travis's face.

"I'll walk ahead, you two can drive up and meet me there. Just follow this road, it leads to the hotel's driveway. Park under the carport, at the entrance," Martin instructed.

Martin started jogging towards the hotel, his back to the lodge. He did not trust them enough to get in their car. He was sure that they would take him up on his offer but, was not certain. He was putting his trust into strangers based on their appearance.

He heard the car doors shut behind him. They would be at the hotel before him. He turned to look back. The car was still in front of the lodge. He could tell by their actions that they were having an animated discussion.

He assumed that Claire was probably just trying to convince the kid to go to the hotel. This would be the first opportunity they had to be alone to discuss Martin's offer and maybe even evaluate him as a person to be trusted.

Martin continued jogging towards The Grand. He could not hear the car driving so he stopped. He was almost at the bend in the road, the hotel entrance a hundred yards ahead of him. The car pulled to the exit of the lodge parking lot, then turned right, the opposite direction to the hotel, the way they had come.

He started waving his arms to get their attention, but they kept on driving, the car getting further and further away, then disappeared around a curve in the road.

Feeling dejected, Martin's arms dropped, his shoulders slumped. He was surprised that he felt disappointed that they did not join him.

He walked back to the hotel and sat down on a bench outside the front entrance. He reviewed the conversation in his head. He did not think he said anything wrong.

As he sat there, he noticed how unkempt the property had become. He had not spent much time outside in the front doing yard maintenance. Bits of paper, and other garbage had blown on the property, some collecting in the overgrown shrubs that lined the walls of the building, some caught in the gardens. He decided to walk around and tidy up.

Five minutes later he heard a car engine. Looking up, he saw the Volvo coming down the road from the other direction. They must have backtracked, taking the other end of the road to get to the hotel.

Martin met them under the carport at the entrance.

Claire and Travis stepped out of the car. Claire had a smile on her face that expressed relief.

"I thought you guys had changed your minds," Martin said.

"We wanted to make sure you weren't running back to get your posse," Travis explained. "We were watching you from the corner up the road."

Claire added, "Sorry, we just wanted to make sure it was safe. Then when we saw that you didn't go rushing into the hotel, your actions led us to believe that you probably are just alone."

"Ya, it was like, this fool's just out there picking up garbage," Travis added.

"So here we are!" Claire said.

"Let's get you inside," Martin offered.

Martin led them into the lobby, "Welcome to The Grand Summit Place."

They both looked around at the grandeur of the lobby. Even with the lights off, the lobby had the power to impress.

"I thought you said you had power," Travis prompted.

"I do, but I shut it down for the day, I didn't want this place standing out like a Christmas tree. I saw you guys last night but didn't know if you were friendly, or how many were in your group. As a precaution I turned the power off."

"You better not be lyin, " Travis threatened.

Martin ignored the hostility.

"You saw us last night?" Claire asked.

"Well, actually yesterday afternoon. I saw your headlights in the distance as you were coming down that sideroad, then I saw that you stopped at the cottage for the night."

"If you give me your word that you are alone, I can turn the power on. Show you to your room. You can have a hot shower."

"At least I know there are no other cars, with you. And it's not like you can call anyone else on your cell phone to give them a heads up on your new location," Martin added.

"We are alone. Just us two for weeks, you have my word," Claire said.

"Ya, just us two, okay?" Travis agreed.

"We're just going to have to trust each other. Wait here while I go turn the lights on. Make yourself comfortable on the couches over there. I will be back in about five minutes."

Martin left, waited a minute in the hallway, then backtracked to the entrance of the lobby. He peered around the corner to see what his new guests were doing. He found that they had not moved. Both were still sitting on the couch where he left them. In silence, they were looking all around the lobby as they waited.

Satisfied that they were being sincere about being alone, he went down to P2 and turned on the generator. The hotel sprang to life with the surge of electricity.

The lobby resumed its cheery appearance. Martin lit the fireplace to add to the atmosphere.

"I haven't seen lights in weeks," Claire said in awe.

"Let's get your car underground, then it will be easier to get all your bags. We can park right beside the elevator."

"Ok, but let's all go, I don't want you driving off with our stuff," Travis said.

Martin held up his hand motioning Claire to wait. He went across the lobby to the bar, and grabbed a can of Budweiser from the mini-fridge. As he passed the couch that Travis was sitting on, he handed him the beer.

"On the house," Martin said.

Travis looked up at Martin, semi-stunned. Then grabbed the cold beer, and managed to mumble a "thanks."

"I'll just wait here after all," Travis said as he opened the can.

Martin led Claire out to the car. She handed Martin the keys. "You might as well drive, you know where we're going," she said.

Five minutes later the car was safely parked underground, the garage door was locked again, and they were heading up the elevator. Claire had grabbed a couple of bags to bring with her.

They retrieved Travis then went back on the elevator.

On the way up, Martin checked his notebook to see which rooms he had most recently cleaned. "I am going to give you each your own room on the fifth floor, same floor as me."

For the time being, he assigned them each a standard suite, same layout as his; with a queen sized bed, a couch, TV, full bathroom and a small kitchenette. He used his own keycard to let them in.

"All the rooms are in perfect shape, ready and waiting for guests. You'll find anything you need, towels, toiletries, even a bathrobe. I will leave you for now. Let you get cleaned up, then we can get acquainted later. You can find me in the lobby when you are done."

Travis seemed happy to get rid of the two of them, and quickly closed his door without saying a word.

Claire stood at her doorway staring at Martin, unsure what to say. It seemed like she had the urge to give him a hug in gratitude. Instead, she gave a heartfelt "thank you", then slowly closed the door.

Both rooms were just a few doors down the hall from his own room, so Martin could keep an eye on them, and also be available for help if needed.

Martin stuck around the fifth floor hallway. He wanted to see if they were just going to stay in their rooms and get settled or were they immediately going to leave their room now that they had gained entry to the hotel. He kept busy by dusting the door threshold to each room in the corridor.   When he passed Claire's room he could hear the shower going from inside. It was strange to hear sound made by someone else after all this time. For months he had roamed the silent hallways. When the hotel was occupied, he could always hear people inside their rooms talking, or the TV going.

After ten minutes when neither Claire nor Travis had left their room, Martin returned to the lobby, and turned on the reception desk computer. He encoded a room key card for each of them. He gave them only limited access as a security measure. The card would work only for their own room, and the regular hotel amenities such as the exercise room, and the indoor pool. The card would deny access to any staff area, storage room, or utility room. They would be limited like any other guest.

Martin stayed on the main floor, dusting furniture and vacuuming the already clean oriental carpets in the lounge areas and at the front desk. He also swept up the dirt the two had brought in with their shoes.

Within an hour of showing them to their rooms, Travis came down to the lobby. He had showered, but had put on the same grimy clothes he was wearing earlier.

"Have any more beer?" Travis asked walking to the lobby bar.

"How old are you?" Martin inquired.

"Get real, there's no rules anymore. Anyways, I'm twenty-one. Legal. And it ain't like I haven't been drinking for a few years already," Travis informed him.

Months ago Martin had locked away all the alcohol bottles that were in the bar. Originally, the bottles had been neatly displayed against the window making them visible from the outside to entice patrons to come inside for a cocktail. Martin put them away after he was alone, so the sight of all that alcohol did not advertise that the hotel was well stocked with supplies, and attract thieves passing by. Now the bar appeared to have no alcohol at all.

"What kind of bar is this, where's all the booze?" Travis asked when he saw the empty glass shelves behind the counter.

"It's all gone, whatever alcohol was left was taken home by managers, and there were no suppliers to deliver new shipments after the virus hit," Martin lied, "and I don't really drink, so I never restocked."

"Those greedy bastards," Travis exclaimed, he seemed to think this explanation was plausible.

"I do have a few beers left," Martin said, and got a can from the mini fridge and handed it to Travis. "There's an arcade down the hall if you want to check it out."

"You got money for me to play?" Travis asked.

"I rigged the token machine so you can get coins for free."

Travis took off down the hall, already drinking from his beer.

Claire came down. She too had showered. She was wearing different clothes, but they were dirty; black form fitting yoga pants, and a peach coloured hoodie sweatshirt and New Balance jogging shoes.

"Feeling better?" Martin asked.

"Ninety-nine percent. When I get into actual clean clothes, I will be one hundred percent. Unfortunately everything I own is soiled and getting ratty." she said. Her hair was still wet and pulled into a pony tail.

"If you want, tomorrow I can take you into the village and you can get some new clothes," Martin offered.

"Are you kidding? Of course, that would be fantastic," Claire exclaimed.

Martin looked at his watch. "It's quarter after three already, we have about three more hours before the power shuts down for the night. I turn the power off before dusk so there's no chance that any lights from the hotel can be seen from anywhere out there. I don't want to advertise that I'm here."

"How about a tour?" Martin offered. "We can pick up Travis on the way, he's at the arcade."

As they passed the arcade, Travis was playing pinball, the beer can sitting on the glass top.

"Want to join us for a tour?" Claire asked.

"Not really," Travis responded, and turned back to his game.

Martin and Claire continued on.

"Is he always this snarky?" Martin asked.

"Only when he's awake," Claire replied with a laugh.

Half an hour later, Claire had viewed the entire hotel. She was most excited about the hot tub and the exercise room. "I'm used to going to the gym three or four times a week, I am out of shape. I've lost weight and muscle tone from not eating properly," she told Martin when she saw all the exercise equipment.

Martin thought different, she still looked fit. She was probably about five-eight in height.

"Why don't you relax. I will fix dinner," Martin offered.

Claire hesitated, but then agreed. "It's been so long since someone offered to make me my meal that I can't resist. I do most of the cooking. Travis's idea of making a meal is opening up a can of baked beans. Maybe I will go back to my room. Have a quick nap. That bed looks comfy."

"I will call your room when dinner is ready," Martin told her.

Martin walked past the arcade on the way to the restaurant kitchen. Engrossed in a driving game, Travis was sitting in a plastic car seat, holding onto a steering wheel attached to the video game console. The beer can lay crumpled, and discarded on the floor beside him.

"I'm making dinner. I'll get you when it's ready," Martin informed him.

"Good, I'm starving," Travis responded without taking his eyes off the screen in front of him.

Over an hour later, the three of them were seated around an oversized coffee table near the fireplace in the lobby. Martin had pulled two leather couches and a large armchair in close to the table so they could all sit comfortably while they ate.

"I was caught off guard when you called me in my room," Claire said. "I just sort of stared at the phone at first. The sound of the phone ringing has almost become foreign. It's been a long time since I used a phone, so the ringing was kind of eerie. Same as going in the elevator. It was almost surreal, all these weeks without the conveniences of modern living, then today here I am with electricity, a hot shower, phone, elevator."

"Why do you think I live here?" Martin said. "Everything anyone needs to live comfortably is right here."

He then went on to explain how the restaurant had a large walk-in freezer and fridge, both fully stocked towards the end of the virus, and since there were very few people using the restaurant, the food inventory stayed full.

"I also stocked up on frozen meals, fries, and vegetables when the power shut down in the area and it seemed that it was not going to come back on. The stores had already been abandoned by their owners by that point. I had to do it quick though, before all the frozen stuff went bad. The maintenance man warned me that we could lose power for good if things really went bad," Martin said.

"We've, like, been eating mostly canned food," Travis told him, "heating it up with one of those camping burner things you hook up to a gas cylinder. Most homes have a gas barbeque in the backyard, those will work, unless of course the tank is empty. Or we would find a house with a gas stove. They still work too. But searching a house you sometimes find the owner stiffed out. The stench is too much to stay around too long."

Claire added, "We've become experts at determining if a house is empty. We still look through the garage window to double check for a car. If there is no car, most of the time that means no one is still in the house. Sometimes we are wrong. We have never come across anyone still alive. If the house is empty, we will sleep there for the night, see what food they have that is still safe to eat."

Martin proceeded to tell them about his involvement with the hotel. "This place has been my home for a few years now," he said proudly.

"I've been keeping myself busy, maintaining the building, keeping up the standards. Actually, I rarely even leave. Only to go on supply runs to nearby stores."

"Well, the place looks amazing," Claire said.

Travis was surprised, "You mean you spend your time cleaning the hotel? You could just be hanging around, doin nothin all day, drinking beer, playing video games. You're like Paul Blart, from the movie *Mall Cop*. You take your job way too serious."

"Ya well, I love this place and don't plan on leaving, so I want to take care of it. You know how in those apocalypse movies, people always leave their homes, then are stranded out in the unknown, getting in life threatening situations, getting chased by zombies. After the virus killed everyone I thought, 'there is no way I am leaving this place.' I have everything I need right here. Even if some violent gang comes here, I have a million places to hide, and would probably see them coming in the first place. Besides the potential to meet some lunatic out there, you have to deal with the weather; like in that book *The Road*. That scared the crap out of me. The dad and the boy walking across the US in the cold, and the rain. Braving the elements dressed in rags and sleeping outside.

"Sorry to inform you, but there are no zombies out there," Travis said. "The virus did not turn people into brain eaters, and there are no gangs of raiders roaming the wasteland like in Fallout 3."

"The video game?" Travis explained when Claire gave him a blank look.

"I have seen some evidence of violence, but not recently, a burned out car, smashed windows in buildings, some signs of looting from stores. But never did meet anyone with threatening behaviour," Claire said.

"Well, I had no idea what it was like out there, just what I have seen in the neighbouring villages, which are still in perfect condition, just deserted and untouched."

"I had one visitor in the winter, and none since then. I've not spoken to anyone, or even seen any evidence of another human being until I spotted you two last night."

"You ain't missin much. Boring as hell. One shitty dull, day after another," Travis informed.

Claire added, "Everywhere is deserted. You would think that everyone just disappeared off the face of the earth."

"Until you go into a house and see them dead, rotting in their bed," Travis pointed out.

Claire took her turn to tell her story. "I'm from Burlington. All that human loss in a big city like that. I just had to get out of there. I had no destination in mind. I just wanted to get into the country."

She explained how she was a speech pathologist. Her husband was a financial advisor. He had died halfway through the virus. They had no children.

"A couple of DINKS, rollin' in the dough," Travis said. "Double Income No Kids."

"Ya, well, I still had family. Like everyone else, I lost all my relatives, parents, a brother, sister, nieces, nephews, friends," Claire said.

She abruptly got up, walked a few steps then stopped. With her back to Martin and Travis, she rubbed her eyes. She returned a minute later.

"Sorry," she offered, when she returned to the couch, her eyes red and her cheeks wet.

"I left the city alone in my Volvo. At first I stayed with a cousin for a month or so. He lived in a small town. But then he got sick, and told me to leave for my own sake. By that point there weren't too many people left, places were empty. Soon after leaving my cousin's the power went out everywhere. I'd stop at different places for a couple days, especially if it was a nice house. If I came across a home with all gas appliances, I would stay for a week. Most nights I slept in the back seat behind a store. The standard option of renting a motel room was out the window, since the owners weren't around anymore, unless I broke into the room of course, which I did do a couple times."

"I found Travis about a month ago. He was stranded at the side of the road with a flat tire."

Travis stepped in, "I was bent over the jack. Didn't even hear her drive up, or else I would have hidden. Scared the shit out of me."

"We decided to stick together. Some days we go without hardly saying a word. I mean, what is there to say when you're with someone twenty-four hours a day, day after day. We just keep driving, waiting for something to happen. We still don't know where we are going. We just wake up, look at the map to see places within the day's driving distance," Claire said.

"Ya," Travis interjected, "It's not like in the movies, where you hear about some safe haven or get this emergency message on the radio tellin' you to go to some secure community that has started up. There's nothing out there. Any survivors are left on their own. The government didn't do nothin'"

"I've only seen a handful of people since I left my cousin's months ago, and except for Travis and now you, I have not seen any survivors for weeks," Claire said.

"Looks like Solara wiped out ninety-nine percent of the population," Travis added.

"Why didn't you catch the virus?" Travis asked Martin.

Martin explained his blood disorder and how that must be the reason for evading the infection. "I was around hundreds of people, different people every week when the virus was rampant. Some even came to the hotel sick. I was even around a few bodies at the hotel. So my blood disorder is the only thing I can think of that saved me. Unless it is the medication I am on, which I assume is not used by many people, since it is a rare disease, so it would be hard to prove either way."

"I don't know why I'm still here," Travis said. "I don't have a disease or nothin. My mom died when I was young. Doctors didn't know why. Maybe she had something like you. Maybe it's in my DNA. I'm not on medication, so it ain't that. I'm healthy."

Claire was just as perplexed as to why she had survived. "It's a mystery to me too, why I am still alive while so many others died. The only thing I can think of is that I've always had a hyper immune system and rarely get sick."

Martin looked at a tall grandfather clock standing beside the fire place. "We have about half an hour before the electricity cuts out."

Turning to Travis, Martin said, "I shut the power off for the night just before dusk. I don't want to attract any undesirables."

"Too late," Travis said with a grin. "Claire 's already here."

"I usually go up to my room. Read. Or go to the gym until it gets too dark outside and I lose what's left of daylight." Martin said.

Martin did not want to tell them about how he used the small generator in his second room at night. He was not ready to share the evening huddled in the small den with his new guests. He had visions of Travis taking over the TV, playing video games non-stop.

"We can go up to my room. I have the curtains blocking off the patio door, so I can at least light some candles or have a lantern going. No light can be seen from the outside." Martin said.

He then quickly added, "That's about the only rule I must enforce. If you use candles or a lantern, all your windows must be completely covered so no light gets out. Like I said, I could see the light from your cottage last night. Except for the stars, it was the only light out there, so ya, it was easy to spot."

"Forget it. I'm going to my own room. I charged up my PSP as soon as I got here. I'll just play it, hang out in my own room," Travis told them.

"Aren't you going to help clean up?" Claire asked Travis.

"It's Paul Blart's hotel, let him clean up," Travis said and got up to walk away.

Claire was about to respond, when Martin raised his hand, "Let him go." He was already growing tired of Travis.

Martin and Claire quickly gathered up the dishes and returned them to the restaurant so they could be washed in the morning.

"Do you have any red wine?" Claire asked.

Martin got her a bottle from the storage room in the kitchen. "I'm no wine expert", but "I think this is good. It's from Niagara, Ontario."

"Just let me lock all the doors, then we can go up. We better take the stairs. Don't want to get stuck on the elevator until morning. Not like there's someone to rescue us."

"Mind if I still come to your room for a visit? It's been ages since I had an adult conversation. Being with Travis is like being with a spoiled thirteen year old."

Once in his room, Martin demonstrated to Claire how to completely cover the balcony door so no light gets out. Then he lit a couple large candles and a small battery powered lantern. Claire got comfortable on the couch while Martin poured them each a glass of wine. Martin sat in an armchair opposite her. They just got settled when the power turned off, leaving them in the warm glow of the candles.

"Do you think Travis would have remembered to bring a lantern or candles?" Martin asked.

"I doubt it. He's probably sitting in the dark with the only source of light being the little screen from his video game. He is not much of a planner," Claire said.

"I think I'll go check on him. I also want to make sure he did not open the drapes," Martin said. "Just relax, I'll be back in a minute."

Martin knocked on Travis's door.

"Ya?" Travis yelled from inside, not bothering to come to the door.

"It's Martin, can I come in?"

"Ya, whatever."

Martin entered the room using his own key card. He found Travis just as Claire had said. The only light in the room was the feeble illumination of the handheld PSP video game screen. Travis was stretched out on the bed leaning against the headboard. Still wearing his running shoes, he was resting on top of the white duvet that covered the bed. A six pack of beer sat beside him on the end table. A couple cans had already been taken out of the plastic holder. The curtain covering the patio was still pulled across just as Martin had left it when he last cleaned the room days ago.

"Here's a lantern for you, just don't open the curtains and let the light out."

He set the battery powered camping lantern on the kitchen table.

"You might need this when you go in the bathroom."

Travis mumbled a "thanks," then added, "you're about two minutes too late. I just put the PSP on the sink counter for light while I took a piss. I think I might have missed the bowl a couple times."

"Claire over at your room?" Travis asked.

"Yes," Martin said.

"Good luck Andy."

"It's Martin," he corrected Travis.

A minute passed. Martin stood by the door in the awkward silence. Travis was ignoring him, staring at his video game.

"Well good night," Martin said.

Travis did not reply.

Back at his room, Martin revealed to Claire that she was right.

"I'm not surprised that he had no light. I usually organize everything. He just waits for me, or nothing happens. He has no initiative."

"At least he did not open the curtains," Martin said.

"It's probably a case of it taking too much effort for him to walk over to the other side of the room and open the curtains," Claire said. "What did he say when you gave him the lantern?"

"Not much, I think he mumbled a thank you, not really sure," Martin answered.

"You might have to confront him on his attitude towards you," Claire said as she sipped some wine.

"I'm not good with conflict. The hotel has conditioned all the staff that the customer is always right. Even if a guest is treating you like garbage, you respond with a courteous smile and a positive attitude. We have to maintain The Grand standards."

"Well, I am just letting you know, you don't have to take his abuse. Don't think of him as a paying guest," Claire said.

Martin knew it would be hard to break out of his conditioning.

Claire refilled her empty glass. Martin had barely touched his wine.

He talked further about the resort area and they talked about going shopping in the village.

Martin was getting anxious to go on the balcony as part of his nightly surveillance. He explained his routine to his guest. "It's how I kept an eye on you guys last night."

She was curious to see the view at night, but when she stepped out into the cold air on his balcony and saw only complete darkness below, she was satisfied and returned back into his room shivering.

"You can get your coat if you want. I usually spend a little while out here, and then go across the hall to see that side of the world.

"Thanks, but the wine has made me tired, so I think I will just go to bed," Claire said, then added after a pause, "You seem like a nice guy. But I am going to tell you the same thing I told Travis when I first met him. You try anything, and I will chop your balls off when you're asleep."

Martin was shocked by her threat, but appreciated her stance. He took a sip of his wine. He did not know how to reply.

She turned, grabbed the almost empty wine bottle and cordially said goodnight as she left his room.

Martin went back out to the balcony. The rest of his night was uneventful. He was happy that no other light appeared in the distance and that he could now assume that Claire and Travis were indeed alone.

15

When Martin woke up, regret began to permeate his thoughts. After months of being alone, he was suddenly back in the role of catering to guests. Before the virus, Martin's job as Houseperson would involve delivering a bathrobe, or making sure the pool changeroom was clean, or tidying the lobby, or collecting the dirty linen after guests had checked out; simple tasks. Now, he had to assume all the hotel roles. Added to the hotel roles, he was also caregiver and provider. His actions would directly impact the lives of the two guests under the roof of the hotel, under his roof. Now, he was obligated to provide the basic needs of life; heat, shelter, food. Being the sole remaining representative at The Grand, he could not abandon this responsibility.

Then he re-evaluated the situation, "I don't even know if they are staying. They might just continue on their way in a couple days, leaving me alone again."

This muddied his feelings, so he decided to get out of bed and do some work, maybe clean up from last night's dinner. He was sure that moving around the hotel would make him feel better.

It was still early, only 7:30. He had no idea what time they would get up and leave their room, especially the kid. Maybe Travis would stay in bed all day. He had no intentions of waking him up early, the kid was surly enough.

After Martin washed the dishes and pots from their meal the night before, he moved to the lobby to tidy up there. He was in the middle of pushing the sofas back into their proper spots when Claire came walking down the hallway. Her long hair was wet, and she was wearing the same clothes as the night before.

"Good morning," he greeted her.

"Good morning," she replied. "I couldn't help it. I just had to have another shower. Hot water is such a luxury. I could have stood in there all day. Usually my only recourse is to wash my body with cold water and a face cloth."

She noticed that he was looking at her clothes. "Ya, I need a new wardrobe. I have about four changes of clothes. I think Travis might have two changes of clothes, at the most. I don't think he cares though."

"I could have slept in, but I was too excited about going shopping," Claire said.

"Let's get you some breakfast and then we can get going if you want," Martin suggested.

Martin showed her the restaurant kitchen. "Sorry, there are no fresh eggs, or fruit, or bread. About the only quick things I can offer you is cereal with powdered milk, or frozen waffles," Martin said.

Claire had a couple waffles and coffee.

"It's slightly disturbing that the cream does not have an expiry date," Claire remarked as she poured the contents of the little creamer pots into her coffee.

She quickly finished her meal.

"Either you are really hungry, or you really want to go shopping," Martin joked, then he paused, "but do we still call it shopping if we are actually breaking into the store and taking stuff ?"

"I think calling it shopping sounds more civilized," Claire said.

"Well," Martin started, then looked around, as if he didn't want anyone to hear, "I sometimes still leave money behind when I am taking stuff. Don't tell Travis. He'll think I'm a geek."

"You are a good judge of character, Travis would crucify you if he heard that. I don't need the extra negativity, so I won't tell him a thing," Claire said. "It just shows that you're an honest person."

"So, you ready to go, should we get Travis?" Martin asked

"No, he is probably still sleeping. I had to drag him out of bed every morning to get going. Then he would just berate me. It was like waking a teenager up for school. Except he is not even my kid. No, I think I could use some time away from Travis," Claire confessed.

Ten minutes later they were ready to go. They both donned fall jackets. Hidden in his duffel bag, Martin had some tools, bottled water and the pistol crossbow. He did not want to divulge that he had weapons in the building. He had learned from movies that once you introduce weapons into a weaponless community, only bad things happen. So for now he was going to let it be his secret.

Claire however was curious "What's in the bag?"

"Just tools and a couple bottles of water for us."

Changing the subject, Martin said, "I thought we would drive. I know we could be there in about five minutes walking, but with a vehicle you can bring home more stuff."

"Sounds like a perfect plan," Claire replied beaming.

"I'll be back in a minute."

Martin went into the valet office and returned holding a set of car keys.

He led her down to the Porsche Cayenne in the parking garage.

"There should be just enough gas left to get us to the village and back. Believe it or not, with the way the roads are laid out, it actually takes longer to drive to the village than it does to walk."

"Nice car," Claire said impressed.

"Ya, but Porsches are a dime a dozen here. The norm is Porches, B'mers, Audis, Mercedes, Jags. This one belonged to a guest." He paused, Martin did not feel he had to elaborate further.

"One time I used this thing to pick up a drum of diesel fuel. Even though it is a sport utility vehicle, I don't think the owner ever envisioned it to be used to haul grimy gas cans around. I think a shopping trip to the mall is much more what this SUV is used to."

As they left the parking garage, Claire was surprised at the extent of Martin's security measures to keep the doors secure.

"I don't want anyone sneaking in the back door," he told her.

Ten minutes later, they were approaching the shopping village. Martin drove directly through the centre of the huge, empty parking lot.

"I still find it unsettling when I see these big parking lots totally empty. It's not right. It should be full of cars," she lamented.

"I know what you mean. During peak season this lot is full, so full that additional guests have to use an overflow parking across the way there. Even when all the shops were closed for the day, there were always still a lot of cars here belonging to people staying in the timeshare condo suites above the stores," Martin said. "It is eerie seeing the lot empty."

"In our situation though, we won't be using the parking lot. Hold on tight. Let's see if this SUV is good for off-road or if it's just a sissified, city SUV."

Martin drove the Porsche up a small grass incline and onto a portion of the paving stone sidewalk. He stopped in front of a pet accessories boutique.

"The whole retail village is for pedestrians only. That is the closest visitors can get with their cars." He pointed to the parking lot they just drove through. "But, I like to keep the car as close as possible, so we will just continue on driving down this cobblestone promenade."

He put the SUV back into gear and drove parallel to the store fronts.

The village resembled an old European city, with narrow avenues, lined by shops, cafes, and restaurants. Above the businesses were three stories of timeshare condos with balconies overlooking the action below. The condos had the appearance of Bavarian architecture with peaked roofs and dark ornate trim on a white stucco facade. The village had a central square with a small covered bandstand and a fountain. One end of the square opened onto the base of a ski run.

In the winter it was common to see skiers walking through the village, or relaxing on a patio in the warm sun enjoying a pint of beer or an exotic coffee still wearing their ski boots and goggles. Instead of a bike rack, a rack for skis and snowboards sat outside most shops where customers could leave their equipment while they browsed for a new equipment, or get a vente non-fat no foam caramel macchiato. In the summer and fall, it was common to see mountain bikers pushing their bikes down the cobblestone streets, both rider and bike splattered with mud after a day's ride around the mountain trails.

Now the village was deserted. All the store fronts were intact, no broken windows, the glass front doors not smashed. Chairs still sat arranged around tables in the patios outside the restaurants and pubs. Only a couple chairs here and there had blown over by the wind.

Looking around, Martin remarked, "You can tell by the flowerbeds, that no one has been here for a while. There was a fulltime landscaping crew for the village. Usually the flower beds are lush with colours, even this time of year. Now they are just beds of dirt and weeds. No one around to even plant the flowers in May this year."

"Sorry," he apologized. "I don't want to put a downer on the day."

Claire replied, "no worries, nothing can get me down today."

"I have keys to most of the businesses here. After everyone departed, I broke into the property manager's office. I had befriended the manager a year ago, had been in his office, and had seen him use the keys. He needed the keys to all the businesses for security measures. Plus, he needed to let owners in their own stores when they forgot their keys at home."

Martin showed her a large ring of keys. Each key had a white sticker with a name printed on it.

"I figured, there are two ways to get inside a store, the civilized way using a key or even picking the lock, which I'm not really good at, or the barbaric way which would be just smashing the front door and walking in."

"At least we don't have to wait for the shops to open," Claire said looking at her watch. It was only 8:45.

Martin parked mere feet from the front door of a store. Claire barely gave the SUV time to come to a complete stop before she jumped out her door in excitement. They had stopped in front of a Lululemon clothing outlet. Martin had seen the familiar logo countless times on guests at the hotel. The yoga wear was almost a uniform for the female guests that frequented The Grand.

Martin found the proper key, and unlocked the front door. Claire rushed in. He followed her inside and walked around the store, then checked the rear storage area. The back door was still locked. The store was the same as it had been left months ago when the lone remaining employee left on what would be her last shift. Garments were still neatly arranged in coloured piles on tables and or hanging on the walls.

"Take your time, I'm going to sit in the SUV and keep my eye on things," Martin said.

Twenty minutes later Claire came out with three large bags bursting with clothes. She threw the bags into the back seat.

"Onto the next place," she said with a huge grin on her face.

Martin led her into a shoe store. He thought that most of the shoes in the display window, high heels, open toed flats, thin strapped sandals, were impractical for the current situation, but did not say anything.

"While you look at shoes, I'm going across the way to the coffee place there," Martin pointed to a cafe twenty feet on the other side of the lane.

As soon as Martin opened the door of the cafe, he was hit with the stench of rotting food. Behind a baker's style glass display case sat a selection of what would have originally been fruit pies, cakes, breads and pastries that had been left out for sale. He only knew this because he often came in before to buy treats. Now, the desserts were unrecognizable after months of decay, the plates holding flattened black blobs. On the counter sat a large bowl filled with a chunky pool of sludge, which must have been a fresh fruit arrangement at one time.

Although the food had long since stopped rotting, the absence of air circulation trapped the stench inside the shop. In the cold October temperature, only a few hearty fruit flies still flittered around the counter.

He knew that the owner ran the cafe basically by himself with the help of a couple part-time staff. The owner must have died suddenly, and did not make it back to his shop the next day after baking and displaying all the treats. As was the case for many businesses during the outbreak, the owners stuck around while the part-time staff went off to be with ill loved ones. Many of the smaller businesses owners, despite being sick could not afford to miss any work, or shut the store down even for a day. A lot of them still came to work with symptoms of the virus. But being winter, it was the busiest time of the year, the time to make money even if Solara had slowed down the amount of visitors.

Martin pulled the collar of his shirt overtop of his nose and went further into the store. There was a small dining area where patrons could enjoy an espresso with a homemade sandwich or have a latte and a pastry after a barista carefully spent five minutes concocting the beverage. Martin went to a row of wood

129

shelves with various take home products. He filled a bag with packages of free trade gourmet coffee. He picked up a tin of shortbread cookies imported from Scotland and checked the expiry date. They were still good for three more months. He added four tins of the cookies to his haul. He also took a couple boxes of biscotti, the contents still wrapped in cellophane. He looked around, nothing else was salvageable. If he needed more coffee in the future, he would just come back. The stench hastened his decision to leave the store.

He met Claire at the SUV.

"I managed to find some Sketchers, a pair of Blundstones, and a couple other items," she announced proudly. "I got them for a real bargain, too," she joked.

They spent another hour shopping for Claire in other stores. Claire shared the philosophy of only taking what you need, but she still picked up a few of what she called "irresistible" items like a Coach purse.

When she was done, she had a whole new wardrobe including a swimsuit, and a couple winter coats. She showed him a long puffy black coat made by The North Face, which looked more like a sleeping bag, and a Spyder brand ski jacket with a price tag of $1300.

From where they were standing he could see the top floors of The Grand, only a few hundred yards away. It made him want to return home.

"Since we are here, let's check out the village grocery store. It's handy for guests, so they can bring food back to their room without having to leave the resort. Of course everything is about fifty percent more expensive than buying the same thing at a store back home, but I guess it's worth the convenience."

They drove around the corner to the small grocery store, The Ski In Market. Martin unlocked the door. He forgot to warn her about the foul smell of rotted food. When they opened the front door, Claire took a step back, "Oh my god!" she exclaimed, her words muffled as she had her elbow covering her mouth and nose.

"Sorry, I should have given you a heads up. This food has been sitting in here for all these months," Martin apologized.

"I did come here to get some food the day after the electricity went off for good. Of course by that time there were no people around. I loaded the trunk up with frozen pizzas, lasagna, Hungry Man meals, and some bags of frozen vegetables. But I could only take as much as my freezer would hold."

"The smell is unbearable," Claire said. "I'll make you a deal. I'll make us spaghetti tonight if you let me go back outside while you get the food. See if you can get the ingredients for a spaghetti dinner."

Martin agreed. Claire waited outside in the fresh air while Martin made his way through the dark store. When he was done, he had filled an entire shopping cart.

Claire was beaming all the way back to The Grand, delighted with her new wardrobe. Her mood warmed up the Porsche.

Once back at the hotel, Martin and Claire loaded up a luggage cart with all the items from their outing.

"Just let me freshen up, then I'll come down and start supper," she told Martin as she dropped all of her shopping bags onto her bed.

Martin returned the luggage cart to the lobby where a half dozen other carts sat waiting for guests that would never arrive.

There was still no sign of Travis.

This gave Martin an idea. He went down to the housekeeping office and took three Motorola walkie-talkie two-way radios. They were already fully charged from sitting in a charging station for weeks. Martin made a quick tour of the main areas of the hotel looking for Travis but did not see him. Then he knocked on Travis's door. It was already mid-afternoon. There was no answer. He knocked again.

"Hold on," was the annoyed response from the other side of the door.

Travis opened the door halfway. He was wearing a soiled white t-shirt and boxer shorts covered with Harley Davidson logos.

"Ya?" he said to Martin.

"Just checking in," Martin said. "We're back."

"Back from where? I just woke up."

Martin could smell stale cigarette smoke from inside the room.

"There's no smoking in the rooms," Martin informed him.

"Sorry, I didn't, know that."

"What do you mean Travis? Considering that people can't smoke anywhere these days, I never thought to tell you that all the rooms are non-smoking. Plus there is a no-smoking sticker on the back of this door."

"OK, I'll keep that in mind. I thought there were no rules now," Travis said.

"No rules?" Martin asked.

"Ya, it's like, the end of the world you know, I thought I wouldn't have to follow any rules."

"Well at least in this hotel there are some rules, and one of them is no smoking anywhere," Martin repeated.

Martin handed Travis one of the Motorola radios. " Here, keep it on and I will call you when it's time for dinner. All you have to do is press this button on the side to talk. Then let go to listen again. This way I can reach you anywhere in the hotel and don't have to wander all over the place looking for you."

Martin was fuming but didn't want to get into an argument with Travis. Smoking in the rooms was one of the things that irritated Martin the most. It required a great deal of work to get rid of the smoke smell and it also showed disrespect for the hotel and staff. All it took was a hint of the remnants of cigarette smoke for a new guest to complain about the room. Management then had to accommodate the disgruntled guest with a room discount or amenity coupons, all of which cost the hotel money.

Martin was on the elevator when he heard a crackly voice coming from his radio, "Martin?"

Martin responded, "Go ahead, Travis."

"You're an asshole," Travis said on the other end.

Martin was caught off guard, and before he could say anything, Travis said, "Just testing to see if the thing works. See ya later."

Martin did not reply. He didn't know Travis well enough to know if he was joking or taking the opportunity to say how he really felt about him.

When Martin got to the lobby, he took a can of Coke from the bar and sat in one of the armchairs to relax until Claire came down.

Martin felt someone shaking his shoulder. He had fallen asleep. He could smell Claire's sweet perfume even before he opened his eyes

"Why do men find shopping so exhausting?" she laughed.

She was dressed completely in Lululemon gear, black tight yoga pants, and a pink hoodie overtop a black t-shirt.

"I got these to walk around the hotel in."

She lifted up one foot to show off a bright yellow flip flop, with what looked like a braided towel material running over the top of her foot and the familiar green alligator logo. "Way more comfortable than wearing socks and shoes."

"Well, you look and smell refreshed," Martin said.

"Oh ya, I found some Chanel Chance perfume in the last store. I couldn't resist. I have some at home but forgot it. It was Philip's favourite."

Martin assumed that Philip was her husband.

He led her to the restaurant kitchen and showed her how to start the gas stove and use the convection oven. Claire insisted on doing everything else herself and kicked Martin out of the kitchen.

Less than two hours later, the three of them were enjoying Claire's vegetarian spaghetti dinner at a table in the centre of The Innsbruck's dining room.

"Well, this is a nice treat," Martin said. "It's been a long time since anyone cooked for me."

"That's because everyone but us in the world has been dead for, like, ten months," Travis replied.

"I mean even before the virus started. I can't remember the last time someone cooked for me, " Martin confessed.

"Sorry there's no meat in it. Spaghetti is one meal you can make that doesn't necessarily require meat. I used frozen vegetables, just to save the meat we do have."

"It's delicious." Martin said.

"Garlic bread would have been nice," Travis suggested.

"Actually, I was thinking along the same lines," Claire said. "At home I had a bread maker. All you do is throw the ingredients in the machine and an hour later you have bread. It's simple, basically all you need is water, bread flour, bread yeast, and of course the bread maker."

"That's an excellent idea," Martin agreed. "Looks like another shopping day tomorrow. We will have to go into town though. There is a hardware store in Odgen Marsh that probably will have a bread maker. It's about twenty minutes away."

"Want to come Travis?" Claire asked.

"Are you kidding, shopping for bread makers with you two dorks," Travis replied.

"Whatever," Claire said, "see if we give you any bread."

Travis poured himself another glass of wine from the bottle Claire had set out. "I don't usually drink wine, but you gotta take what you can get right?" Travis said.

"They got any video game stores in that town?" Travis asked.

"Ya, they have a Radio Shack, it has video games. Pretty sure they sell systems too," Martin said.

"Maybe I will go with you. Get a PS3 or Xbox 360," Travis said.

Martin took the opportunity to ask them a question that had been on his mind.

"So, what are your plans? I mean, you're welcome to stay here as long as you want, but we never really discussed if you're going to continue on driving, or if you're staying for a couple days, or a week, or whatever."

"Travis and I never really discussed it," Claire said.

"Just a warning, winter comes early around here. The snow will start flying in less than a month, and without snowplows to clear the roads, you could be stuck wherever you happen to have stopped for the night. You wake up one morning and there is a foot of snow. In the blink of an eye you go from fall to winter. I will be basically trapped inside here for six months, but then again, I am not going anywhere anyways, but at least I will have heat, power, and food. I can offer you that much," he said.

"Ya, and a hot tub, an arcade, and booze," Travis added.

"That too. It's your call," Martin said. A thought flashed through his mind, trapped here with Travis for six months.

"Maybe you should have headed south. I don't think people realize how soon winter comes to this area. Most people who don't get much snow, think winter starts around Christmas time. And I know some of the nearby cities don't get much snow, even though they are only a two hour drive away. We've had snow start as early as mid October and not go away until the end

134

of April. So really, we could only have a couple weeks until permanent snow, " Martin said.

He was suddenly hit with the urgency of the timing. With winter coming, he had to make a lot of preparations in the next couple weeks. He started to get an anxious feeling.

"Well I ain't got nowhere to go," Travis said without consulting with his travelling companion.

"I would be happy to stay here," Claire agreed. "I didn't have a destination in mind either. I'm getting tired of scrounging for food every day, and not knowing where I will sleep at night."

"Well, let me know for sure in the morning. You can sleep on it." Martin said.

"You have your Motorola?" Martin asked Travis.

"No, it's up in my room," he said.

Martin rolled his eyes in frustration.

Turning to Claire, Martin held up his Motorola. "I came up with a way we can stay in contact with each other. The hotel uses these radios. Staff used them to talk to each other from anywhere in the building, and even outside the building. Usually it's the front desk asking us to deliver towels to a room, or unclog a toilet, stuff like that. If you carry your radio with you, we can be in contact at all times. It is fully charged. Keep it on station two. All you do is press the button on the side and talk. Let go to listen. If you want to speak to someone, you say, 'Travis come in', and Travis would respond, 'Go ahead, Claire' and then you just say what you want. At the end you say 'copy' to let the person know you heard and understood the message. I already gave Travis his radio."

He handed Claire her radio.

"You really are Paul Blart," Travis said. "It's just us, we don't have to say copy, and go ahead, and all that shit."

"I guess not, it's radio etiquette," Martin said, "but I probably will still say copy, and go ahead, out of habit."

Claire took her radio.

Claire asked Travis to clear the table of the dirty dishes. He reluctantly agreed.

"Hey at least there's a dishwasher," Martin said. "You have two hours before the power shuts down."

"I think I will go do a work out," Claire said.

"That's not a bad idea. It's been a few days since I went on the treadmill," Martin said.

Soon they were jogging side by side in the gym. Claire had changed into a different Lululemon outfit and had on a new pair of pink Saucony jogging shoes.

When she first got on her treadmill, Claire instinctively pressed the power button to turn on the small TV screen attached to the treadmill. The screen powered up, but only fuzzy static appeared.

"Um, there is no cable," Martin reminder her.

"Oh, ya how stupid. Just natural reaction I guess", she said embarrassed.

While they jogged, Martin explained his theory on building your endurance and that he got the idea from a zombie movie. Claire mulled it over, and then agreed it was a smart idea to stay in shape just in case you had to evade a hostile person.

After fifteen minutes, Martin was tired but did not want to show it. Claire kept going strong.

"I think I've had enough," he said when he saw that she still had twenty minutes left on the timer for her run.

"Ok, when I am done here, I might use an elliptical machine, then the Pilates ball. Even if the power goes off, I can still do Pilates," Claire said.

Martin handed her a flashlight he had hidden in a small storage closet at one end of the gym.

"Here, take this so you can find your way back to your room. The hallways are pitch black after the lights go out. Just remember to turn it off when you are near any windows. I'll talk to you later," he said as he left the gym.

Martin went down to The Innsbruck to inspect the young guest's cleaning attempt. Travis had finished, and was nowhere in sight. Martin lifted up the stainless steel door on the commercial dishwasher. The rack of dishes was still inside, unwashed. Travis had not bothered to scrape off the plates. Remnants of noodles and sauce clung to the plates. Martin sprayed the plates off, then started the dishwasher. On the whole, Travis had done a better job than expected. He did not wipe their table down, but at least it was totally cleared.

Martin called on the radio, "Travis, come in?"

"Ya?"

"Thanks for cleaning up."

"Ok."

"What are you doing tonight?" Martin asked.

"Nothin, stayin in my room, playing a game. Have a couple beers."

"OK, talk to you later." Martin left it at that. He did not really want to hang out with Travis anyway.

After another shower, Claire met Martin in his cozy room to relax with a bottle of wine. There was a pause in the conversation as both sat quietly sipping their wine in the candlelight.

"Do you hear that?" Martin asked.

Claire shook her head.

"There's like, no sound at all. We're not talking. The heat's off, and with the power off, none of the appliances are humming. It's one of those rare times when you are with someone else and there is no sound at all."

"I didn't notice."

"Silence is a true example of natural perfection."

"Pardon?" Claire asked.

"Silence is a true example of natural perfection," he repeated.

"What's that from?"

"Nowhere, I made it up. When you're walking around the empty building you notice things like how quiet it can get and I was thinking, and I know this sounds strange, but how much effort it takes to have silence. If you think about it, there's always some sound, even if you are in a room alone, there is always white noise going on in the background. So I was thinking that absolute silence is rare, like some sort of perfect thing. Then I thought about how it would make a good quote, like people put up on *facebook*. It took me awhile to get the words right, but then I put it together, 'Silence is a true example of natural perfection'. I don't know, maybe it's corny."

"No, I like it," Claire said. "You should've been a writer."

"I always wanted to write a novel or something, but never got around to it. I guess it's too late now."

"It's too late for a lot of things now," Claire added.

16

The next morning, Martin was thinking that the idea of using the radios was looking more and more like a brilliant idea. He could do his own thing, but still stay connected with the others. He was in the guest laundry room making sure all the machines were operational, when Claire called him over the radio around ten o'clock. She had checked the lobby for him, then after making herself frozen waffles at the restaurant, she knocked on his door to find him not there either.

Martin responded. "I usually get up around seven. My body is still on a work schedule."

"I'm ready to go into town whenever you are," Claire said.
Martin called Travis, "Travis, come in?" Martin waited thirty seconds, "Travis, come in?"

A groggy sounding voice answered, "Jesus, what?"

"We are leaving to go to town soon. We will wait in the lobby."

"What?" Travis asked confused.

"We are going into town, you said you wanted to come to get an XBOX."

"Oh, ya," Travis said. "Wait a minute. You woke me up."

Claire joined the radio conversation, "Just get down here Travis."

Martin quickly retrieved a coat and his tool bag from his room. Before returning to the lobby, he went down to the parkade to take inventory of the available cars and try to remember which one had enough gas to get them to town and back.

Martin returned to see Claire leaning against the reception counter. Travis had still not come down. Martin got a set of keys from the valet office then called Travis on the radio again.

"OK, relax, I'm on my way," Travis replied.

Travis was down ten minutes later. The trio walked through the parkade, passing one empty parking spot after another until they turned a corner and all the remaining cars came into view.

"Holy shit!", Travis exclaimed, suddenly awake.

Frozen in place, Travis's gaze moved from car to car, choosing which luxury model they should take. Martin explained that most of the cars belonged to rich guests who had passed away.

"Let's take the yellow Porsche," Travis said after a moment, indicating the bright yellow Porsche 911 sports car.

"Um, we're taking the silver Mercedes over there," Martin said, pointing to a four door Mercedes sedan.

"Are you kidding me, that grandpa car?" Travis protested.

"That Porsche only has two seats, and not much cargo space. There's three of us, remember?" Martin said. "If you want, we can take the rusted out maroon Pontiac Sunfire there, it belonged to a valet guy."

Travis did not say anything for a few seconds. "OK, we'll take the Mercedes, but you owe me a ride in that Porsche."

They reached Ogden Marsh twenty minutes later. It was a typical small rural town. County Road 7 passed right through the centre of Ogden Marsh, briefly became Main Street for five blocks then continued on as County Road 7, which was the biggest road the county had to offer. The locals called it "the highway" because it was the main artery in the area, and the route used by all the tourists to reach the resort area. It was also a well maintained two lane thoroughfare, which compared to many of the country gravel roads, or pot holed filled side streets, did seem like a highway.

For travellers, Ogden Marsh was more of an inconvenience, forcing them to reduce their speed or sometimes even stop at one of the two traffic lights in town. It was viewed as an annoying hindrance that put them behind schedule in reaching their final destination, the resort.

Main Street was complete with two banks, a funeral home, The Winchester Tavern, Cormac's Family Restaurant, McCarthy's Hardware, a Radio Shack, and a few other businesses, including a combination convenience store, bait shop, and video rental store.

The only gas station within a twenty minute drive was on the edge of Ogden Marsh. A full service station, the owner or one of his sons would pump the gas for the customer, then wash the windshield. The tourists enjoyed the rustic charm of the service, and for some it became a traditional stop on the way to the resort. Locals resented the fact that the inflated price of gas here was geared to the carefree tourists.

Martin parked the car in front of McCarthy's Hardware.

"I get shotgun for the ride home," Travis announced as he climbed out of the backseat.

Out of habit, Martin almost put change into the parking meter. He looked up and down the street. It was still a strange feeling to see the main drag deserted, no one on the sidewalks, no cars driving through, all the stores dark. There were only two cars parked on the street, both dusty, and both probably belonging to someone who had lived in an apartment above one of the stores. There were no signs of looting anywhere.

The big plate glass window on the hardware store had a thin layer of dust making it hard to see inside. The neon "Open" sign on the other side of the glass seemed anaemic without electricity to provide its bright colours.

"Wait here," Martin said to Travis. "We're going to find a way in."

He motioned to Claire to follow him. They took an alleyway beside the store to get to the rear. A driveway used for deliveries and staff parking at the back of the stores ran the length of the block. A weather beaten wooden fence separated the driveway and the backyards of the houses on the next street. The bare branches of the oaks and maples planted years earlier in the properties matched the stark image of the lifeless row of houses.

In one of the backyards, the top of a swing set could be seen above the fence line. A candy cane striping of bright red and purple on the swing set's frame stood out on the grey day. "Looks new" Martin thought to himself, assuming that it was probably put up in the summer a year ago for the kids that used to live in the house. The parents bought it with the idea that their children would get years of enjoyment out of the swing set. He did not want to say anything to draw Claire's attention to the depressing sight.

Martin surveyed his options about getting into the hardware store. Metal double doors seemed to be the best route inside. A small faded metal sign on the door read *Deliveries 3 pm-5 pm*.

He was pulling a crowbar out of his tool bag, when he was startled by the sound of breaking glass.

Claire shot Martin a scared look. "I think that came from the front!"

Wielding the crowbar, Martin bolted to the front of the store with Claire close behind. Travis stood on the sidewalk, looking pleased with himself. McCarthy's large plate window was shattered. Broken shards of glass strewn across the sidewalk. Shards were also sprayed inside the front display area of the store.

"Thought I'd speed the process up a bit," Travis boasted. "Missed the target though," he pointed to an "X" he had marked in the dust on the glass door with his finger.

"I could have done that!" Martin yelled.

"What's the big deal?" Travis asked agitated.

"We're trying to keep things civilized here. Do you see any other stores with the windows smashed in?" Martin asked.

"Well, we're in now," Travis mumbled.

Claire was still silent, not sure what to say.

The opening still had jagged pieces of glass sticking out of the frame on the bottom. Martin ran the crowbar along the frame to break off all the shards of glass, making it smooth. The top still had shards hanging down, like piranha teeth.

Martin went to the trunk of the car and pulled out a sleeping bag. "The owners had this in their trunk, part of an emergency road kit I guess, for the drive from the city into the wilds of the resort area."

He laid the sleeping bag across the open frame of the window.

"So you don't cut yourself when you crawl in to unlock the front door," Martin said to Travis.

Travis looked at Martin, then looked at the laid out sleeping bag, then gave a sigh of disapproval. After uttering something under his breath, he reluctantly crawled up into the window frame and onto the display area.

A tiny pink bike with tassels on the handle bars and training wheels sat in front of a four foot high Christmas tree. Other toys were on display as well. Under the tree, presents with sun faded wrapping paper completed the scene. Travis pushed the tree over to get it out of his way scattering ornaments everywhere. He picked up a present and tossed it behind him onto the sidewalk.

"Here Martin, I got you a present, it's only been sitting here for, like, a year."

Travis unlocked the front door, then turned back into the dark store to look around. It had a distinguishable musty smell due to the lack of air circulation for months.

"This place smells like my grandma's dank basement," Travis remarked.

McCarthy's was a traditional small town, main street hardware store that had been family run for decades and was set up to sell almost everything. It had the role of catering to a rural area that did not have a department store, or a big box hardware outlet. Merchandise was arranged on the three aisles that stretched to the back of the narrow floor space. Shoppers could find everything from a toothbrush, to an electric drill, to bird seed, to a mop. At the back of the store was a small toy section which must have sold many a Christmas and birthday present over the years. The store had one solitary checkout counter at the front.

It only took them fifteen minutes to find the items they needed. Martin got batteries of all sizes, and two more camping lanterns. Claire got a bread maker and a stainless steel water bottle. The store was full of other everyday, useful items, but everything they needed was already in abundance at the hotel.

"I got razors," Claire said, "I haven't shaved my legs in a couple months. Why bother right? Besides I didn't have hot water. But now that I might be putting on a swim suit again I thought I should pick up a pack of razors."

For Travis however, after quickly discovering that the store's small electronics section did not have video game systems, he waited impatiently outside. Every couple minutes he would bang on the glass of the front door or yell in the gaping window, "Yo, you guys done yet?"

To appease Travis, they drove the two blocks down the street and parked in front of Radio Shack.

"Why'd we drive?" Travis asked, "thought we were trying to save gas."

"For protection. I like to keep the car close. I don't like the idea of having to run far to get to the car in case of an emergency," Martin said.

142

Travis looked in both directions down the empty Main Street. "Whatever."

Martin took Travis to the back of Radio Shack. He pried the rear door open with his crowbar to gain entry.

"That is how you can get in without smashing the front window," Martin said.

"Claire and I will be across the street at the grocery store. We'll meet at the car. And please leave the same way we came in. Use the back door," Martin pleaded.

Beside Radio Shack was a small community policing office, CAPTAIN TRIPPS was painted in gold lettering on the front window. Like everywhere else, the police office looked like no one had been there for a long time.

Martin and Claire went across the street to the Super-Duper Mart, one of the last remaining stores in a once large national grocery chain which was slowly being beaten down by the larger big box grocery outlets and super sized multiservice department stores. With only five aisles of food, it was just the right size to serve the sparsely populated area.

"Let's make this quick," Martin said. "It shouldn't be too hard to collect edible food, all the fresh stuff will be long spoiled."

"Not looking forward to this," Claire said as she pulled the collar of her top up over her nose and followed Martin in through the delivery bay door. Both of them took a shopping cart.

Like the small market at the resort, all the fresh food had been rotting for months. The smell of rancid food was mixed with another stench however. As they walked through the first aisle they felt something crunching under their shoes. Martin shined a flashlight on the white linoleum floor to reveal what looked like black pieces of puffy rice scattered everywhere.

"Great, mice droppings" he said.

"What?" Claire said, looking at the feces. She sounded slightly panicked but stayed calm. "Mice I don't mind, snakes are what scare me."

Droppings were also on the shelves. The mix of decaying mouse feces and the rotting food was unbearable. Martin shone his flashlight onto a shelf with boxes of breakfast cereal. A couple mice scuttled away.

A mini deli was situated at the back of the store. A selection of cold cuts were still behind the glass counter. The rolls of meat were now shrivelled logs, covered with a green moss of mould. One wall of the store was taken up with floor to ceiling glass freezer units. The dark units were still fully stocked with food in brightly coloured cardboard boxes.

"That's a shame. All that food spoiled. We could have lived off this for months," Claire observed.

They were also dismayed to see that even most of the non perishable food was made unsalvageable by the infestation of mice. Boxes of instant potatoes, crackers, and cookies had the corner chewed off so the mice could get at the contents inside.

"We should take whatever we can now. We can't leave some for next time, there won't be any left," Martin said.

When he went past the dairy section, he could see that some of the plastic jugs of milk had exploded out of the top lid from the summer heat, then dried on the shelves over the past couple months. The smell of rancid milk still lingered, making him gag. He quickly moved to the next aisle.

It didn't take long for the pair to fill two shopping carts each. They took any remaining items that the packaging had not been compromised.

When they got to the car, Travis was already sitting inside. Half of the back seat was loaded with Radio Shack bags filled with video game cases and a couple boxes with gaming consoles. A long box with a picture of a cheap looking plastic guitar stood upright on the floor. Beside the bags, stacked on top of each other were two cases of Budweiser cans.

"Got my stuff. Got an Xbox 360, but they didn't have a PS3, only a PS2. I haven't played PS2 for, like, three years. I grabbed one anyway. Got Guitar Hero Metallica, and a guitar. And made a trip to the convenience store to stock up on beer, and JD." Travis said as he held up a brown paper bag for them to see.

"And yes, I went through the back door of the store. I used a rock to smash off the door knob. I even closed the door behind me when I left." Travis's mood had noticeably improved.

"We got necessities of life," Claire said.

"I guess I'll sit in the back with my stuff, look through the games," Travis said, not catching on to her inference.

Once the groceries were put into the trunk, Martin pushed the shopping carts back across the street to the cart corral in the Super-Duper Mart parking lot.

"This guy is nutty," Travis said as he watched Martin return the cart.

"Ya, I have concluded that he likes things in their proper place," Claire said.

On the ride home, Martin noticed that Claire was silently starring out her window as they passed one abandoned house after another. He knew what she was thinking. He had the same thoughts of regret every time he left the hotel. He wanted to turn on the radio. Music would be a distraction, but knew all he would get was static.

Travis was busy opening up his video game cases, throwing the cellophane wrapping on the floor by his feet.

When they got back to the hotel, Travis immediately took his stuff up to his room, leaving his companions to unload the food and supplies.

"I think I will make us some homemade bread," Claire announced after they had put away all the food into the restaurant pantry.

"Ok, I am just going to do a walk around. I like to check the entire building every day. Start at the top floor and then make my way to the lowest level. It's my way to make sure everything is ok."

Their supper was not the most exotic, frozen chicken fingers that were on the restaurant's kids menu, french fries, and peas from a can. The best part was the fresh bread, still warm.

"You know, I haven't used the hot tub yet," Claire said, "but if the power is off in a couple hours, I guess it won't be much good."

"Ya, if we keep the jets going until the power shuts off at least the water will be hot," Martin said, "but with the jets off, it's kinda like you're sitting in a bathtub with other people."

Travis raised his head to stop eating for a second. He usually didn't contribute much to the conversation when they were all together. "I saw on the internet, you know, like how people send pictures around of stupid stuff. This was rednecks. One showed how they attached a boat motor to the side of an above ground pool to make it into a hot tub. You can do that."

Martin thought of a better idea but kept it to himself for a moment. He looked at Claire to gage her reaction before he spoke.

She rolled her eyes, "I'm not that desperate for a soak in a hot tub."

"I could just hook the electrical up to small portable generator, and then we could be in the hot tub when the main power goes off. A small generator might be good for a couple hours with the amount of power the hot tub uses."

As soon as the words were out of his mouth, he regretted putting the idea out there. He was waiting for the light bulb to go off in Travis's head, but Travis finished off his fries, then got up from the table.

"I might join you," Travis said. "After the power goes out what the hell else am I going to do? Might as well sit around in the tub, have a couple beers."

He got ten feet from the table, stopped dead in the middle of the restaurant dining room, and turned around.

"Crap, here it comes," Martin thought.

"Hey, I could set up one of those generators in my room, then I could play video games all night."

Martin nodded, and dropped his head in defeat. He could not say no. "OK, I will do it if you can wait until tomorrow. I have to scrounge up another portable generator. Then I will get it set up in your room. Tonight I just want us to all relax in the hot tub."

17

The hot tub sat in one corner of the indoor pool room. The pool itself was the standard rectangle shape. It was not as popular as the outdoor pool, catering mostly to seniors who did not want to get a chill by going outside or parents who in the winter time were not as brave as their children to go swimming when the pool was surrounded by snow. The swimming pool water was murky but not as bad as the outdoor pool which was exposed to the elements.

Tall tinted windows made up the outside wall. Wicker lounge chairs were arranged around the pool. Each chair had a Hawaiian theme cushion on top. Potted fake palm trees were placed in the corners to add to the atmosphere.

Martin got the generator running and hooked it up to the hot tub. To cut down on the noise, he put the generator in a small storage room that housed the hot tub's pump and filtration system. The exterior of the pump room was fabricated to look like a garden shed with cedar shingles, and wide, rough hewn planks.

Claire sat patiently stretched out on a lounge chair watching while he worked away. She was wrapped up in a fluffy white bathrobe, *The Grand Summit Place* stitched in gold thread across the front.

"That's loud," Claire said when he cranked up the generator.

Closing the door to the shack helped to dampened the noise.

Claire stood up and let the robe drop to the ground. She was wearing a modest one piece black swimsuit.

Martin had to admit that he was slightly disappointed that she was not wearing a bikini. In her swimsuit, he could see that her body was well toned, her stomach flat, but the suit was not overly exciting.

She stepped into the hot tub and placed a bottle of champagne on the ledge. She sighed with relief as she sank down and the bubbly water came up to her shoulders. She tilted her neck back

147

until her head was resting on the tub's edge. She closed her eyes and sighed again. "Nice," she purred without opening her eyes.

The hot tub was designed to look like a sunken tropical pool, complete with greenery, and at one end, a faux cliff rose six feet above the ground. A waterfall feature allowed water to gently cascade down the cliff into the pool.

Martin joined her in the tub, taking a seat on the opposite side.

Travis walked into the pool room wearing only green boxer shorts with pictures of Homer Simpson dressed up as Santa Claus. The colours were faded. Without his shirt on, Martin noticed he looked more fit than he appeared with the layers of clothes he usually wore. He was short, around five-ten, which worked to his advantage to make him look muscular.

"Am I interrupting?" Travis asked, then laughed, "No, not Andy."

Claire opened her eyes and turned to Travis, "Uh, no way, no way are you coming in here in your underwear. Who knows when last time you washed those things!"

"What? It's not like I threw a bathing suit into my survival bag with me when I left home," Travis protested.

Martin intervened, "Why don't you go to the Wave Shop. It's the small store beside the change rooms leading to the outdoor pool. It has a selection of bathing suits, hats, suntan lotion, goggles, all that stuff. Go pick out a suit."

"I'll pay for it myself," Claire said smirking.

"I'm surprised he has a change of underwear, yesterday he had different boxers on," Martin said.

Travis gave Martin the finger, then headed off to the Wave Shop.

Ten minutes later, Travis returned wearing a new swimsuit that came to his knees. It was black with photographed gold fish repeated as a pattern throughout. "You, owe the shop $110 Claire. Can you believe that shit? Like, they are Billabongs, but a hundred and ten bucks?"

He had grabbed a six pack of beer along the way. "I thought I'd join the party," he said nodding at the bottle beside Claire.

Travis just got into the hot tub when the electricity went off for the night.

"Just in time," Travis said looking up at the ceiling.

The only remaining light came from the setting sun coming through the large windows at the other end of the pool room.

Claire peeled off the foil wrapped around the top of the champagne bottle, and twisted the wire that secured the cork.

"Wow, the cork is made of like, real cork, not plastic. Ritzy shit," Travis said.

Claire kneeled on her seat. With the bottom of the bottle against the rim of the tub, she pushed under the edges of the cork. With some effort, it slowly moved, then burst out of the bottle with the distinct pop sound. Champagne came frothing out like a weak fountain. The cork sailed across the room and landed in the swimming pool.

"We should offer some to the hot tub gods," she said and poured some into the water.

"I forgot glasses. I guess we will have to drink it right out of the bottle."

She took a swig, and handed it to Martin.

The glass of the bottle was cold against his hot hands. It felt comforting. He took a swig, then another. He liked the bubbly sweetness of champagne, much different than the bitterness of wine.

"Slow down Andy," Travis said.

"What are you talking about?" Claire asked.

"Oh, nothing," Travis replied with a smirk. "I'll take one drink. Don't want to be rude. Then it's me and my six friends." He held up the six pack of beer cans linked together with a plastic holder.

The three sat in silence enjoying the soothing bubbling hot water. The room slowly became dim as daylight turned to dusk. Steam rose from the surface and disappeared a couple feet in the air.

Travis quickly finished two beers. Martin got the sense that Travis had already started drinking before he came downstairs, maybe even having his first drink in the early afternoon. Martin and Claire passed the Champaign bottle back and forth.

As he crumpled his third empty beer can and dropped it off the edge of the tub, Travis broke the silence. "I was thinking, like, everyone did all this stuff to save the planet, like recycling, car pooling, sorting your garbage. What a waste of time. Look at the world now, no one around. Children are our future, what a crock of shit."

"Well, who knew right?" Martin said.

Travis chugged from a new beer. "Anyway, I didn't bother I always just threw everything into the same garbage bag. I mean why should I go out of my way? There's countries in like, Asia with millions of people, none of them do nothin'. They all keep on polluting, and we're here in North America bustin our balls trying to save the planet."

Claire said, "I did my part. I had a composter in the backyard, tried to buy things with minimal packaging, even rode by bike instead of driving sometimes. Whatever I could do to reduce my own carbon footprint on the world."

"Forget that, I ain't riding no bike when I got a car. Like, how much is that going to make a difference?" Travis said.

"It was all about doing what was socially responsible," Claire replied.

"Whatever, was still a waste of time now," Travis replied.

Travis noticed a sign that warned bathers about hot tub use:

WARNING: Pregnant women and the elderly should consult their doctor before using a hot tub. Alcohol or drug use could impair your judgment, causing you to become unconscious and drown. Do not use a hot tub if you are taking any medication that makes you drowsy or affects your circulation. Soaking in the warm water can dehydrate you, which could lead to nausea, dizziness, or fainting. Take breaks from your hot tub and drink water before getting back in.

"Blart, aren't you going to warn us about alcohol use in the hot tub?" Travis asked Martin.

Martin looked at the sign above him. "Well, you're an adult. And you just proved you can read. So I will let you decide what to do. And if you do get sick, you can sue the hotel."

Turning to Claire, Travis continued without skipping a beat, "Ok. And I don't suppose you're pregnant with Andy's love child?"

"You're an ass!" Claire said. "Why can't you just get along with people? And what's with calling him, Blart and Andy. Who the hell is Andy.?" Claire asked.

"Relax, just kidding around," Travis said. "I already explained Paul Blart, but he also reminds me of Andy, the guy from The 40 Year Old Virgin."

A slight grin came to Claire's face. Martin noticed.

She also thought Martin did have a slight resemblance to the movie character Andy in appearance and demeanor. "Try and be nice. He has done nothing to you."

"I'm going to get a drink of water, cool off," Martin said. He got out of the spa and left the pool room.

Martin returned with a bottle of water, and two vodka coolers. As he descended the steps into the tub, he turned to Travis, "I'm already tired of your crap. My name is Martin, unless that's too hard for you to remember."

"Ok...Martin," Travis said with a smirk, emphasizing the syllables.

"Now don't make me call security on you," Martin said in an attempt to alleviate the conflict.

Travis took a long drink of his beer. The three of them continued soaking in silence, until Travis announced, "well, this is boring, I'm going to play my PSP. At least I don't need power for that."

"How did you put up with him?" Martin asked Claire after Travis had left the room.

"Mostly we didn't talk. I guess with you here, he is trying to be the dominant male."

"But I am older and this is my place. Maybe I am old fashioned, but I think he should show some respect."

"Well, at least for now that might be a lot to ask," Claire said.

"But what's his deal, why so angry?" Martin asked.

"I blame his upbringing. Like he said, his mother died when he was young. He was raised by his grandmother, who was single. His father was out of the picture, so no male role model around. By the sounds of it, he was spoiled by his grandmother who felt bad for him. I think he was allowed to do whatever he wanted, plus he was an only child. Used to being the centre of attention, selfish. In a way I feel sorry for him, but I still believe that you choose your own attitude. You can't blame everything on your past, or someone else. Geeze, I'm starting to sound like one of those quotes people put up in *facebook*."

Martin laughed. "I guess he is still young, but as he gets older, and interacts with more people he will soon realize that not everyone will not put up with attitude. In this new world, if he meets up with new people, he will either find himself alone, or get beat up a few times, or worse."

Martin took a long drink from the bottle of water, and then opened up one of the vodka coolers. Claire finished off the champagne.

Claire held up one her hands, "look my fingers are all pruney."

"If you're going to nurse those coolers, I'll have one," Claire said.

Martin could tell that the alcohol was starting to affect Claire. Her thoughts were becoming more random.

"So, one day, we're startin out, looking at the map I see this place called Utopia. An actual town called Utopia! I couldn't believe it. So I says to Travis, 'We gotta go there.' Of course the moron didn't know the concept of a utopia. So I explain that it's more like a idea. A place where everything is supposed to be perfect. I say maybe a higher power intervened to save the good people of Utopia. Deep down I knew that it would be like all the other places, deserted and creepy. Travis thought I was stupid. 'It's just a word' he said. 'Just because some crappy town is called that, doesn't mean all the people aren't going to still be dead.' The little moron was right, it was deserted, but with a name like Utopia we couldn't pass up the chance to at least check it out."

"Between the steam and the darkness, I can barely see your face," Claire said.

Night had fallen outside leaving the pool room without any lighting.

"I know, with those huge windows I don't want to use a lantern," Martin said indicating the windows at the end of the pool.

Claire emptied the last sip of her cooler.

"I'm just about asleep anyway," Claire said.

She stood up, swayed, caught her balance then went up the steps of the hot tub and walked unsteadily to where she had left her robe. Martin followed her. When she bent over to pick up her robe, she staggered forward, and fell onto the soft cushion of the lounge chair. As she fell on the lounger, the cooler bottle flew out of her hand landing five feet away. Glass shattered everywhere on the tiled floor. Martin picked up the robe and put it over her shoulders. She stood there teetering back and forth like a thin tree in the wind until Martin grabbed her shoulder to steady her.

Both dripping water as they walked, her slim wet footprints beside his, they left a watery path on the ceramic floor in the lobby. He walked her to the closest suite on the first floor. In her intoxicated state he did not think she could walk the five flights of stairs up to her room.

"You can sleep in here tonight. We're on the first floor," he reminder her, as he led her into the dark room.

He sat her on the edge of the bed then opened the curtains to let the moonlight brighten the room.

"You should get you out of your wet suit though. I'll wait in the bathroom while you undress."

He stood in the bathroom waiting. He could hear the rustle of clothing.

"Claire?" he inquired.

She did not answer.

"Claire, you ok?"

Claire still did not answer. He walked out into the room assuming she was already passed out.

She was slumped backwards onto her bed, her feet still touching the carpeted floor, with her soggy swimsuit around her ankles. The robe was pulled over her naked body like a blanket.

Martin climbed onto the bed and pulled her by her shoulders until her whole body was now on the bed. He put a pillow under her head, and pulled one side of the duvet over to cover her up. He pulled her swimsuit off her feet and threw it into the bathtub. It hit with a wet plop sound. Before he left, he closed the curtains across the patio door and felt his way through the darkness, touching furniture and the wall to get to the front door of her suite.

Martin went back to the pool room and shut off the generator. He would clean up the broken glass in the morning when he had light.

On his way up the stairwell to go to his own room, he spotted a flattened beer can Travis had stomped into the second floor landing. A small puddle of beer had dribbled down the steps and filled the hallway with the smell of Budweiser. With every step, he felt more and more dizzy from the alcohol. He exited into the third floor corridor and entered the suite across from the stairwell. The room was still high enough to see the area. He was buzzing, but was alert enough to remember to complete his nightly duty of surveying the outside.

With the duvet from the room's bed wrapped around him he stood there looking through the glass. With his mind groggy, time seemed to lose meaning. Had he been staring outside for two minutes? Ten minutes? An hour? He did not know. He did not see any lights outside. He did not bother to look out the other side of the building.

He plopped down into the bed in room 313, took his wet bathing suit off and dropped it on the carpet beside the bed.

18

The next morning as promised, Martin went to set up a portable generator in Travis's room so he could use the TV and video game systems after the power went out for the night. When he walked into Travis's room Martin was appalled. It smelled like a mixture of body odour, beer, and stale cigarette smoke. The garbage cans were overflowing, wet towels were thrown all over the bathroom, and empty beer cans and junk food wrappers were scattered all around the carpeted suite. It had only taken the new guest four days to turn his room into a dump.

Martin immediately turned around and refused to set up the generator until Travis had cleaned his suite.

"You're not a paying guest you know. You have to clean up after yourself." he reminded Travis.

"Whatever," Travis replied, "How much does this room cost anyway?" he asked.

"It's the off season, so around $225 per night."

"Are you serious? This is a normal hotel room. I could stay at the Super 8, for like, $120."

Martin mumbled under his breath, "Super 8 sounds about right for you."

Martin made Travis thoroughly clean the room to the exact condition he had found it when he moved in. Once Travis was finished, Martin completed a full inspection of the suite, including looking under the bed for garbage. He then provided fresh towels and linen. Martin even made sure that Travis had the towels folded and hanging on the towel bar in the correct fashion. It took Travis most of the day to get the room back to meet The Grand Summit Place's standards for cleanliness. The entire time, Travis was whining about the futility of the exercise, arguing that there were plenty of other rooms and no one else was coming to the hotel anyway.

That night, as soon as the power went out, Travis cranked up the generator. It was irritatingly loud. Martin could clearly hear the motor pumping through the walls of his own room two doors down. Into the night, the generator kept pumping out noise. Martin fell asleep to the mechanical rhythmic pounding of the generator, then woke up at 3:34 to hear the generator still thumping. He eventually fell asleep again.

The next morning Claire complained about the volume of noise.

Travis's second night of having the generator was a repeat performance. Tired, grumpy, and wanting to go to sleep, Martin banged on Travis's door around midnight after first trying to get him on the radio. When he did not answer the door, Martin let himself in with his master key card. The dark room was illuminated by the flickering glow of the TV. Travis was sitting on the sofa playing a video game. Over the roar of the generator he yelled at his young guest to go to bed.

Travis was angry about the intrusion. "What the hell man, you can't just barge into my room!"

"I can hear the generator coming through my walls. I want to go to sleep," Martin yelled over the noise.

Travis argued, but they came to an agreement that he could keep it on for another half hour. Travis stuck to his end of the bargain, and with only one more reminder from Martin, the hotel fell silent around one in the morning.

The next day, Martin offered to move him to the other end of the hotel into a one bedroom suite with an attached den. The move would allow Travis to make as much noise as he wanted and neither Claire nor Martin would hear him.

"Before I move you, you have to totally clean this room again. Once this room is done, you can move, and stay up all night for all I care. I won't be able to hear you," Martin told him.

With a smirk on his face, Travis walked back into his room, leaving Martin waiting at the door. When Travis returned, he handed his host an envelope with The Grand hotel logo on it.

"Here, now I'm a paying customer. There's $3000, that should cover my stay so far, plus a few more days, maybe even a tip."

Martin looked down at the envelope in disbelief. Travis had obviously misconstrued what Martin meant when he said he was not a paying guest. Martin's intention was to make his young guest realize there is no free ride and he would have to help out.

Travis changed it around so that he could pay the money, and would not have to do anything.

Martin felt defeated, and could not help but think it was a demeaning gesture. He was torn between throwing it back in his face and accepting it as genuine payment for the hotel.

"Where the hell did you get all this money?" Martin asked.

"Savings," Travis replied curtly.

Martin did not believe it for a second but kept quiet. He opted to take the money and just put it in the hotel cash box. At least this way he could avoid having an altercation with Travis every time he asked him to clean his room.

"By the way, the new room I am putting you in is, $400 a night. That's for the off-season. It has a separate bedroom, a living room, and a separate TV den. Once the snow flies it goes up to $600 a night. Hope you can afford it."

The price did not seem to faze Travis even though it was illogical to charge the inflated peak rate given the current scenario. Travis was right, there was not going to be a sudden influx of people coming to the hotel, ski season or not.

Once Travis was set up at the other end of the floor, Martin and Claire could no longer hear the generator from their end of the building.

After a week at the hotel, boredom set in for Claire. There was a limited amount of activities to do inside the hotel to keep her entertained. To keep busy during the day, Claire was starting to help out around the hotel doing odd chores.

She was amazed how Martin had kept the hotel in mint condition. She respected that he made the effort even though he did not have to.

Soon, two weeks had passed since Travis and Claire had moved into The Grand. Everyone was settling into the new living arrangement. Travis had taken to mostly isolating in his room, opting to spend his days, sleeping, and playing video games.

In the two weeks since they first met, the temperature had dropped dramatically. The sky had changed from a deep blue on that sunny fall afternoon to a steel gray most days. The air was routinely cold and damp. Martin had warned them that the first sign of snow could be any day. Sure enough the day after he spoke those words, he woke up to see a sparse amount of small unassuming snowflakes falling lazily to the ground. He knew from that point, they might not have much time before they could be snowed in and unable to leave the hotel except on foot, or take one of the resort's snowmobiles.

The first thing he did that day was go down to the parkade to check on the fuel truck. He knew before he got there that there was not enough fuel left in the truck's cargo tank to supply the main generator for the entire winter. Checking the fuel level gage on the side of the truck confirmed that the tank was less than a quarter full. He went immediately upstairs to get ready to head back to Frank's Fuels. He thought this would be a good job for Travis to assist with.

"Travis, come in?" he called over the radio. It was still before noon and did not expect him to be awake. Travis was routinely sleeping in until well into the afternoon.

"Travis come, in?" he repeated. On the third call Travis answered, still half asleep.

"Get up, we have a little job to do."

"Are you kidding? It's too early," was the reply.

"If you know how to drive standard, I will let you drive the yellow Porsche."

Travis became suddenly alert."You're going to let me drive the Porsche? Why?" he asked with his usual skepticism.

Martin explained that they would drive to the fuel yard together, then he would drive a new tanker truck back to the hotel while Travis returned in the Porsche.

It did not take long for Travis to meet Martin in the parkade.

Martin disliked the feeling of not getting along with the people around him. In the past if he was having problems with a guest he knew it would only last until the guest departed. If he was having problems with a co-worker, at least he would only have to endure them during work hours, even then he could keep his distance from the person by avoiding them. With the current situation at the hotel, he was around the same two people 24/7. The only respite was when either of the guests went into their room for the night. Martin preferred harmony over conflict, so he thought letting Travis drive the Porsche might improve their rapport. As it was, Travis was barely civil to Martin, and was only slightly more cordial to Claire.

Claire said she wanted to stay back at the hotel to exercise, but her true intent was to give the two guys a chance to be alone, hoping the time together would help them bond.

As Martin drove the Porsche to the fuel depot, he attempted to make small talk with Travis. Travis said that his car back home was a Honda Civic, with a standard transmission, so he would know how to drive the stick shift in the Porsche. After a couple minutes, Travis put on a set of oversized Skull Candy headphones and listened to his IPod, ending any further attempts at conversation.

When they got to Frank's Fuels, Martin was relieved to see that all the remaining trucks were still there. He searched the tankers to find one that had a full cargo of diesel.

The snow had turned to drizzling rain, the temperature was still just around two degrees. Cold and damp, it was worse than being dry and below zero.

When Martin went into the office to get keys, except for the accumulation of a little more dust, everything was the same as when he had last been there months earlier. There were no signs that anyone had been around, and all the keys were still accounted for.

Martin found a truck slightly bigger than the one sitting at The Grand. He was already stressing about having problems driving the big truck. He tried to start the engine on the tanker. When he turned the key, nothing happened. The engine did not even attempt to turn over. The truck had not been started for over ten months, and the battery was completely dead. Martin had not anticipated this. He would have to boost the battery.

Travis viewed this as a huge inconvenience, and a delay in getting to drive the Porsche. "I don't have the patience for this shit," he grumbled. Rain drops were spotting his black hoodie. "I'm going to wait in the office while you get it going, it's friggin cold out here."

Travis turned and went inside.

Martin found a set of grimy, oil covered, booster cables behind the driver's seat in the truck. He did not want to damage the Porsche in the attempt to boost the big tanker and leave them stranded there with no ride home. It was only a twenty minute drive, but a two hour walk back in the cold rain. And he would have to listen to Travis complain every step of the way back to the hotel.

Martin stepped out of the cab of the truck and looked around. Parked behind the office was a large pickup truck, a black Dodge Ram with the Frank's Fuels logo on each door. He could only hope that the Ram's battery might be more durable. It would not only need to have enough juice to start the Ram, but also enough power to charge the tanker's battery.

Martin got in the Ram's driver's seat. He paused, he almost did not want to put the key in the ignition, wanting to avoid the bad news if the engine did not start. He turned the key. The Ram's engine chugged struggling to turn over, but after a couple tries, it came to life. Martin leaned back, closed his eyes and sighed with relief.

After letting the pickup run for ten minutes to give its battery a better charge, he had no problems boosting the tanker's battery.

"Finally," Travis said emerging from the office, "Now, we can get going."

Martin said, "Go ahead, but wait for me on the road by the entrance, then you can follow me home."

Travis turned and got into the Porsche. He started it up, and bolted off, the rear tires spitting gravel.

This was the moment Martin had been dreading, driving a big truck again. Having to drive with Travis watching elevated his anxiety. He did not want to look stupid or embarrass himself with his poor driving skills.

It took him several tries to get it into first gear. Each failed attempt lurched the truck forward before it stalled, giving Martin a minor jolt. Each time he had to restart it. Although it was cold enough in the cab of the truck to see his breath, Martin was sweating from nerves. Finally he coordinated the clutch pedal and the gear shift to get the truck moving. He reached the gate, and stopped the truck on the road outside. He got out and latched the gate closed.

Back in the truck, he managed to move forward. He got the truck up to the peak of first gear. The engine revved at 6000 RPM, screaming for him to shift to second. Martin pulled the shifter back to second, the gears grinded, the truck stalled and shuttered to a stop. He looked in the side mirror. The yellow Porsche was waiting behind him.

Martin got the truck started, drove for a couple hundred feet, managed to get it into second with only a minor retching of the gears. But when it came time to shift to third, he got it stuck in neutral, the engine screamed again. He stepped on the break, and shut it off. His neck was starting to hurt from being thrown forward from stalling so many times.

Travis got out of the Porsche, and walked up to the truck. Martin rolled down his window "Sorr.." he started to apologize.

"What the hell man, can't you drive that piece of shit?" Travis asked. "I'm in one of the world's fastest cars, and I'm stuck going, like twenty."

"You go ahead. I'll meet you at the hotel," Martin said.

"Good, if you don't turn up by supper, I'll send a search party after you," Travis said without hesitation.

As he was walking away Martin heard Travis say to himself, "What a pussy!"

Travis passed the tanker, quickly accelerated, and sped off around a turn, heading in the direction of The Grand.

Forty minutes later, Martin showed up at the hotel. He parked the truck parallel to the tanker he had gotten months earlier.

Travis was sitting at the bar having a beer when Martin came into the lobby. Claire was on one end of the bar reading an issue of Vogue from December.

"You just got here?" Travis asked.

Claire looked up from her magazine.

"Ya," Martin said, eyes down, feeling a little sheepish.

"It took you this long?" Travis reiterated.

Martin's embarrassment turned to anger. At that moment he knew he would never like the kid. He was like an irritating, little bully that always ended up in your class throughout your school life. You hated him but had no choice but to tolerate him. Out of instinct he raised his hand to wing the truck keys at Travis's head, but Claire was quicker to respond. She rolled up her magazine and whacked Travis in the back of the head.

"Ow, what's your problem?" Travis asked indignantly.

Travis saw that Martin was going to throw something.

"Jesus, relax man," Travis said. He jumped off the bar stool and headed towards the elevators, "Screw you guys!"

Martin explained to Claire about the drive home.

Consoling him, Claire said, "I guess driving big trucks is just not your thing."

It helped slightly, but he did still feel pathetic. "What kind of a man am I?" he thought.

"I'm going to take the Porsche back down to the garage," he told her. Travis had left it parked at the front door, the keys still in the ignition.

After supper that night, Martin and Claire worked out in the gym again. Travis did not come down to eat. Martin was happy that he did not have to look at him.

While working out, Claire talked about her husband, their busy lives, and how they had grown apart due to work. Now she really missed him. She wished they had spent more time together when they had the chance.

"We took our relationship for granted. We thought we would have a lifetime together," she lamented. "Some nights I would be upstairs on the computer and he would downstairs watching hockey, or The History Channel. It's not like we didn't get along, just we got to that point in our relationship that that we did our own thing at home. Now I wish I could just cuddle on the couch with him, have a glass of wine and watch a movie. Or go out to a restaurant. Just the two of us, having a conversation and enjoying a nice meal together for a couple hours. When you are at a restaurant, the focus is on you and the other person. For two hours you have their undivided attention, you talk, laugh, get caught up. That's what I miss too."

Afterwards, Martin went straight up to his room. He told Claire he was tired. Martin was happy to get to the solitude of his room. After being alone for months, socializing with others was still an adjustment, and an endeavor he found to be taxing.

Martin was in his room reading *Fahrenheit 451* by candlelight enjoying his peace and quiet, when he heard a soft knock at his door. He sighed, plopped his book down on the coffee table, and went over to his door.

He paused, collecting himself before answering. He opened the door halfway.

"Hey," he said, he did not open the door further, and did not move aside, instead stood waiting, to see what Claire wanted.

"My lantern battery is out of juice, it died late last night, and I just went to sleep after that. Also I ran out of matches for my candles. I don't know where to get some more."

"OK," Martin said, he held the door open for her while he got his keys and flashlight."Follow me to the storage closet."

They walked down to the hall and stopped in front of a door, marked "Electrical". Martin took out a key ring and opened the door.

"Some rooms are locked with a hard key. Only a few staff have access or else stuff gets stolen. You'd be surprised what staff will take home; light bulbs, toilet paper, garbage bags."

He opened the door, and shone the light to reveal a long, narrow storage room. He grabbed a box of Redbird wooden matches, and a large square battery.

He walked her back to her room. He did not indicate that he wanted to stay. "That should do ya," he said, still standing in the hallway.

"Er, thanks," Claire said. She could sense his stiffness, and his eagerness to leave.

"You ok", he confirmed.

She nodded. "Ok, good night," he turned away.

"Thanks again," she said. As she shut her door, Martin was already at his own room.

19

Martin slept in the next day. He did wake up on time, but in the darkness of the early morning, decided to just stay in bed. He was not motivated to get up. As the days passed, the hours of daylight were dwindling. It stayed dark until almost eight in the morning, which meant the generator did not turn the power on until nine. Once December hit, it would start getting dark around five o'clock. Martin did not bother to observe daylight savings time, and there was no government body to enforce the time change. So, the clocks stayed the same as they had been since January.

When he did get up and look outside through his patio door, he instantly regretted spending the extra time in bed. The lawn had a thin layer of snow. The tips of individual green blades of grass could be seen poking out from the white carpet. The snow had already melted on the road, the black asphalt glistening wet. The ski runs were solid stripes of white, edged with the mix of leafless maples and birches and the green of pine trees. The snow on level ground might melt by mid day, but the snow of the slopes would stay as a warning that winter had arrived.

He knew that it was quite possible to wake up to a foot of snow the next morning. If more snow did come overnight, it might melt again, but there were no guarantees. With that much snow, driving would be difficult. They would have to make their own path down the roads. There were no plows to clear the snow off the roads, no sanders to salt, so the roads would be slippery. It would be safer to just go out today. He had to be prepared for the possibility that the outdoor conditions would make him and his guests basically house bound for the next five months. This was not the time to procrastinate. He had to build up the food and supply inventory now while he could still get a vehicle out. After the snow fall he would still be able to get out by foot, or by snowmobile, but would be able to bring home only whatever supplies he could carry.

Martin called Claire on her room phone. It rang several times before she answered, "Hello?"

"Claire, its Martin, have you looked outside yet?"

"What? No, hold on," she put the phone down.

"Oh my God," he heard her say from the other side of the room.

"Where did that come from?" she asked, when she picked up the phone again.

"We have to go grocery shopping as soon as possible, like now," Martin said, "Can you meet me at the front door in half an hour?"

Claire agreed without hesitation.

Martin put on his winter clothing and went down to the parkade. He drove the Land Rover outside. Just as he remembered it only had a quarter tank of gas which would not be enough. He drove it to a maintenance garage which housed the resort's utility vehicles and a couple pickup trucks used for landscaping. Inside the garage were five full drums of gasoline. On top of each drum was a hand pump to extract the gas. He filled up the tank of the Land Rover then parked it out front of the hotel.

He returned to the parkade and picked out the biggest vehicle in the group, a black Chevy Suburban with tinted windows. The Suburban had seating for eight plus ample storage space behind the last row of seats. Chevy products were not the usual type of manufacturer found at The Grand Summit Place, but this particular one was top of the line, had a lot of custom add-ons, and probably cost more than some of the Audis and BMWs that came to the hotel. Martin had never driven it. Starting it showed that it had half a tank of gas. He assumed that although it probably got poor gas mileage, there would be enough in the tank for the trip today. He parked it behind the Land Rover.

Claire was already waiting in the lobby for him, dressed in her North Face coat, a pink toque, and ski gloves.

"Sorry to call you on your phone, I just didn't want to attract Travis's attention by using the radio. I don't want to deal with him today. The whole time he would be complaining," Martin said.

Claire nodded in agreement.

Martin explained the plan. Claire would drive the Land Rover, and he would drive the Suburban. They were going to drive to the biggest town in the area, Hemingford. With a population of 6,000, it had the largest grocery store around. They were going to fill up both vehicles with as much food and supplies as they could hold.

"The Suburban is a beast of a truck, we should be able to fit a lot of food in it," he told her.

Claire followed the Suburban through winding roads until they got to their destination. Hemingford was as it had been the last time Martin was there to visit King's Sporting Goods, deserted and untouched.

They passed a McDonald's. The iconic golden arches sign was a drab yellow without the electricity. The interior of McDonald's looked somber without lights.

When they came to the grocery store, they parked in the rear and used a crowbar to get into the staff entrance door.

"Hope there's no mice at this one," Martin said.

The store was a full size national chain with nine long aisles. It had a bakery, seafood counter, butcher, pharmacy, health food section, and produce area. Eight checkouts sat empty, the cash registers unmanned, waiting for customers.

Before they went in, Martin gave Claire a respirator mask to put on. "We use these at the hotel for painting. It should cover the smell of the rotting meat and vegetables inside."

They went to the front of the store and each got a shopping cart. The front area was illuminated by the large windows, but as they got to the back of the store, the dimness made it hard to see. With the lights off it felt like they had been locked in the store after hours. It felt unnatural to be in the store that was normally bright with the overhead fluorescent lighting. At this time of day the place was usually busy with customers, listening to cheery elevator music as they walked up and down the aisles getting food for their families. The darkness created an anxious, unwelcome feeling.

As they passed the produce section, Martin pointed to a sign that said "Fresh!!!" The fruit and vegetables sitting on the counters had turned into undecipherable mounds of green mould. The meat sitting in the refrigerated bunkers had turned

166

green underneath the cellophane wrapping. From experience, they knew to avoid this section and quickly headed to the aisles which would have non-perishable items.

"I feel like a squirrel gathering food for the winter," she said, her voice muffled by the respirator.

They were glad to see that no mice had ravaged the store and everything was still intact.

It took them over an hour to fill three shopping carts each with food. They tried to grab everything in bulk sizes. When they were done, groceries were stacked almost to the roof of each SUV.

When they got back to the hotel they parked right beside the elevators. Claire thought they should ask Travis to help them unload. Martin did not think it would be easy to persuade him to help out.

"Travis, come in?" Martin called over the radio.

"Ya?" Travis replied.

"Can you come down to P2 by the elevators and help unload groceries? We went shopping."

"Ya, I'll be there in a bit," Travis replied.

Claire said to Martin, "that means he will come down when he feels like it."

She then picked up her radio and called Travis herself. "Travis, if you ever want to eat again, I suggest you get your ass down here now!"

"Ok, Ok," he replied, obviously feeling put out.

Travis came down within five minutes. "Holy shit!" he exclaimed when he saw the two SUV's loaded with groceries.

The three of them started filling two large Rubbermaid laundry carts to transport the food back up the restaurant kitchen.

"You two reek. You smell like garbage," he commented after being in their proximity for only a few seconds. The smell of rotting food from the store had permeated their clothing and skin.

Claire sniffed her coat sleeve and winced.

It took four cart loads to transport the groceries upstairs.

They got large cans of chilli, ten pound tins of ham, corned beef in a can, and other foods that Claire thought she would never eat in her lifetime.

At Claire's suggestion they got two twenty pound bags of basmati rice, whole wheat pasta, couscous, organic caraway crackers, fortified soy beverage, enriched rice beverage, and an assortment of other foods Martin had never heard of. The organic caraway crackers looked like piece of tree bark and probably tasted like it too Martin thought. From the picture on the box, the soy and rice "beverages" looked like milk. Martin hoped that they tasted better than the powdered milk he had been drinking for the past few months. He liked that their expiry date was a year away. He was happy that tofu has to be refrigerated and had gone bad months ago, or else Claire probably would have taken some of that as well.

As a precaution they got medicine, vitamins, and first aid supplies from the in-store pharmacy.

Travis took some bags of cookies, and potato chips directly up to his room.

At eight o'clock Martin called Travis and Claire on the radio, asking them to meet him down in the conference room area for a surprise. The hotel was dark, but a bank of windows in the conference lobby let in the small amount of light shining in from the almost full moon.

Ten minutes later, he saw them come out of the stairwell exit door together. Martin asked them to shut off their flashlights since they were now in an area with windows. Claire complied.

"Aw come on, it's pitch black in here," Travis exaggerated, "no one is around to see anything from our little flashlights."

"Just turn it off," Claire demanded, showing more frustration than anger in her voice.

"Ok, whatever. What are we doing down here anyway?" Travis asked. "I was about to level up in Fallout."

"Is that popcorn I smell?" Claire asked.

Martin led them through a set of double doors into a small conference room. Several rows of chairs were set up to face a white screen at the opposite end of the room. In one corner was a replica, antique-style street vendor popcorn maker. Freshly made popcorn could be seen through its glass windows.

"I thought we could watch a movie," Martin said as he closed the doors behind him. There was a second of complete darkness in the windowless room before he turned on the camping lantern he was carrying.

"In the busier times, like around Christmas, and March Break, when there were lots of families in house, we would set this room up to be an impromptu movie theatre. There is a DVD projector there," he said pointing to a black box suspended from the ceiling.

"Ideally, we want guests to rent movies from their room's TV at $8 a pop, but this is a free perk that families seem to love. So, I thought we could sit back, relax, and watch a movie with popcorn. I have the whole thing hooked up to a portable generator and since this room does not have any windows, we don't have to worry about the light from the movie screen or even the lanterns when the doors are closed."

Martin had even hooked up a small heater so they would not be cold. With the power off, the temperature dropped to an uncomfortable level quickly.

Claire looked around in awe.

"What movie did you get, *Wizard of Oz*?" Travis asked sarcastically.

"No, *My Diary of Venice*. It's a new release. Well, you know what I mean. It was a new release in November last year. I haven't seen it. It's supposed to be funny."

"Sounds lame. Is that guy, Hugh Grant in it? I ain't watching no chick flick for like, the next two hours," Travis said.

"I don't think it's a chick flick," Claire said, "I think it's more like a romantic comedy."

"Same thing," Travis said. "No real dude wants to watch that." He filled a bag of popcorn, then said "I'm going back up to my room."

"No big loss," Martin said as he started the movie.

Turned out that Travis was right, the movie was basically a chick flick but Martin enjoyed the experience of watching a movie on a big screen in a theatre style environment and having popcorn.

When the movie was over, Claire gave him a hug in gratitude and thanked him for being so thoughtful. She also apologized for Travis.

"No need, he's not your responsibility," Martin said.

They decided to clean up in the morning when they could turn on the overhead lights and use the vacuum to get all the popcorn crumbs off the carpet.

Claire sat outside with Martin to watch for signs of life in the darkness. She made hot chocolate with Kahlua to warm them up. There was enough to fill a large white coffee carafe.

"You know, it's been over a year since the news of Solara broke," Claire observed.

"I was thinking about that yesterday," Martin said. "What a difference a year makes. Last year at this time the hotel was full of staff running around getting ready for the ski season. I think we had a few small conferences going on, so there were guests in the hotel too. News of the virus was just picking up steam, but around here, Solara was just another headline on MSN. Even when news of the first confirmed deaths became public, we were all too busy to give the news any weight."

"It was big news in the city," Claire said. "It was more in your face, because you couldn't go far without seeing someone coughing or looking sick. Also the papers had headlines daily, and the Public Health started putting up posters everywhere."

"Halloween should be soon, I guess," Claire said.

Martin thought of how all over the country little kids with their best friends, would go from house to house trick-or-treating. They would be dressed in their costumes going to every front door in the neighbourhood for candy as their parents waited and watched on the sidewalk. He thought of how that did not happen this year, how that would probably never happen again.

"Um, Halloween was a couple days ago," Martin said.

"Really?" Claire asked astonished. "Are all of the holidays going to pass us by?

"Not if we make a conscious effort to watch the dates. I guess we can celebrate Christmas still," Martin said.

Claire lamented, "I completely lost track of the date a long time ago. I guess I should have kept a calendar or something from the beginning. The days just flow into each other. You don't know what day of the week it is. The bigger question is, does it really matter now what day of the week it is? I don't know maybe it does."

"For Thanksgiving, Philip and I always went to my parents. My whole family would be there, my siblings, their kids, sometimes my aunt and her family. We'd have the traditional turkey dinner, even pumpkin pie. Then the next day, we would repeat the whole thing over at Philip's parents'."

"Sounds nice," Martin said. He glanced over at Claire as she wiped a tear from her eye.

They continued looking out into horizon in silence, caught up in their own thoughts of their losses in the last year.

20

Martin now felt confident that the three of them could remain in the hotel and survive the winter. Together they had addressed all their needs. They ensured they had enough fuel for the generator to provide heat and electricity and along with what was already in the restaurant's inventory, they had gathered enough food during their last outing to feed themselves during the coming months without having to ration meals. They even had pharmaceutical supplies including Tylenol, antibiotics, penicillin, and an extensive first aid kit if a medical situation arose.

When Martin thought of this, he was happy that he could return to the simple task of just maintaining the hotel. "We only have to survive each other's company for the next five months," he thought to himself.

He liked Claire, but he was just not accustomed to sharing time with someone seven days a week, and although he did not physically see them at all hours, it seemed like Claire and Travis were in his presence twenty-four hours a day.

The day after the shopping trip to Hemingford, it snowed again. This time three inches of damp snow covered everything. Travis was upset that Martin and Claire had not brought back beer, so he took the Land Rover on his own to drive to the village market. Martin gave him the key to get in the front door of the store. As Travis drove away from the hotel, the SUV left a trail down the middle of the road, two black parallel lines in the whiteness covering the asphalt.

Following that, a two day blizzard blanketed the area. With no one to disturb the snow by driving or walking, the snow remained untouched, covering everything like smooth white frosting on a cake. Everything was levelled out with the snow. Sidewalks and flower beds were indiscernible beneath the flat sea of whiteness. The curb was reduced to a mere dip above the white road. Travis's tire tracks on the road from his trip a mere two days earlier were completely filled in.

Claire moved into a one bedroom suite a couple doors down from her first room, giving her a much more spacious living area to enjoy over the coming months. They cleaned her old room together, returning it to check-in condition.

Martin felt there was enough snow that he and Travis could go get a couple snowmobiles from the maintenance shed on the other side of the resort. A small fleet of snowmobiles were used by the Ski Patrol team to monitor the slopes and provide first aid to injured skiers.

Martin had to give Travis a staff-issue winter coat, gloves and toque for the trip to get the snowmobiles. He found a pair of boots left behind in a valet's locker, which he gave to Travis. Travis had not gotten around to picking up winter clothing for himself in the weeks leading up to the first snowfall.

It took them twenty minutes walking through the snow to reach the shed that housed the snowmobiles. With their heavy duty deep stroke batteries, the snowmobiles started with no problem. Once Martin filled the fuel tanks, they grabbed helmets and rode to the retail village.

From a ski shop, Travis got some new winter gear, including boots. He selected his clothes based on style, picking up a bright, busy patterned, multi-coloured, Burton snowboard coat and matching snowboard pants.

When they got back to the hotel, Travis was obviously enthralled about driving the snowmobile. He was like a child with a new toy on Christmas morning. He changed into his new snowboard gear and went right back out on the snowmobile for a joy ride around the hotel property.

He returned two hours later with frost bit cheeks, but still thrilled. Martin parked both machines beneath an overhang at the entrance to the parking garage and covered them with a large white tarp.

A week passed, bringing seven more days of snow. When Travis woke up he begged Claire to go out for a ride with him. It was a beautiful day, deep blue sky and a bearable five degrees below zero. She reluctantly agreed to go on the ski-doo. She had witnessed Travis ride. He rode fast and was careless. Travis had been going out alone every day, but he was always pestering Claire and Martin to go out with him. Claire had no interest in driving a snowmobile herself but did go out a couple times as a passenger with Martin. Travis's new favourite riding area was the golf course across from The Grand. He loved to use the mounds around the greens as ramps or drive in and out of the snow filled sand traps.

"As long as you don't drive like a maniac," she conceded, agreeing to ride with him as a passenger.

Martin wanted to stay back at the hotel to take care of a few small jobs. From the lobby, he watched them ride across the road and onto the golf course. Claire holding on tight with her arms wrapped around her driver's waist. Martin turned away when they got out of sight.

He made his way down to the guest laundry room. Claire had mentioned that one of the washing machines was making a grinding noise. He pulled the front cover off the machine, and found the problem, a bobby pin was caught in the agitator. The bobby pin was now all contorted and rusty. The washing machine sounded normal when he put it back together.

He noticed that Claire had a load of wet clothes in one of the washing machines. He took the clothes out and threw them in the dryer so they would be ready for her when she got back later.

Next, he mopped the stairwell that Travis used all the time. From going outside, Travis's boot prints left circular stains on the concrete steps all the way up to the fifth floor. He also found some chocolate bar wrappers that Travis had dropped along the way.

Martin was mopping the tiled floor by the front desk when he heard the double doors at the entrance slide open. He looked up. Travis walked into the lobby. His pants were wet up to his waist. Snow was caked from his boots to his knees. He was hunched over with his arms crossed against his stomach. The sleeves of his coat were wet too. He did not have his helmet with him. He had no gloves on. His bare hands were red and swollen.

Martin looked past Travis out the front door. Claire was nowhere in sight.

Their snowmobile was not there.

Travis did not say anything. He did not even seem to see Martin standing there, ten feet away. Travis appeared to be in shock. He silently sat down on the closest couch and stared at the oriental carpet at his feet.

Martin dropped the mop. It hit the ceramic tile with a clatter.

"Where is Claire?" Martin asked, and looked back out the front doors again, but there was still no sign of her.

Travis looked up from the couch. His lips were blue, his cheeks and ears where bright red. He was shivering. "She...we...we sunk," he answered, stuttering.

Travis looked like he was going to pass out.

"What? Where?" Martin yelled.

"Pond,...golf course," Travis answered, then flopped over on his side and passed out leaning on the arm of the couch.

Martin grabbed a winter coat, and leather gloves from the valet office. He put the coat on and pulled on the gloves as he ran down towards the exit door by the parkade entrance. He hopped on the one remaining snowmobile and headed in the direction of the golf course.

Martin had an idea which pond Travis was talking about. The golf course only had two water hazards, one was small, only thirty feet long, the other was more like a small lake which was over a hundred yards long and half as wide in the middle. Regardless, he would have to ride by the small pond, the bigger pond was around the fourth hole, one of the furthest holes away from the hotel.

He rode over the road and right onto the 13th fairway directly across from the hotel. Snowmobile tracks zigzagged in the snow everywhere.

Within two minutes he was coming up to the small pond. Ahead he could see the three foot tall cattails and reeds lining the fringe of the pond sticking out of the snow. He pulled up alongside it. There were tracks going across it, but the ice was not broken.

He cranked the throttle and sped off. A couple minutes later he was approaching the larger pond. Even from a distance he could see a hole in the ice surface. He did not know how deep the lake was, but he knew from playing golf there, that you could only see the bottom the first ten feet from shore, after that, the bottom disappeared into a murky darkness.

Martin stopped by the edge of the pond. A thin layer of snow covered the ice. No sign of the snowmobile or Claire. He stepped down onto the ice with one foot, then the other, carefully. It was solid enough to hold his weight, but he was not going to take any chances, he wanted to distribute his weight the best he could. He went on his hands and knees and crawled. Every once in a while the wind would pick up creating dancing swirls of snow in the air just above the surface of the pond. The hole was almost right in the middle, at least fifty feet away. He did not get far before he could feel his knee caps burning from dragging them over the craggily ice that lay hidden beneath the snow. The frigid wind whipped snow across his bare face as he inched slowly forward. So far, the ice was not cracking beneath him. The tips of his fingers and heels of hands were tingling with the cold. His knees felt as frozen as the ice he was crawling on.

When he got within five feet of the hole, he heard a crack beneath him. The crack sound continued past his feet. He did not move. He lower himself onto his stomach and with his legs stretched out behind him, he dragged himself forward by using only his forearms. He tried to crane his neck high so he could see into the hole. The surface was calm. Small chunks of floating slushy snow were trying to seal the entire opening. Looking into the hole, he could only see the grey blue water, no sign of the bright yellow snowmobile or Claire's pink Spyder jacket and snow pants in the depths. He knew it was futile. She was somewhere in the water, trapped under the ice with no way of getting her out, possibly drifting away from the opening. He saw marks in the snow where Travis must have crawled out of the water, and then his boot prints walking away from the hole.

Only one set of boot prints.

Martin rotated his body around and started to crawl back to the shoreline, trying to balance his weight evenly. He was cognizant of every movement he made, trying not to put too much weight on his feet or his knees touching the ice. When he thought it was safe, he stood up and shuffled to the edge of the pond. As he crawled up over the bank, one hand plunged down through a foot of snow, pulling his sleeve upwards. The snow on his bare wrist felt like icy razor blades cutting into him. He turned around and sat on the edge of the bank, staring back at the pond in a daze. His feet were frozen in his black, uninsulated work shoes.

Time seemed to stand still. Only the utter cold woke him from his trance. He pulled the back collar of his coat up to shelter his neck. He rubbed his knees to try to create some heat. They felt like balls of ice in the middle of his legs. He took his gloves off, and one at a time blew into them to warm the inside with his hot breath. He pulled them back on tight. He started up the snowmobile and followed his tracks back to the hotel.

Martin pulled the snowmobile up to the front door of the hotel. He sat there hunched forward, his entire body shivering, his joints stiff from the cold. He looked through the front doors of The Grand. He could see the welcoming glow of the fireplace lighting up the lobby.

He walked inside. He was instantly warmed physically and emotionally. Travis was still passed out awkwardly on the couch. Martin ran to the closest guest room, pulled the thick feather duvet off the bed, and then ran back into the lobby. He laid Travis out flat on the couch, yanked his boots off, removed his wet snow pants, then opened up his jacket and pulled the coat off from underneath him. He covered him up with the duvet. Some of the colour had returned to Travis's face but he now had white circles on his cheeks from frostbite. The tips of his ears were bright red and puffy.

He knew he had to wake Travis up. Travis had to get up and get the blood circulating. Martin slapped him on the cheek. He slapped him maybe harder then he should have.

Travis shuddered awake. Groggy, he slowly opened his eyes. It took him a second to realize where he was and what had happened. He sat up.

"You need to get out of those clothes and warm up," Martin said bluntly. "I'll take you to your room."

Travis stood up, with the duvet draped over his shoulders and shuffled towards the elevator.

"I, I`m sorry," he mumbled, still shaking, "... went down so fast."

Hunched over, he got in the elevator. Only Travis`s sniffling runny nose broke the silence on the trip back to his room.

Martin felt the same way towards Travis as one feels about a drunk driver who has killed someone in an accident. It was a reckless, unnecessary tragedy.

"Get changed and then get into bed under all the blankets. Do not have a shower. Hot water will only make it worse, shock your system. I'm going to make you something to eat."

Martin kicked an empty beer can out of the way as he left Travis's room.

Martin returned with comfort food, a pot of tea, and a big bowl of Kraft macaroni and cheese. Travis sat up in his bed. He was looking slightly better. He ate without stopping, shovelling the noodles into his mouth.

Martin turned on the fireplace.

"What the hell happened out there?" Martin asked abruptly. He knew the answer but wanted to hear why Travis would do something so stupid.

Travis looked up, startled by the question. Then he quickly looked back down, staring into his empty bowl. "We were having fun. I wanted to try to skid on the ice. I hit the brakes and we skidded to a stop. Then the back end broke through the ice. Claire let go of me when the ski-doo started sliding backwards into the water. I jumped off and landed on the edge of the ice with my legs still in the water. I pulled myself out."

"I was lying on the ice. Then the front went under water, the rest was already sunk. All I could see was the pink of Claire's coat beneath the water, like a blur. I stuck my arm in to try and grab her, but did not feel her, she was out of reach. She was way beneath me, then disappeared. I was scared. Then I walked back, before I died too."

Martin stood up. Without a word he walked away.

"Martin?" Travis pleaded.

Martin slammed the door shut behind him. He was not going to give Travis sympathy. He was sure that Travis felt remorse, but was not in a disposition to show sympathy towards him at this time.

Martin went back down to the restaurant. He ate the rest of the Kraft Dinner.

For the first time since his guests had arrived at the hotel Martin went into his other room and cranked up the generator. He closed both doors, sealing himself in the TV room for the night. He opened up a bottle of wine, then sat down to play a video game. He just wanted to get drunk and immerse himself in the world of the game he was playing. He did not want to think about Claire. He did not want to think about Travis.

After a couple hours his vision was blurry, and he was feeling drowsy. He could barely keep his eyes open. Soon he passed out, slumped sideways on the couch, still holding onto the XBOX controller. The TV was on. His game character was standing still waiting for him to touch a button on the controller. In the game, life around him in the vibrant city was still going on, people walking by, cars driving around, dogs barking.

21

In the morning, still laying on the couch in the den in his second room where he had passed out, Martin fabricated various possible conversations with Travis. Martin was not convinced that Travis would accept responsibility for his actions. It was more probable that he would blame "the ice", or "the snowmobile wouldn't move fast enough" or maybe even blame Claire, saying something like, "but she was having fun too."

He contemplated whether his perception regarding Travis's culpability should change. Martin had a long, deep sleep induced by the alcohol, but his empathy for Travis had not wavered. He had no proof that the kid would react this way, but had been around Travis long enough, and young guys like him to know that they had an, "it's not my fault" mentality. The more Martin thought about it, the more his anger elevated.

After having a shower, Martin's attitude shifted slightly. To be fair, he decided he would try to give Travis the benefit of doubt.

Martin tried to get Travis on the radio. "Travis come in?" No answer. "Travis come in?"

"Um, go ahead," Travis responded.

Martin paused. This was the first time that Travis had used the proper radio etiquette. "So, he had been listening when I told him how to use the radio," Martin realized. Travis had just made a conscious effort not to follow as instructed.

"Are you ok?" Martin inquired.

"I'm a little, like, stiff, but feelin better."

"OK, I am going to bring you some breakfast."

Travis had been left alone for over twelve hours. Martin was sure that he did not have severe hypothermia, possibly a moderate case at worst, which he would quickly recuperate from.

Martin prepared doubles of toast, coffee, oatmeal, and orange juice, and brought it up to Travis's suite on a room service cart.

He wanted to use this as an excuse to see how Travis would respond to the accident.

He knocked on the door. He thought he heard movement from inside before Travis said, "come in."

Martin pushed the cart into the room. He rolled over an empty bag of chips, and then one of the wheels go caught on a wet face cloth lying in front of the kitchen sink.

Travis was in bed sitting up. After clearing a collection of garbage off the bedside table, Martin set the tray of food down.

"This should perk you up."

"Thanks." Travis took a sip of the coffee and closed his eyes with relief. "This is good."

Travis looked out his window as if to see what the weather was like. It seemed like he was not going to bring up the accident.

Martin was not sure if Travis was in denial, or just did not want to deal with it.

Martin initiated the conversation. "I went out there after you passed out. I could not see Claire at all. I couldn't even see the snowmobile."

"It happened so fast. One moment we are, like, sitting there, then the ass ends falling through the ice." He paused to take a drink of coffee. "The water was so cold, like I never felt before. I tried to grab her. I was too slow."

Travis took a bite of toast. "I thought the pond was solid, the ice should have held us, it was cold out."

Martin had to step in "It's hardly a pond, more like a small lake and it has to be really cold for a long time for that much water surface to freeze. You need many days of below zero temperature."

Travis looked up, and in a hushed voice said, "I didn't know. I thought it was solid, the little pond was solid."

"I'm still tired," Travis said.

His breakfast was half finished. He looked up at Martin. His silent expression indicated that he wanted his host to leave. As far as Travis was concerned, the conversation was over for now.

"Ok, I'll see you later," Martin said when Travis leaned back on the headboard and closed his eyes.

Leaving the bedroom, Martin walked through the den. The green power light on the front of the Xbox 360 was lit, but the

TV was off. The 360's controller power light was on too. Martin knew that after ten minutes of non-use, the controller automatically shut down and the green power light would turn off. Travis had been playing video games before Martin came up. "He must have had the volume down low so I wouldn't hear it when I came to the door," Martin surmised.

Martin went to the lobby and sat down on one of the big couches. The hotel seemed even quieter than when he was alone for all those weeks. The building had lost a measurable level of energy that Claire emanated. She had a positive aura about her that must have helped her to be successful in life.

Martin thought about the term *"grief stricken"*. He felt sadness, a feeling of separation, but he really had not known Claire for very long, and did not think he was grief stricken. But he did miss her. Sitting there having a coffee, he thought of how it was such a waste. She had been immune to the virus while thousands around her died. She survived for weeks being homeless, travelling the countryside alone, at least until she met Travis. Then, just when she had a safe place to stay in a comforting environment, she dies in a senseless accident.

Martin's attention then turned to his young guest, and wondered what he was doing right at that moment. Was he in bed recuperating like he was supposed to be doing, or was he on the couch playing video games in the den? Maybe even having a beer already. Martin would secretly check later.

The weather seemed to mimic the mood of the day. Outside, it was grey, dismal, overcast, with no trace of the sun. The snow had turned to drizzling rain, which would make everything ugly outside. This was the worst kind of winter day, one that would spoil a skier's plans. A combination of the dampness from the rain and the cold, made the thought of going outside undesirable for most vacationers. Even when the most dedicated went out on days like this, their jacket and gloves would be soaked after twenty minutes of skiing down the slopes, their pants wet from sitting on the chair lift.

Usually the weather had no impact on Martin's mood, in fact, most days he was so busy that he barely even took notice of the conditions, and could go an entire day without even stepping foot outside. Today however, as he sat in the usually inviting lobby, the daylight coming through the ample windows seemed drab and meager, creating a depressing feeling in the room.

He kept thinking about Claire. Although he had not been there to witness it, his mind had vividly recreated the scene. It plays out like a slow motion sequence in a movie:

Travis and Claire are seated on the stopped snowmobile in the middle of the pond. Travis in front, Claire is behind him. The ice breaks. A hole appears at the rear of the machine. The back of the snowmobile drops into the water like a trap door has suddenly opened. Still on the ski-doo, Claire is flung backwards blindly like a scuba diver dropping off a boat facing the sky. Her arms stretch out as if she was making a snow angel. The snowmobile starts to sink. Her head and shoulders above water, her arms start flailing, frantically trying to grab onto something that is not there, just splashing the surface. The front of the Ski-doo is still on the ice but is tilted, quickly sliding backwards. Then the heavy machine drags her entirely under the cold, dark, water. The front end follows, pointed towards the clouds like a sinking ship. Only a single, thin white hand is left above the surface, clawing at the air before it gets pulled downwards too, and disappears below.

The scene then changes to an underwater view. In Martin's version, the water is not dark, but deep blue, like salt water in a tropical sea. Claire has no helmet on. She becomes free of the ski-doo, which sinks faster than she does. Looking upwards towards the light created by the hole she had just fallen through, she tries to swim up. Her clothes are too heavy.

Her eyes close. She becomes limp, lifeless. Her long blonde hair is floating above her as she sinks. She goes deeper. It gets darker as she descends further from the light, further from the hole.

Back on the surface, chunks of ice and clumps of wet snow are working to seal up the hole, bobbing in the remaining ripples.

The ripples stop, the water is calm.

Then the image pulls out so Martin sees the entire pond from the bank. The surface is barren, thin snow covering the ice. Far away, in the middle is indent where the hole is. The hole appears grey, dark.

This is how Martin envisioned the accident. For whatever reason Claire has no helmet on, no hat, no gloves. After the ice breaks, Travis is no longer in Martin's interpretation.

Martin had to get up from the couch, do some chores, and get his mind off continuous recycling of this movie his mind had fabricated.

Martin would have to clean Claire's room, but not now. Completing the task today would be too emotional. Maybe he would ask Travis to help, but then again, it would best to pretend that he was cleaning a stranger's room rather than gathering up Claire's possessions. He had to try to think of it as cleaning any unknown guest's room after they had checked out and gone home.

He spent the rest of the day doing mundane chores to divert his attention. He tried to come up with tasks that involved problem solving to keep his mind focussed on the activity instead of Claire.

Around four, he wanted to see what Travis was doing but he wanted to be sneaky about it. He took the elevator up to the fifth floor and stood outside Travis's door. He could hear the TV going, the familiar sounds of a video game; gun fire, shouting, loud explosions, police sirens, and pulsating background music.

Martin went into the stairwell and descended one flight of stairs to the landing between the floors. He called Travis on the radio. On the second attempt, Travis responded. There was no TV sound in the background.

"Feeling any better?" Martin asked.

"Sort of, but still in bed, still tired," Travis replied.

"OK, I'm in the kitchen," Martin lied. "I'll bring you some food in a little while."

Martin walked back past Travis's room, at first it was still quiet on the other side of the closed door, but then the TV turned back on, and the sound of video game mayhem came droning out into the hallway.

"Caught cha," Martin said to himself.

Martin made chicken nuggets and french fries for the both of them. He ate alone in the empty restaurant at a booth, then got his guest's tray of food ready.

Vacancy

When Martin went back up to the Travis's room, the kid was prepared. He was sitting in bed waiting. The TV was off. The den had no lights on.

"You look much better," Martin said.

"Ya, feelin not too bad, but not hundred percent."

"I'm going to have to clean Claire's room," Martin said, "Get it done tomorrow."

Travis did not acknowledge the comment and did not offer to help. Maybe he was still thinking of it as Martin's duty as staff to clean the room

"Still can't believe the ice gave way like that," Travis said.

Martin thought to himself, "Well, when you try to drive a five hundred pound piece of metal onto a thin layer of frozen water, it's not going to hold. Common sense."

Martin could never understand it, every year he heard stories in the news about snowmobilers drowning after falling through the ice on lakes. There are hundreds of square miles of land and even groomed trails to ride on, yet they have to ride over lakes.

"It was still risky," Martin said.

"Ya, well you don't know what it was like out there. It looked solid. It was solid. Look I'm sorry it happened," Travis paused, "it's something I will have to live with for the rest of my life."

Martin studied his expressions as he spoke. He did not know if Travis was genuine. The last line did not sound sincere. It sounded rehearsed. It sounded more like a quote Travis might have remembered from a movie.

Martin stood up to leave. "Maybe tomorrow you can get out of your room. Walk around, maybe help out with stuff?"

"We'll see how I feel, " Travis said.

Martin left and did not talk to him for the rest of the night.

185

22

The next morning Martin called Travis on the radio at 9:30. He woke him up.

"Thought maybe you could do some vacuuming, maybe mop around the hot tub and pool room."

Martin knew that Travis wanted to say no but did not decline, placating Martin out of guilt. Martin set him up with a mop and bucket and left him to wash the floor in the pool room. He also let him vacuum the long gathering area outside the conference rooms. Travis did not object, but he did not show any eagerness either.

While Travis was busy cleaning, Martin turned his attention to Claire's room. It was imbued with the enticing fragrance of the perfume she had gotten on their shopping trip during her first full day living at the hotel. Claire had worn the perfume every day since. The lingering scent was going to make it more difficult for him to pretend that he was cleaning a stranger's room. He had a history with the clothes in the room also. He recognized many of the clothes that Claire had brought home from the village on the very same shopping trip.

Her room was relatively clean. Garbage was in the garbage pails. All towels were hanging neatly in the bathroom. Her dishes were washed and back in the cupboard. Her bed was made.

Martin started collecting all the towels and linen, put them all into one big bundle then dropped it in the hallway outside her room to be sent down the linen chute later.

Some of her clothes were hung up in the closet, he took them off their hangers and put them into a black garbage bag. All the clothes in the dresser drawers were neatly folded and organized. Her clothes were not still sitting in the suitcase like guests do when they are only staying for the weekend.

On her bedside table sat a framed family picture. The photo was of Claire, a handsome man who must have been her husband, and two older people, maybe her parents. Everyone was dressed up, probably attending a wedding. One of the few occasions families took the time to get together. Everyone in the picture looked happy.

She was making the room homey.

Martin filled three garbage bags with her clothes and possessions, including her make-up, a knapsack he did not open and other things she had brought with her. He would later take all the bags to lost and found, not that she would be returning for them, but it seemed a waste to throw away all of her belongings.

Up until last year, "lost and found" was nothing more than a plastic tote bin filled with items forgotten by guests. It was a collection of swimsuits, single socks, toys, ski gloves, phone chargers, and the occasional pair of underwear that was found at the bottom of the guest's bed in the sheets. These were mostly things that people had inadvertently left behind, and would not bother to claim once they got home.

Once Solara started claiming victims at The Grand, Martin had to convert the ski locker room into a lost and found storage to accommodate all the items left behind. Now however, the items were not "lost" but were things still around after the guests or staff had passed away in their room. The lost and found now was filled with items no one would consciously leave behind. There was a $600 snowboard, several full suitcases, skis of all sizes, a couple laptops, a travel DVD player, iPhones, even a little pair of pink ski boots that looked like they would fit a five year old. The lost and found room was getting full. He had enough equipment to open up his own used sporting goods shop.

When Martin was finished in Claire's room, he sprayed a deodorizer to eliminate the smell of the perfume. It was now returned to just another anonymous room in a hallway filled with other identical vacant rooms.

An hour into cleaning Claire's room, he got a call from Travis saying he was finished his tasks.

Since he already had the housekeepers cart out, Martin thought he would take it down to Travis's room. The room was going to get cleaned one way or another. It had been a couple weeks since Travis had given him the money, and lodging payment was due if he wanted to continue the charade of being a guest and Martin being the housekeeping staff who catered to him.

Martin could hear the TV going. He knocked loudly, loud enough that Travis would be able to hear over the TV. The TV volume cut out and Travis answered the door.

"Your room is due for a cleaning, are you going to do it or am I? If you want me to do it then you owe about $2000 for your stay since the last payment. If you don't have the money, I will leave the housekeeper cart right here for you to clean it yourself. It has everything on it, including new sheets, towels, chemicals, even a toilet brush."

Martin was really hoping that Travis did not have enough money. He wanted to see Travis kneeling down on the tiled floor of his own bathroom scrubbing the stains off the toilet.

Travis looked at the cart, "wait here," he said.

He returned a couple minutes later with a wad of cash and handed it to Martin. "This should cover it."

As he took the money, Martin tried to project indifference, but inside he was seething. It seemed like Travis had no intention of cleaning up after himself.

Martin convinced him to leave the room and go down to the kitchen while he cleaned his room. "Give me an hour," Martin said. "It's going to take me that long to clean this sty."

Travis went to say something, but changed his mind. Maybe he thought he had better not press his luck at this point in time.

Martin made the bed with fresh sheets and gave him all new towels.

While cleaning up the den, Martin noticed a small hole in the wall beside the TV stand. The hole was smaller than a fist, and higher than if someone had kicked the wall. Then he noticed a smashed Xbox controller. Travis must have gotten angry while playing a game and threw the controller at the wall in a rage.

The kid was slowly destroying the room. There were now a couple stains on the carpet from spilled drinks, one was unmistakably a red wine spill. Usually guests were charged a fee when damage was found. Hotel management would take pictures as proof in case the guest made any denials.

Martin filled two bags of garbage, one of which was half filled with empty beer cans.

While vacuuming, he hit something under the bed. He bent down and saw a duffle bag close to the edge of the bed frame.

He went back to the front door and looked down the hallway to see if Travis was coming. When he saw that the hallway was empty, Martin pulled the housekeeping cart across the doorway to block entry into the room.

Martin went back to the bedroom and dragged the duffle bag out. He unzipped it and looked inside. It was filled with money, countless bills of all denominations. The bills were not neatly stacked, but just thrown in the bag haphazardly. There were only two ways to get that much money, either you withdraw your life savings from the bank, or you rob a bank. Since Travis had told them that he was not working before the virus struck, it was obviously not his own hard earned cash. No, Martin assumed that Travis must have been stealing money in his travels since hitting the road, taking money here and there from empty stores, and houses. The money must have come from cash registers or safes if he could get them open. Maybe even people's homes, going through purses, wallets, jewelry boxes of the deceased. He must have done it secretly, though because Martin did not think that Claire would have allowed such behaviour. There were quite a few hundred dollar bills, also fifties, but mostly twenties, tens, fives and one dollar bills.

The bag however was too heavy to be just full of money. Something else was in there. He dug around in the cash and felt something hard and cold at the bottom of the bag. His hand froze. Without even looking , he instantly knew what it was. He pulled out a small pistol. It looked to him like the kind police use. He looked in the cylinder. It was fully loaded, six bullets. He put the gun back in the bottom of the bag and carefully buried it beneath the bills again then put the bag back in the spot he had found it.

Martin went white when he felt the gun. He did not like the idea of Travis having a gun.

Martin unplugged the vacuum and left the room. It was clean enough.

This amplified Martin's misgivings about Travis. It was like finding out that the classroom bully now carried a knife. It added value to the bully's already existing menace. He was not

189

scared of Travis, but did not trust him. Of course there was no reason to think Travis would ever use the gun. He was certainly verbally belligerent, but had never shown signs of physical aggression. It could be there for personal safety. Still, Travis was basically a stranger, and Martin did not know what he was capable of. An image of a drunken Travis staggering down the hall waving the gun around went through Martin's mind.

He did not think that Travis had used the gun to rob stores to obtain the money. He did not have the backbone to rob people at gun point, he was more the type to slink in when there was no threat, and take whatever he wanted.

Martin returned the housekeepers cart to the storage room and put all the dirty laundry down the linen chute.

He went down to the lobby. He wanted to test Travis. While at the front desk he called Travis on the radio and asked him to meet him there.

Travis came from the direction of the restaurant. "Ya," he asked

Martin went in the reception office and held the door open for Travis to follow as he continued to talk. "Just wanted to see how you were doing. Also, see what you wanted for supper. Since you were down here I thought I would see you in person, instead of asking a bunch of stuff over the radio."

Travis followed him into the office. Martin made it obvious that he was putting Travis's wad of money in a metal cash box he got out of the manager's desk drawer. He opened the lid to reveal a large amount of bills already in the box. He added the new payment amount then closed the box back up.

"Thought we would have a good meal to raise our spirits. Maybe roast beef. Make us feel better," Martin said.

Travis did not take his eyes off of the cash box.

"Raise our spirits?" Travis asked.

"Ya, make us feel a bit better about Claire," Martin explained.

"Oh... ya, sounds good," Travis said, with all the aloofness of a monotone teenager.

Martin closed the box but did not lock it, and put it back into the drawer. He then locked the drawer with a small key. He put the key back under the phone. Martin did not attempt to hide his movements. Travis continued to watch every action.

As they left the room, Martin said "Your room is waiting. Nice and clean. I'll call you when supper is ready."

On his way to the kitchen, Martin walked with Travis and watched him get on the elevator to go back to his room. Martin found a small roast and put it in the oven.

Martin returned to the reception office opened the lock box and counted the cash inside, noted the exact amount on a yellow sticky note, then put the note in another drawer. He returned the cash box back to the drawer and locked it up again. If his guest was going to steal any money it would be a discernible amount, not just a couple hundred dollars. Martin would check the cash box again in a couple days.

He then went down to the laundry room and emptied the chute of dirty linen from cleaning Claire's and Travis's room. As he handled the linen he got whiffs of Claire's perfume, then Travis's body odour.

By the time dinner was ready, the power had already gone off. They ate by candlelight in a corner of the darkened restaurant. Martin selected an out of the way booth that did not have any windows nearby. They enjoyed a nice home cooked meal with roast beef, gravy, carrots, and baby potatoes that were round and perfect looking. Travis was surprised that the potatoes came from a bag and had been sitting in the freezer for the past eleven months.

After eating, Travis offered to clear the table and take the dishes to the kitchen.

23

In the week following the accident, things returned to normal. Travis returned to isolating in his room doing his own thing and kept socializing with his host to a minimum. Travis started making his own meals which were mostly frozen dinners or chicken nuggets. Travis no longer offered to assist with chores. It was as if he had paid his debt for Claire's death with the few meager tasks, had been nice to Martin for a couple days, and therefore felt he could now return to his own routine of staying up late, drinking, playing video games, and sleeping in until after lunchtime.

Martin recalled the phrase "Time heals all wounds". It seemed to him that it took very little time for Travis to heal from Claire's death. Travis was back riding the one remaining snowmobile within three days of the accident. On the first ride after the accident, Martin had gotten a quick call over the radio from Travis informing him that he was going out, and would be back in a few hours. Martin was shocked. He went out the front door just in time to see the snowmobile disappear, racing across the golf course.

Martin checked the cash box a couple days after he had shown it to Travis, sure enough over $3000 was missing. The amount of bills looked the same, but the twenty and fifty dollar bills had been replaced with fives to make it appear that the same number of bills were still in the box. Martin did not confront Travis, but stored the information away in his mind.

One morning, Martin came down to the lobby to find Travis passed out on a leather couch. Martin had given him free reign of the hotel. He had trusted him to behave in a civilized manner. The table that was in the middle of the area had been pulled close to the couch. On the table were several empty cans of beer, an empty bottle of rum, and the handheld PlayStation video game. There was a dried pool of vomit on the oriental carpet beside the couch. Travis lay on his side, facing the back cushions.

Martin pushed on his shoulder, "Travis, wake up".

He did not stir. "Wake up !"

Travis turned over to reveal that he had also thrown up into the corner of the couch and the vomit had gone down behind the leather cushions. Martin gagged at the rancid, sour smell.

Travis shielded his eyes from the light, "Wha...What, where am I?" he asked slurring his words, his blood shot eyes barely open.

Travis slowly sat up, and looked at the table. "Oh, ya, " he said and laughed.

His guest's lack of concern raised Martin's ire, "You're cleaning this shit up!", he yelled.

Travis sat up, leaned forward and put his head in his hands.

"No way man, that's your job. Do you make regular guests clean up after themselves? I don't think so."

Martin knew that his young guest had been drinking to excess and had been helping himself the small stash of alcohol at the bar that Martin had set up once Claire and Travis arrived.

Martin left the lobby without a word, then returned five minutes later with a Rubbermaid tub cart. He pushed it up to the bar and started hurling the few remaining beer and wine bottles from the shelves into the plastic cart. The bottles smashed as they hit each other in the bottom of the cart. Travis looked over in horror when he heard the sound of smashing bottles.

Travis sprung from the couch enraged, and darted towards the bar. "What the hell are you doing?" he screamed.

He reached across the bar counter to try to grab at Martin, but Martin quickly stepped back. Travis was left grabbing at the air, his stomach against the edge of the counter restricting his reach. Martin threw the last bottle into the bin. Travis tried to catch the bottle in mid air but missed. The bottle hit the inside of the cart and smashed.

"That's it, the last of the alcohol," Martin lied. He still had some locked away in the restaurant kitchen that Travis did not know about, but there were no more bottles behind the bar.

Travis stepped back and looked into the bottom of the cart, hoping to see an unbroken bottle. A defeated look crossed his face.

"Asshole!" he yelled and kicked the cart.

He stormed off in the direction of the elevator. A second later, Martin heard something crash. Martin ran around the corner just in time to see the elevator door close. A small round table was lying on its side on the floor, the glass top had smashed, spraying tiny shards all over the carpet.

He now had proof that Travis could easily lose his temper. Martin's thoughts turned again to the gun Travis had in his room.

Martin returned to the bar and sat down on one of the stools to cool down. A sickly sweet smell of beer and wine permeated the area from the broken bottles.

He wanted Travis to clean up the vomit in the couch but he did not think he would do a thorough job. Two hours later with the help of a steam cleaner, chemicals, and a lot of air freshener, Martin had the oriental carpet and the couch totally clean.

Martin felt nauseous himself after smelling the vomit for so long. Cleaning up vomit was a task he was unfortunately far too familiar with for his minimum wage position. It was quite common to get a call to go to a guest room to change the bedding after a child had thrown up all over the duvet and sheets, or clean up the carpet in the hallway outside the restaurant, or go to a room after a group of young partiers had checked out. With the absence of guests, Martin was just beginning to enjoy the thought that he would never have to clean up someone else's vomit ever again.

Martin called Travis on the radio. "Travis come in?" He waited ten seconds, and tried again. "Travis come in?"

He repeated calling Travis every ten seconds, for two minutes. Nothing was more annoying then someone calling your name over the radio repeatedly and not giving you enough time to answer.

Travis answered, "Jesus Christ, what the hell do you want, I'm sleeping?"

"You need to come down here and clean up the broken glass, from the table you threw over.

"Screw you!" Travis replied.

Not wanting to drag the kid out of his room, Martin relented, vacuumed up the broken glass himself with a Shop-Vac, and took the table to a storage room that housed damaged furniture that could still be repaired.

Martin left Travis alone for the night and did not make him supper. Travis did not come down to make his own meal either. Martin assumed he probably had chocolate bars, and chips for supper or maybe even just slept the evening away to recover from his hangover.

The next morning Martin came down to find Travis sitting on one of the stainless steel food prep tables in the restaurant kitchen having a bowl of Fruit Loops. An open tin of Carnation condensed milk sat beside him.

Travis looked up when Martin came near him. "I know what you're gonna say, but I ain't leaving. I'll keep paying like a regular guest. You can't kick me out into the cold."

He did not apologize for his actions the previous day, and did not thank his host for cleaning up the mess.

Travis slid down from the counter, put the dirty bowl by the dishwasher, and then walked out without saying another word.

Martin sat down in a booth to have a couple waffles and fresh coffee. He found that the confined solitude of the booth was a spot that he did his best thinking. He had to review, to plan. Different thoughts went through his head. What if he did kick Travis out? He doubted that Travis would go peacefully and honourably agree to never come back. He did not want to live with the paranoia that at any time, day or night, Travis could try to break in, smashing a window to gain entrance. It was highly conceivable that Travis would return and try to claim the hotel for his own. Martin had set The Grand up as possibly the only place left that had electricity, heat, running water, and a well stocked kitchen.

On the other hand, if Travis did stay, Martin did not think that his behaviour would change.

So, he was stuck with Travis. It was still November. The snow was piling up outside. He would be housebound with the kid for the next five months, five months at least, the snow could last longer, maybe even into May.

Martin mumbled, "Stuck with Travis for five months, and can't even stand being alone with him for a week."

Then a thought struck Martin. Travis had not given any indication that he even wanted to leave the hotel. Travis had said that he was happy at the hotel. Up to this point, for whatever reason, Martin had assumed that it was the cold weather that was keeping his guest at the hotel, but if Travis was happy here, he may never leave. Travis probably felt the same way about the hotel that he did. Travis was living the good life now at a five star resort hotel. Why would he want to change his living situation? He probably felt like he was in a rap video or something, Porches in garage, hot tub, booze, everything but girls in bikinis.

Even if he did not see Travis much, the thought of him in the hotel made him uneasy. It was like having a mouse in the attic. It was always in the back of your mind that this vermin was in your space. Sometimes you could hear it scurrying about, and your anxiety went up. It kept you on edge. It was an intrusion on your solitude.

When his breakfast was finished, Martin got up from the booth, went back into the kitchen and pushed the dish rack with his dishes and Travis's empty bowl into the dishwasher.

After lunch, Martin was in the laundry room, when he got a call from Travis.

"Hey, what's for supper?" Travis asked.

Apparently, in Travis's mind he had made his case for staying as a paying guest, and the conflict was over.

"Don't know, I'm busy washing sheets. Don't think I will have time to make us supper," Martin said even though it was early in the afternoon.

"Fine, I'll make my own then." Travis replied.

When all the laundry was done and neatly folded, Martin went to the engineering office. On a shelf behind the manager's desk sat a collection of binders, manuals, and catalogues. He pulled out a binder labelled *Otis Elevators: Maintenance Schedule and Operational Manual.*

He returned to his room, he heated up a microwaveable meal and spent the rest of the night reading over the elevator manual.

24

Martin had a fitful sleep, waking up several times during the night and then going over things until he fell asleep again, only to wake up a little while later to repeat the same thoughts. He had formulated a plan at some point the previous day while doing the mindless task of folding laundry. Since then, he had wrestled with the scheme. Once he got out of bed he felt slightly nauseous. He was not sure if it was due to hunger or if it was anxiety related. Eating breakfast did not help.

The day involved taking care of some routine monthly tasks. The first thing he did was go down to the parkade, move around all the vehicles. It was beneficial to start the cars periodically to get the parts moving so nothing seized up. He wanted to make sure that any and all cars were operational, mostly for his own selfish needs, however, a part of him held onto the idea that someone, maybe a family member of the car's owner, would come to claim their vehicle. For future reference, he logged in his notebook the amount of fuel each vehicle had in its tank.

While he was at it he decided to give the dirtiest of the cars a wash. High pressure water taps were built in intervals around the parkade. He washed the Land Rover, the Porsche, the Suburban, and a Hyundai Accent that belonged to a room attendant.

He then checked the level of the generator and topped up its fuel using the tanker truck's supply. To make sure that the fuel would last the entire winter, Martin decided to further increase the energy conservation strategies he had already put in place. At this point, the main sources of energy consumption were lights, the heating system, laundry machines, the elevators, and all the appliances used in The Innsbruck's kitchen.

He went to the only other parkade level, P1, and shut off all the lights for that level. He rarely went to P1 and there was no need to keep the lights on all day. He shut off all the lights for the second, third, and fourth floor hallways as well. He could just carry a flashlight when walking these areas. All the lights in the guest rooms had already been shut off. The only guest rooms in the entire hotel that had power constantly running, was his and Travis's room.

By that time he was ready for lunch. He made himself a peanut butter sandwich with bread he had made a couple days ago.

His next task was to deactivate all the guest elevators. He had restored service to two guest elevators after Travis and Claire came. Standing in the elevator maintenance room he shut down service to the guest elevators. With the Otis maintenance book in hand, he made some adjustments to the service elevator.

Martin then went to the lobby to have a rest. By this time his nausea had changed to stomach cramps. His anxiety had increased to the point that he felt like he could not sit still. He tried to relax for a couple minutes but could no longer remain idle, so he got up. He knew how to alleviate his anxiety.

He took the stairs up to the fifth floor housekeeping linen room which accessed the service elevator on this floor. He turned the lights off. The room was now only illuminated by the daylight from the sole window on the wall opposite the door. It was gloomy outside, which made the interior dim.

Martin left, and stood in the hallway outside the room.

It was time.

He called Travis on the radio. "Travis come in?"

"Um, ya?"

"You up?"

"Ya, been up for a couple hours now, why, what do you want?"

"I felt bad about getting rid of all the alcohol so, I tracked down a case of beer from the restaurant storage. Come with me and I can show you where it is."

"Can't you just bring it up to me?"

Martin had not planned for this response, though he should have expected it. He paused, "No, Travis I have things to do. Just come, it won't take long."

"You mean go all the way down to the first floor?"

"Yes!"

"Ok, whatever, I hope the beer's cold."

Martin sighed. The kid really was not going to change.

"I'm by the elevators down the hall. Meet me there."

Five minutes later Travis came walking down the hallway, wearing only a pair of boxers, and a stained t-shirt.

"We have to use the service elevator. I'm trying to save energy so I shut down the other elevators. We have to go through here," Martin said as he used his key card to let them both into the linen room.

"Why the hell are the lights off?" Travis asked.

"Save power," Martin quickly replied.

"What's the use of having power, if you don't use it, this is whacked," Travis replied.

They walked towards the elevator. Martin let Travis walk ahead. Travis pressed the button and stood in front of the door, eager to get to his case of beer. As the elevator was making the trip from the first floor, Martin's heart started pounding.

Martin took a step backwards.

The elevator chimed to announce that it had arrived. The stainless steel door slowly slid across to reveal total darkness. The elevator cab was not there. Just the gaping black chasm of the shaft was in front of them. Travis paused, was puzzled. He started to turn his head as if to question Martin. Martin with both hands pushed on Travis's back as hard as he could. Travis lurched forward from the force. He tried to grab the side of the elevator door frame but it was smooth, rounded, with no edges to grip. Travis fell forward into the darkness of the open elevator shaft. His body soon disappeared into the black abyss.

He screamed as he fell, screamed all the way down the dark shaft, a plunge of seven stories down to P2. His screaming came to a sudden, blunt stop when he hit the bottom. The screaming was replaced with a sickening splat.

The gleaming stainless steel elevator door slid across and closed in front of Martin.

He turned and vomited into a garbage can that was sitting nearby.

He stood up and pressed the button again. The elevator door immediately opened to reveal the dark shaft. He took out his flashlight and shone it upwards. The bottom of the elevator cab was four feet above his head, just as planned.

His anxiety was gone.

Martin took the stairs down to P2 and went directly to a large housekeeping storage room where they kept all the bulk chemicals along with personal safety equipment for handling hazardous materials. He put on eye goggles, a respirator, a long rubber apron, and thick black rubber gloves that came up to his elbows. He picked up a large, tightly sealed pail labelled sodium hydroxide, left the room and took the stairs to P1. He pushed the button for the service elevator and waited for it to come down from the fifth floor. When the door opened, the shaft was empty in front of him. The elevator had stopped one floor above again. Even from this level, it was too dark to see the bottom of the shaft and he was grateful for it. He did not want to see the bottom of the shaft's grisly contents.

Martin pried open the lid of the pail. The contents looked harmless, a pail full of small white flakes with no odour. Staff used the sodium hydroxide to make up their own batches of drain cleaner, or used it to get rid of oil stains in the parking lot. He knew that it was a powerful corrosive material which could dissolve proteins, fats, grease. He remembered a movie, in which a killer had used it to get rid of a body.

He filled a plastic scoop and scattered the flakes into the shaft, letting them fall to the bottom. He tried to cover the entire area, tossing heaping scoopfuls of sodium hydroxide into all the corners of the shaft's floor. He did not know how far the mess would be spread out.

He had been at the bottom of the elevator shaft before to pick up things that had fallen down the thin crack between the elevator cab and the elevator doors on each floor. He would find coins, room keys, valet tickets, food, and small pieces of garbage. There were no mechanical parts or wiring at the bottom. It was basically an empty room, with a bare floor and cinderblock walls. It would have the effect of being a concrete pool that would contain the corrosive chemical and allow it to do its job until Travis's remains were totally dissolved.

By the time he was finished, half of the pail was empty. He dragged a hose into the elevator vestibule from the parkade and let a fine spray of water fall down into the shaft. The chemical only needed a small amount of moisture to start the corrosion.

He returned the pail to the storage room and took off all of his protective equipment.

He then went to the elevator mechanical room on P2 and reset the service elevator. He walked around the corner and pressed the button for the   elevator. He was now standing mere feet from the bottom of the shaft. The door opened to reveal the elevator cab, just as how it should be. Invisible vapors were starting to come up through the opening in front of the elevator threshold. It had   that familiar smell like when he was using Drano to clean out a clogged sink. He decided that he would not use the elevator for a few days. He would wait until there was no evidence of the caustic smell.

To test the elevator he got in and pressed button 5. When the door opened again, he was standing in the fifth floor linen room again. Everything was back to normal.

Martin had contemplated simply shooting Travis with his hunting rifle, but then reconsidered when he realized it would be much more graphic. He had envisioned the scene; Travis lying in the hallway, half leaning against the wall with a bullet wound to the chest. A pool of blood soaking into the carpet, splatters of blood on the wallpaper.

Martin saw pushing Travis down the elevator shaft as a no muss, no fuss solution. He would not have to see Travis's body. He would not have to physically handle the body. He did not want to have the picture of a bloodied Travis etched in his memory for the rest of his life.

Martin spent the next three hours thoroughly cleaning Travis's room. He put all of his possessions into garbage bags, mixing them with the other trash he picked up. Garbage was under the bed, on the carpet, on the bathroom floor, behind the couch. He found garbage everywhere. It took a total of seven large black trash bags to clean out the entire room. He kept the video game systems but put them in the lost and found to be used later if needed. He would store the pistol in his own room. He put all of Travis's money into the front office cash box.

By the time he was finished with Travis's room, he did not have much time before the lights went out. Martin would have to return the next day to steam clean the carpets. Several holes in the wall, evidence of Travis's aggression would also need some attention, requiring multiple layers of drywall compound, then a repaint.

Martin had a hot shower, then cooked a microwave meal. He ate his meal in the lobby, sitting on one of the large leather armchairs in front of the fireplace.

When he finished his meal, he stretched his legs out onto the coffee table in front of him, leaned back and looked around the entire lobby. He felt like he had reclaimed the hotel. A wave of comforting calmness overcame him. A sense of affinity returned that had been absent since Travis and Claire arrived.

Instead of isolating in his room like he had been doing lately just to avoid seeing Travis, he decided to stay in the lobby for the evening. He laid stretched out on one of the plush leather sofas, his head resting on one of the ends and just enjoyed the silence of the hotel. Soon the power went out, but he was content and watched as the daylight dwindled, leaving him in the warm glow of the fireplace.

By nine o'clock he was tired and ready to go back to his room. He completed a quick check of the area from his balcony lookouts, took his medication then went to bed.

He fell asleep almost immediately.

25

Opening his eyes, he was greeted by darkness. Light seeping in around the edges of the floor to ceiling heavy curtain at the end of his room told him that it was daytime. Through blurry eyed vision he turned to look at the alarm clock on the nightstand beside his bed. The green glowing digital numbers read 7:13.

To get a better look at the day, he walked across the room to the curtain covering the sliding glass doors of his balcony. He pulled one side of the curtains across just enough so that only his head was revealed. Another perfect winter day, deep blue skies with only a few small white clouds. He surveyed the grounds beneath him. No activity. He pulled the curtain completely closed again, and turned to go back into his room.

From the fridge he grabbed a can of grapefruit juice and a carton of soy milk. He poured the milk over a bowl of Corn Flakes. Having used the last of the milk, he threw the carton in the garbage. From the cupboard he took out a new carton and put it in the fridge.

He sat down at his dining table ate his breakfast. When finished, he quickly washed his dishes and placed them back into the cupboard. After brushing his teeth, he changed into jeans and a sweatshirt, made his bed, and was ready to start his day.

He walked out into the empty hallway. Rows of closed guest room doors stretched out in front of him. He pulled a small notebook out of his back pocket and flipped through the pages until he found the day's date. Handwritten in pen was a list of tasks he had made for himself.

"Let's see what I have to do today" he said aloud, reading the page as he walked down the hall, ready to start his daily routine.

The hotel was quiet. The only sound was his shoes scuffing the soft carpet as he walked. He stopped. Now there was no sound at all. Standing there alone, in the middle of the hallway, he took a second to appreciate the silence.

He sighed, and smiled contentedly.

The End...

The future...

Solara has only been around for one year. What is in store for Martin in the days, months, years to come? Are there any other survivors? Will The Grand Summit Place have any more visitors?

It is as uncertain as the future of a world decimated by the virus.

Footnotes:
Chapter 6, page 57 Toffler quote pp. 356
 page 57 Toffler quote pp. 346

Bibliography:
Toffler, Alvin, *Future Shock.* (New York:Bantam, 1970)

Bryan Coburn moved to the resort town of Collingwood Ontario with his family after living for thirty years in Guelph, Ontario, a busy university city. Although, he has wanted to write a book since grade school, Vacancy is his first attempt at composing a full novel. He had already started another book, when the idea for Vacancy surfaced, and was written since moving to Collingwood. He is considering at least one more book in the Vacancy series, and always has story ideas rattling around in his head.

Made in the USA
Lexington, KY
27 July 2014